Against her better judgment, Akira went to the corner of the room where the chest of drawers stood. The woman in the pictures was more gorgeous than she could have imagined. Her demeanor in the photos displayed intelligence, class, and strength.

Akira's heart sank as she took in a sharp breath. Her happy illusion disappeared into a puff of smoke. She counted the picture frames—twenty of different sizes, shapes, and textures, but they had two things in common. All the frames were laced with gold trim, and the same woman appeared in each photo.

One photo in particular caught her attention. Until she examined the way Roman enveloped the woman in his arms and smiled at the camera, dimples fully exposed, she had hoped that maybe the girl was a relative. Any lingering hopes sank when she found the photo album with page after page of pictures of them together in poses reserved only for lovers. Now that she knew the truth, questions flooded her mind. She should have never trusted him.

Indigo Love Stories

An imprint of Genesis Press Publishing

Genesis Press, Inc.
315 Third Avenue North
Columbus, MS 39701

Acquisitions

ISBN: 1-58571-095-4
Manufactured in the United States of America

First Edition

Visit us at www.genesis-press.com
or call at 1-888-Indigo-1

Acquisitions

by
Kimberley White

Genesis Press, Inc.

Sexual harassment at the workplace can have devastating effects. I hope Acquisitions sheds light on the seriousness of this issue. For more information, contact the Equal Employment Opportunity Commission.

Readers, thank you for supporting my career. I look forward to meeting you on the book-signing circuit. Please drop me a line with your thoughts about this book.

Snail mail: P.O. Box 672, Novi, MI 48376
Email: kwhite_writer@hotmail.com

Special thanks to my family and friends - your support is immeasurable.

Kimberly White

Chapter 1

<u>November 9</u>

Akira Reed froze with her hand poised above the pricing proposal.

Now that noise, she thought, *is not the heating clicking on.*

The quiet engulfing the empty outer office was disrupted by a synchronized snapping—much like the sound a deck of cards makes when a thumb rapidly flips through it.

Akira immediately wished she had shut and locked the door to her office, but at the time, she thought it wiser to leave it open to hear any coworkers who might come in after hours. Another strange thumping sound broke the silence. She could hardly breathe.

Immobilized by panic, she quickly evaluated her options. Should she jump up, run across the room, slam the door and lock it? Could she do that before the intruder realized she was in the office? Would it be wiser to call security?

Akira started to dial the numbers that would summon Officer Diller, the night security officer. *No*, she thought, *he's a little too slow, a little too unconcerned, and a little too interested in catching up on his sleep during the night shift.* He

Acquisitions

tended to forget that the pharmaceutical manufacturing and sales business was often plagued with the threat of stolen formulas and sabotage. By the time he arrived, whoever lurked in the outer office could attack her and be gone.

Akira had never been alone in the office late in the evening; maybe the sounds were normal, or her imagination. Pharmaceutical sales in the western Detroit suburbs covered a large territory and kept her too busy to come in every day, but in her four years at Greico Enterprises, there had never been any incidents of foul play at the office. She needed to stop watching late-night horror movies and succumbing to her overactive imagination. Convinced the sounds were only in her head, Akira replaced the telephone and continued completing the blanks on the pricing form.

A muffled thud—

Akira's head flew up. The pen fell from her fingers and rolled across the desktop, spiraling to the floor. With a jerk, she straightened her back. Her legs wouldn't move. She couldn't run.

Akira remembered hearing on a television news show that if a rapist confronted a woman, one option of self-defense was to challenge him head-on, rattling him enough to make him run. Considering Officer Diller working at the security desk, she didn't have many options. She'd have to get out of the office on her own.

"Is someone there?" Her voice sounded strained, too low to be heard.

Calling out released a bit of the tension that stiffened her body to the point of dysfunction. She called out again, this time louder and stronger. "The office is closed. If you don't answer, I'm calling security."

She sure wouldn't get any more confrontational than calling out a warning. She waited to see if the television news show had given her good or bogus advice.

Footsteps. Moving away from her door. The steps hesitated; sped up. Next, she heard a slight rattling as if someone bumped a desk, causing a lamp to shake.

Akira's heart lurched.

The only way onto the sixth floor was by elevator; the stairwell had been locked at six o'clock. Only the sales staff and security were given elevator access keys. Why wouldn't her co-worker answer when she called out?

The elevator chimed signaling the intruder's escape.

Akira took a deep breath, held it, and squashed her fear as she pushed her chair back. Quietly, she edged across the carpeting while keeping her back against the wall.

She peeked out the door. A lone light glowed across the room in the center of the cubicles used by the telemarketers, dispatchers and secretaries. The height of the sooty-gray cubicle walls made it impossible to see the elevator.

"Hello? Is anyone there?"

Akira wanted to make her way out of the office before the unknown visitor returned. She scurried across the room and snatched her purse from the bottom drawer of her desk. She flipped the light switch and pulled the door closed before racing toward the bank of elevators.

A light came on in the space between Akira's office and the elevator. She stopped, looking left to right. She would never make it back to her office—the door locked automatically upon closing, and her hands were too shaky to search her purse for the key. She would have to make it to the elevator and call security from the phone inside. She ran toward the silver doors, stopping only once to look over her shoulder in the direction of the light.

Akira slammed into a solid mass.

"Hey." Her supervisor, Mr. Johnson, caught her around the waist. "What's wrong?"

Akira clutched her chest. "Mr. Johnson."

"Slow down." His grip tightened around her waist. "What's going on?"

Her lungs pumped rapidly. She took several deep breaths, which brought the fragrance of Mr. Johnson's overly perfumed

Acquisitions

body into her lungs. "Someone was here. Did you see him?"

"No, I didn't see anyone. Let me check it out. Did you call security?"

"No, I thought I'd call from the elevator."

"Stay here."

Mr. Johnson released Akira and moved slowly across the room, weaving his way between the cubicles toward the light. Akira considered getting on the elevator and calling security as she had originally planned, but thought she might be overreacting. She had been working long hours, seven days a week. Fatigue could be making her react irrationally.

Mr. Johnson soon reappeared, strolling through the cubicles with the short strides his stocky legs would allow. "I don't see any signs of anyone. It must have been the cleaning staff."

Akira tried to force a smile. "Yeah, I bet it was the cleaning people."

Mr. Johnson smiled behind his thick beard. "You're shaking. Come to my office and calm down. I'll call security to walk you to your car."

Embarrassment flooded Akira's body and reddened her face. Did her boss have to find her having a complete mental meltdown? Not the best way to win new accounts. Who would promote a shaky woman who hears noises to lead a team of sales executives?

Akira accepted his offer, hoping that she'd have a chance to redeem herself. "I don't want to take up your time, but it would make me feel better."

"Of course it would, Akira." His large hand found the small of her back and guided her through the cubicles.

Mr. Johnson's office severely contrasted with the offices used by the sales executives. The sales teams' shared space was small, used only when dropping in to clarify assignments or complete paperwork on a deadline. His space occupied the entire west corner of the building. His black marble-topped desk sat in front of a picture window that spanned the length of the back wall. The Canadian skyline was visible across the sparkling Detroit River. Evergreen carpeting covered the floor and perfectly matched the drapes at the many windows in the room.

Akira sat down in the overstuffed chair placed against the right side of his desk.

"Would you like a drink? It'll settle your nerves."

"No, sir. I'll be fine. I was a little spooked." She laughed nervously, "I shouldn't be working late alone in the office."

"I wish more people had your dedication."

Mr. Johnson took a seat behind his desk with an iced glass of clear brown liquid. He took a sip and braced himself for the impact. "You didn't see anyone, but you heard noises? It could have been anything. Pipes rattling, anything. What made you so upset?"

Akira shook her head. "No, it definitely had to be *someone*. I called out. Whoever it was didn't want me to know they were here." She glanced over her shoulder in the direction of the open office door. "Are you sure you didn't see anything strange when you looked around?"

"Not a thing." His beard separated with a straight-lipped grin.

An eerie feeling—crawling worms—inched down Akira's spine. "I should be going."

"Before you go," Mr. Johnson said, stopping her as she rose from the chair, "I have a few papers I need you to sign. I was going to fax them to you in the morning, but since we're both here, we might as well take care of it now." He rummaged through a stack of papers on top of his desk. "Here they are." He placed the papers in front of her.

Akira read over the documents as Mr. Johnson finished his drink. The silence made her uncomfortable. She could feel his eyes on her. More specifically, she could feel his eyes locked on her breasts. She twisted auburn streaked locks of hair around her fingers as she quickly skimmed the routine customer agreement.

"May I borrow a pen?" She caught his eyes on her cleav-

5

Acquisitions

age.

Mr. Johnson lifted a pen out of its gold-plated holder in the center of the desk and handed it to her. The pen slipped out of his hands to the floor before she could grasp it. "Sorry."

Before Akira could say anything like, "No problem, sir," or, "I'll get it", Mr. Johnson dropped to the floor with his hand extended between her legs fishing for the pen underneath her chair.

Mr. Johnson looked up, his head between her thighs. "I think I might have it." The bulge of his lips grazed her thigh, swept over her hose and permeated her raw nerves with a scraping sensation.

"Mr. Johnson!" Akira shrilled.

He moved his head vigorously back and forth, rubbing the bristly hairs of his beard against her inner thigh. The rough surface of his tongue darted from his mouth and slathered her hose with moisture.

Akira jumped up, and clutching her purse, darted to the door.

"Akira." Mr. Johnson unfolded his short, stocky body from his crouching position while he brushed his suit clean of lint.

Akira stopped in the doorjamb and turned to face him. Even at that distance, the aroma of his cologne turned her stomach. She tried to slow her breathing, hoping to limit her inhalation of his cologne cloud.

"I want to remind you that I'm the manager of this office; people place a great deal of value on my word. If you want things to go easy for you here at Greico Enterprises, you might want to consider spending a night with me."

"Sir?" Akira's mind reeled, her heart pounded. *What is he saying?* The contents of her take-out dinner pushed up in her throat.

"Don't stand there looking at me like this isn't what you wanted," Mr. Johnson grunted. "You almost knocked me over when I stepped off the elevator." His face softened, and his voice gained a lilt as he rehashed Akira's words. " 'Did you see anyone?' And, 'It'll make me feel better'. Pretending to be shaken up. Please," he sat behind his desk. "I know what you were doing."

"Mr. Johnson, I gave you the wrong impression. I didn't mean—"

"Didn't you apply for the sales manager position at the west suburban branch office?"

"Yes, but—"

He flipped his hand as a gesture of dismissal. "You wanted me to come on to you, but when I did, you tried to play innocent."

"Mr. Johnson—"

"The difference between those who go far in this company and those who fade away is how hard a woman is willing to work to gain my approval—in the office and out."

Akira's mouth dropped. All the comments she regarded as misguided attempts at being friendly rushed at her, producing an explosion in her head. The innocent brushes against her breasts in tight doorways didn't seem innocent now. Even as she watched his coy expression, she felt sure she was misunderstanding him.

Mr. Johnson cleared his throat. "You should take the time to consider my request. I'll certainly consider your answer when I submit my evaluation of who should become the sales manager of the west side office."

Mute, Akira backed to the door.

Mr. Johnson's face erupted into a satisfied smile before turning his attention to the documents littering his desk.

Chapter 2

"Mr. Miller, your next appointment is here."

"Remind me who that is please, Columbia."

"Akira Reed, sir."

Roman searched for the file marked "Reed." Finding it, he flipped it open and scanned the complaint form.

Hunched over his desk reviewing complaints the entire morning, Roman's eyes burned and his shoulders ached. He rubbed his eyes behind the tiny, square reading glasses. He stretched his long arms out from his body. The gesture reminded him that he needed to pick up his suits from the cleaners. When had he become so jaded that his mind wandered to trivial errands when he had a complainant waiting to be interviewed?

The media's recent emphasis on sexual harassment in the workplace had opened Pandora's box at Greico Enterprises. The solution to every problem with a superior became filing a sexual harassment complaint. One false charge jammed the system, making it harder to maintain the impartial attitude he needed to detect the true complaints. Investigating the phony allegations made his work unproductive and meaningless.

Remembering that he would be rewarded with a partnership at Greico Enterprises one day, he rolled his neck to relieve the tension.

Roman's best friend had the right idea. Immediately after law school, Butch started carving out his career path. Making contacts. Going to political parties. Being seen in all the right places. Butch had quickly become one of the top criminal defense attorneys in the state. Having put in all the work at the beginning of his career, he now sat behind a large desk, making obscene amounts of money while ordering the new lawyers on the block to pick up his grunt work.

Instead of following his friend's advice, Roman took time off from his career to travel. He overspent when the banks offered him financing for a new car and pre-approved credit cards. Living the lifestyle of the rich and famous when employed in a pool of lawyers had not been his smartest move. When the opening came at Greico Enterprises—which offered a better salary, bonuses and the potential for advancement—he jumped at it.

Coming to Greico had been in Roman's best interest. Financially, he couldn't complain. He worked independently with little interference from management. The hours were consistent, which meant he could vacation at will. His evenings were free, allowing him to keep a close eye on his grandmother.

Roman reared back in his chair and wondered where this feeling of intense dissatisfaction with his life came from?

Disappointment came when he learned it could take tens of years before he would be able to advance up the corporate ladder; the senior attorneys had held their positions for years and did not plan to retire soon. He often questioned if arguing cases in front of a jury would suit him—as it did Butch. His work had become monotonous. Meetings consumed his days. Paperwork ruled his evenings. During claim investigations, he felt more like a social worker than an attorney.

"Mr. Miller?" The woman's timid voice interrupted his

Acquisitions

thoughts but did not command his attention.

Curtly, without looking up, he responded. "Have a seat."

In a monotonous tone, Roman started his speech, the procedure so routine that he repeated the script without thought. "Ms. Reed, you have filed a sexual harassment complaint against your supervisor, Mr. Johnson. I should warn you that this is a serious accusation, and if there is a hidden motive behind filing said complaint, you should withdraw this matter now before I proceed with my investigation."

Roman marked a three-second pause by tapping his pen against the file folder. "All right then. The complaint will be handled in three parts. I'll review your account of the incident and call you in for further questioning as needed. I'll interview Mr. Johnson to obtain his recollection of the alleged event. I will then talk with your coworkers. Again, I need to advise you that Mr. Johnson can protect his reputation any way he sees fit, not limited to presenting character witnesses on his behalf or to discredit you. Any questions?" He did not wait for her to interject. "I'll be in touch."

Roman began to make note of his initial interview in the file folder. He stopped writing when he noticed Ms. Reed had not moved. He looked up for the first time into the darkest eyes he had ever seen. Vulnerability glistened in the twin pools, and rendered him momentarily speechless. He drew in a long breath along with his professional grit. "Is there something else, Ms. Reed?"

"Yes, Mr. Miller, there is."

Akira's lips were full, framed in burgundy and colored in shiny red. *Kissable.* Roman's eyes moved upward behind his reading glasses to the cute little slope of her nose. Paralyzed by her splendid face, Roman gave Akira the opening she needed.

"Congratulations, Mr. Miller, on making me feel violated for a second time! It seems you have dismissed my complaint without any compassion. You're supposed to help me."

Akira's dark, alluring eyes were locked on Roman in an

icy glower. Pulled back in a tight bun, her auburn-streaked hair made her eyes even more pronounced. Her honey brown skin glowed red with rage. The voluptuous curve of her breasts pulled him into her world and led his eyes on a tour that ended at the hint of cleavage revealed atop the second button of her blouse.

Roman regained his composure and remained firm. "I'm not here to 'help you'. I'm here to investigate a charge of sexual harassment. My findings will reflect the truth—not compassion."

"Don't you have to use a little compassion to find the truth? The decision to file these charges against Mr. Johnson was a difficult one to make and—"

"I'm sure it was."

"Please don't interrupt me, Mr. Miller. I've listened to you lecture me, now you listen to what I have to say."

"Don't get upset. If you have questions—"

"You don't feel I have the right to get upset? Are you really as cold and unfeeling as you seem to be?"

Roman tensed with defensive anger at her assessment of his lack of character.

"As I was saying, filing these charges against Mr. Johnson was a very hard decision for me. But I decided that if I didn't speak up he would threaten more women. I've come to you for help, and you don't even show me the respect of looking up at me when I come into your office. You talk to me as if I'm another piece of paper that you need to neatly file away so that you can leave for the day. Can you see how this has undermined my confidence in your ability to process this complaint competently?"

Akira hiked her purse up on her shoulder. "Mr. Miller—" she made his name sound like a vile curse word—"I'm sorry that my supervisor threatened to fire me if I didn't sleep with him. Believe me it *was not* something I wanted to happen. But also believe me that I will not let him—or you—get away with it."

Acquisitions

"You make it sound as if Mr. Johnson and I are forming a conspiracy against you."

"No, Mr. Miller, you made it appear that way the moment you tried to minimize my situation." She moved to the edge of her seat, prepared to leave.

"Just a minute. You've made a serious allegation that I need to address right now."

Roman put his pen down on top of the documents lining his desk. It spiraled off the edge of the desktop and came to a stop against the tip of Akira's black pumps. Silence engulfed the office as Roman's eyes roamed over Akira's shapely legs. When his eyes met hers, her scowl helped make an instant connection to the occurrence in her complaint. He took in a breath, searching for the right words to clear up the misunderstanding.

Akira held her head high, lifted her nose, and dipped with confidence to retrieve the pen. Her dark eyes flashed cold as she stood and approached his desk. Gingerly, she placed the pen on the edge of his desk. She maintained her dignity in the sassy sway of her hips when she turned and left his office without another word.

The door slammed against the wall. She added attitude to the rock of her full hips and sashayed out of his office. Hypnotized by the movement, Roman's eyes moved with the precision of a pendulum, swinging back and forth with the shift.

Roman removed his reading glasses and deflated behind his desk. *Don't you have to use a little compassion to find the truth?* The betrayal and hurt in Akira's voice awakened his guilt. He came across as pompous and aloof.

Don't you have to use a little compassion to find the truth? When had he lost his empathy? The endless mountain of fraudulent complaints had hardened him over time. Unthinkingly, he had made it necessary for the victim to prove her case instead of impartially listening to both sides before rendering judgment.

And when did he start glaring at the women who came into his office as if he were on the prowl at a single's bar? Hell, he hadn't been attracted to a woman since Sherry left. He'd buried himself in his work and didn't think twice about opening his heart for another woman to fillet.

He couldn't keep his eyes off Akira's intimate curves.

Or the cute slope of her nose.

And her dark, magnetic, defenseless eyes.

Akira knocked him slightly off kilter with his first look at her. Her strong demeanor and mysterious eyes made a striking impression that stirred a familiar sensation in his belly.

Roman admired the way Akira held her back iron-rod straight to display the toughness of her armor even though her voice wavered in anguish. A solidly built lady with the kind of womanly-thickness that made a man want to cuddle her, she stood five or six inches shorter than his six-foot-two frame. Attractive, but not the type to flaunt it unnecessarily, she wore a classic winter-white business suit.

Akira possessed fire but she didn't appear openly suggestive. If anything, she carried herself in a conservative manner. He had learned that many of the tall, shapely saleswomen in the company used their looks as an advantage when making sales calls with male clients. Akira didn't strike him as that type of person.

She had been right to put him in his place.

The faint chime signaling the elevator's arrival shook Roman from his theorizing. He impulsively moved to the door, hoping she had not gotten on the elevator yet.

"Ms. Reed," Roman called as he hurried to catch her. He rushed past the reception area under Columbia's glare of disapproval. He cast his eyes opposite her direction as a sign that he understood his error and did not need scolding.

The silver doors parted. Akira stepped inside the box. Their eyes locked.

"Ms. Reed," Roman called again.

The doors closed in his face.

Chapter 3

"I can't believe what you did." Mr. Johnson entered the storage room as Akira gathered the last of the sample drug packets she would deliver to her clients that day. "Sexual harassment charges? Do you understand the weight of what you've done? I could be ruined." He made a show out of leaving the door wide open and stood at an exaggerated distance. Hard to believe that this could be the same man who blatantly placed his head between Akira's thighs.

"If you admit to what you did, I'll withdraw the complaint."

"What good would that do you?"

"It would give me a safety net if you threaten me again."

"Oh, I see." Mr. Johnson rubbed his wide fingers through the thickness of his beard.

Akira shivered. She could almost feel the coarse hairs grating against her thigh.

"Like I suspected. You're trying to blackmail me into recommending you for the promotion to sales manager. Is that it?"

"Doing that would make me no better than you. I work hard and earn everything I get. But I want to be assured that when I do work hard, I'm judged on those actions only."

Mr. Johnson snaked his fingers through his beard while searching for a response.

Akira moved toward the door.

He blocked her path with his stocky body. "I won't let you get away with this."

"Me?"

"I don't know what your game is all about. I don't want to know. I do know that if this nonsense isn't stopped—and soon—you'll never see yourself as sales manager at any branch of Greico Enterprises as long as I'm around."

"How can you be this way?" Akira asked in an exaggerated whisper. "You and I are the only blacks in the sales division."

Mr. Johnson laughed as if he had uncovered a sinister plot. "Are you playing the race card with me?"

"No," Akira stammered. "That's not what I meant." She didn't expect special treatment from him because they were both black. She expected his understanding of her struggle to make a name for herself at Greico. "I don't want special treatment. I want equal treatment. I want you to respect me for the work I do here."

"Did you file the sexual harassment complaint because you found out that I'm dating Candace—a white woman? Is this why you played hard-to-get in my office? To teach me a lesson? Are you trying to punish me because you don't believe in interracial dating?"

Rumors flew around the office about Mr. Johnson and Candace, another sales rep. Akira had heard Candace brag about it to her groupies in the office, but could care less who he dated. The way he turned the situation around, putting her at fault, chilled her. She hadn't expected him to play this dirty. She figured he would deny the truth, but never imagined he'd blame her.

Acquisitions

"Don't be ridiculous," Akira said.

"Oh, I think I'm on to something. I finally figured it all out. You want me for yourself." Mr. Johnson advanced on Akira with a grin that said his mind often wallowed in the gutter. "Don't worry, there's enough of me to go around."

Akira shriveled back from his creeping, stubby fingers.

"We have to be discreet. I don't want Candace finding out about it."

Shaken by the encounter, Akira darted out of the rapidly shrinking room. She scurried to the elevator, keeping her head down, as she passed gawking coworkers. Rounding a cubicle wall, she slammed into a tall mass of lean muscles. All of the sample drug packets bundled in her arms flew into the air. The secretaries in the cubicles turned their gossip-hungry eyes on her.

"Ms. Reed," Roman said, "I'm sorry. I didn't see you coming."

Akira bent to retrieve the samples. Roman joined her, using his long arms to scoop up the bulk of the packets. A secretary offered her a custom made black net carrying bag with the Greico logo on front. Feeling eyes watching her every move, Akira shoved the packets inside the bag and took off for the elevator again.

"I was on my way to see you," Roman called after her.

"What for?" Akira hit the button that summoned the elevator.

"We need to schedule your interview."

The square reading glasses were gone, revealing fiercely sexy facial features. Roman's smoothly shaven skin glistened with a trace of left behind baby oil. The flash of his long lashes made Akira's mind go blank. She clumsily switched the carry bag from her left hand to her right. Under his concentrated glare, she felt small and awkward. A response she refused to acknowledge moved into the warm place between her thighs. Roman Miller's closeness ripped through the cobwebs protecting her heart. She felt a stirring awakening that couldn't have come at a worse time.

The elevator chimed, and Akira stepped inside the car with Roman close behind.

"I know that I came off rather abrasive in our first meeting. I apologize."

Akira ignored the havoc he caused by standing close to her. She stared at the numbers illuminated above them.

"Can we call a truce?"

Akira dared to glance over at him. Seconds ago Mr. Johnson had her in frenzy. Roman stepped into the picture and blanketed her with a calmness that he seemed unaware he projected.

"I'd like to get this matter cleared up as quickly as possible. Your interview will be key in doing that."

Akira shifted away from the heat radiating from his tight body. "I have an appointment with an important client."

"After your meeting?" Roman's outdoorsy scent consumed the space between them.

The floors passed much too slowly. "I have a full day of meetings." Akira couldn't discern if she was making excuses to avoid the interview or trying to avoid being alone with Roman.

"Ms. Reed, I understand that your salary depends on the amount of successful sales you make." Roman took the Greico carry bag out of her hands. "I won't hinder your work. But we do need to get together as soon as possible." He sounded more understanding than at their first meeting.

As Akira was about to cooperate, the depth of his dimples softened her resolve. Remembering the nature of their relationship, she pushed away the attraction and focused on projecting a stoic attitude. "I don't know when I could possibly squeeze in the time."

The elevator came to a jerking stop and Akira stepped off into the lobby.

Roman followed. "Ms. Reed, only days ago you were scolding me for not giving your case the attention it deserves."

Acquisitions

He stopped, letting his words follow her through the lobby. "Are you intentionally making this difficult? Is there a reason you don't want to meet with me?"

Akira froze. *Yes,* but not the reason he believed. Her thoughts jumbled up when he came near. Inappropriate visions filled her head when she inhaled his scent. The rumble of his voice set her on fire. She babbled and tripped over her own feet when she looked into his sexy eyes.

Roman's long legs brought her to him quickly. Thankfully, no one in the busy lobby paid his accusation any mind.

"I'm not avoiding you, Mr. Miller. It's just that—"

He dipped his head in anticipation.

"This has been a hard day," Akira admitted. "And I do have a busy schedule."

"Well, you have to eat." Roman checked his watch. "How about an early lunch? We could start the interview right now."

Despite the flip-flop of her stomach, Akira couldn't find a reason to ditch the lunch meeting. If she protested too much, he might think she filed a false claim. Taking the meeting out of the building might help keep the gossip down.

"We'll make it an informal interview."

Akira checked her watch. "I can spare one hour."

"Great, there's a café in the building across the street. Let's take these samples to your car, then we'll walk over."

Akira walked with robotic stiffness to her car. Roman followed silently behind her. They placed the bag in her trunk and started for the café across the street. Roman opened the door for her, placing his massive hand in the hollow of her back to guide her inside. Akira felt the heat transfer off his fingertips and sear his brand deep into her bones. The sensation surprised her. She tripped over the mat at the front door.

"Be careful." Roman rescued her from a fall by firmly gripping her arm. This brand would match the one sizzling the flesh of her back.

She avoided looking at his dimpled smile. "Thank you."

A young woman, not more than twenty, hustled up to Roman. She looked the picture of the stereotypical waitress. Popping bubblegum, pencil behind her ear, skirt too short. She presented a big toothy smile for Roman. "Mr. Miller, how ya doing today?"

"Good, Latice."

"Usual table?"

"No. I need a table for interviewing today. Somewhere quiet and private."

Latice assessed Akira with a smirk that said she now understood why Roman had brought her for lunch—business. "One minute, Mr. Miller. I'll take care of you personally."

The waitress' rude dismissal stung Akira. Why couldn't she be the lunch date of someone like Roman Miller? Latice insulted her by not even considering it an option. Not that she wanted to be his date. This was business. Having a fling with the attorney investigating your sexual harassment complaint was definitely out of the question.

"It shouldn't be long," Roman said, again branding Akira with the touch of his hand on her back.

The waitress reappeared and led them to a vacant dining room. She poured their water and gave them menus before disappearing.

Roman answered Akira's silent question. "They open this dining area during the lunch and dinner rush. If I come at the right time, they offer it to me for conducting interviews. Our meetings are confidential and no one will bother us here."

Latice buzzed near their table, hovering in wait for Roman's order. The first time he glanced up from his menu, she hummed over to the table. "What'll you have, Mr. Miller?"

"My usual."

Latice grinned. "Club sandwich, fries and pink lemonade."

"You've got it." When Latice didn't ask, Roman did.

Acquisitions

"What would you like, Akira?"

Akira. Her name dripped with innuendo when it slipped between his dark lips. She peeped over the top of the laminated menu. "Chef salad."

Roman lifted the menu from her hands. "You have to eat more than a salad. Bring her the same thing I'm having, Latice. If you like, Latice can bring a salad on the side."

"No." Akira liked the gentle commanding tone Roman used. "The sandwich will be fine."

Latice popped her gum, cracking Akira's ears before spinning around to place their orders.

"I don't think she likes me."

"Latice?" Roman laughed, "Don't worry about her." He relaxed back in his chair and crossed his arms over his chest.

After an uncomfortable moment of silence, Roman spoke. "I feel I need to apologize again for the way our first meeting turned out. I will give your case the attention it deserves."

"I appreciate that." She did—the apology and his promise to investigate her claim seriously.

Roman's concentrated assessment rattled Akira. She fiddled with the silverware. He leaned forward, resting his arms on the table. "You looked pretty shaken when I ran into you—literally."

Akira pushed a clip of auburn hair behind her ear without answering.

"Did something happen today?" Without his reading glasses to shield her from his rays, the flashes of his long lashes mesmerized her. "I take that as a silent yes. Tell me what happened."

Akira didn't deny.

"Akira, you do have rights in the workplace. One of them is to not be punished for filing a complaint against your supervisor. Tell me what happened. I can help."

Sitting across from him helped. Falling under the suggestive rhythm of his dark lashes helped. The sincerity in his baritone voice helped.

"Akira?"

Her name floating between his lips gave her the encouragement she needed to trust him. "Mr. Johnson gave me a hard time about filing the complaint."

Roman nodded. "I figured it was something like that. I'll take care of it."

"No. It'll only make things worse."

"Greico has guidelines that address this type of thing. Mr. Johnson won't even know that we talked." The comforting dimples appeared. "He won't bother you again."

"Then you believe me?" Akira held her breath, needing to have one person at Greico on her side.

Roman shifted uncomfortably in his chair. "I don't have enough information to form an opinion."

Akira wanted Roman to assure her that she had done the right thing; tell her it would be okay. After her long day, she needed him to reach across the table and cover her hand with his. For one moment, she wanted him to cross the line of propriety their business relationship dictated and provide her the security only a strong man could give. Instead, he switched gears and became the emotionally unattached attorney again.

Roman's lashes dipped. He shifted again. His eyes met hers. "I don't have enough information at this time, but I will get to the bottom of it."

Latice appeared from nowhere with their order. She lingered near their table during the entire lunch. Akira wanted to swat her like the annoying gnat she was. Latice buzzed over, grinning in Roman's face anytime he gave the hint of needing something she could provide. She probably would have tried to feed him given the chance.

Latice's disapproving glances bothered Akira. The obnoxious way she popped a loud bubble whenever Roman let the conversation slip away from business said to Akira, "He's mine." Or she wanted him to be.

A handsome man whose height made him more visible than his competition, Akira could understand all the attention

Acquisitions

Roman received from Latice. Chiseled facial features displayed his serious side, while twin dimples hinted at his playful side. Intelligence oozed with every head-held-high step, but was balanced by his quiet, sexy nature. His suited-down body couldn't hide a firm physique the color of polished saddle leather, the iron hard thighs, or the killer buns beneath the jacket.

Akira, given the chance, would never date a man as good looking as Roman. Constantly fighting off other women could destroy a meaningful relationship.

Latice's open advances and cunning remarks bothered Akira because Latice never considered her a threat. Akira had never been one to turn heads when she walked into a room, but she wasn't a deformed troll either. True, with Eric—her last semi-serious relationship—there had been issues. Issues she knew went directly to the thickness of her thighs and the cushion at her waist. But that was Eric's problem.

Latice's attitude irked her. Roman could have been out on a real date with her. If he hadn't been working on her sexual harassment case. As she stared into his eyes from across the table, Akira had to keep reminding herself of that.

Once she became comfortable with Roman, the lunch interview went well—despite Latice. Although Roman donned his impartial attorney mask when needed, Akira sensed his underlying tenderness. She imaged him to be the type of man never to forget his woman's birthday or a special anniversary. He would support her dreams and always be in the front row of their kid's school functions. He'd make love as slowly as he consumed his lunch. He'd study every curve of her body until he found the combination of actions that satisfied his woman. Akira's first assumption remained—he probably had too many women to count—but she would bet he treated them each as the queen of his harem.

"I feel naked without my legal pad," Roman said, reaching for his lemonade.

Akira choked on a fry. Her mind had wandered onto

images of how Roman would satisfy his lover when she heard him say something about getting naked.

"Are you alright?"

Akira nodded, still choking.

Roman slipped into the booth next to her. "Drink this." He pressed a glass of lemonade to her lips.

Akira let him help her, enjoying having him this near.

"Latice," he ordered, "bring her a glass of water."

Latice popped her gum before moving at a snail's pace to the drink station.

"I'm fine. A fry must have gone down the wrong pipe."

Latice reappeared. Roman took the water pitcher from her and sent her away.

Akira's skin seared with a new brand when Roman brushed her arm while reaching for a water glass.

He poured. "I thought I was going to have to do the Heimlich maneuver on you."

If it meant squeezing her from behind, another fry might be in order.

In the firm commanding tone Roman said, "Take a drink."

She heard, "Take—every—inch."

"Drink," Roman repeated.

Akira did as instructed.

"We can finish up this interview in my office."

"I'm sorry." Scrambling for her composure, "We didn't get much done."

"Sure we did." The dimples. "I learned a lot about your character today."

How had that happened? His questions seemed benign. He asked about her work history. He delved into her duties and responsibilities. Could he have been slick enough to get information from her without asking the questions outright? Had her lips slipped as she daydreamed about him in a horizontal position?

"I'll walk you back," Roman offered.

They parted on the street. Akira went to her car. Roman

Acquisitions

went back to his office.

Akira was still thinking of him when she reached the physician's office for her afternoon appointment. Undeniably, Roman Miller was the finest specimen of man she'd encountered in a long while. After the failure of her last relationship, she hadn't placed much focus on men, but Roman stirred up intimate feelings.

Too bad Roman was the attorney investigating her sexual harassment claim.

"Off limits," she whispered. "I'll have to keep reminding myself of that."

Chapter 4

Roman pulled his Infiniti into the driveway of his grand-mother's home.

"Grandma," he banged on the front door. A little hard of hearing, she didn't always hear the doorbell. "Grandma."

With much protest, he had moved Grandma Dixon into her own condo. Secured in a retirement community, the area off the main street and down a winding road held all the services she needed. The village included a nursing home, senior apartments, convenience store, and a medical clinic. The vicinity allowed her to have other people around for friend-ship, and in case she experienced a medical emergency. Although she would never admit it to her grandson, she loved her new surroundings.

Roman heard several locks click before the door eased open. "Why are you making all that racket out there, boy? My neighbors are probably calling the police."

"Sorry, Grandma." Roman stepped into the house that always seemed too warm. He stomped the snow from his boots and removed his coat before he followed her into the kitchen.

Acquisitions

"Hey." Butch sat at the tiny kitchen table eating from a plate piled high with food. Addicted to keeping the perfect body into old age, it surprised Roman to see Butch consuming the smothered chicken and mashed potatoes with unrestrained vigor.

"You're here more than I am." Roman straddled the seat across from Butch.

"Somebody has to keep an eye on Grandma Dixon."

"Got everything I need." She placed a plate and glass down in front of Roman. "Wash your hands before you sit at my table."

"Grandma Dixon, I'm not hungry."

"Wash your hands, boy. You know your daddy would knock you down on the spot for sassing me."

"Yes, Ma'am." Roman moved to the sink as instructed. He didn't voice his opinion about what his father would or wouldn't put up with—he had no way of knowing. Besides, you could not debate with Grandma Dixon. And don't even think about arguing your point. He was twenty-seven the last time she tried to hit him upside the head with a frying pan for smart-mouthing her.

"Actually," Butch said when Roman came back to the table, "I came by looking for you. I stopped at your house first."

"What's up?"

"Trying to make plans for this weekend."

"No plans for me. I've got to catch up at the office."

Butch made a grumble of disapproval as he lifted his glass to his lips. Over and over, he had encouraged Roman to leave the going-nowhere job at Greico and join his firm.

"How's work?" Grandma Dixon pulled a chair from the corner and fit herself between them. "Tell me about your new cases. I love hearing that stuff. Every time I get together with my friends to watch that lawyer show on TV, I brag about my grandson. Who would've thought you'd end up on this side of the law?"

"Yes, Ma'am." Roman interjected in her pause. His motivation to practice law spawned from her.

"A lawyer that's doing the right thing, too—defending people being pestered by their bosses."

"It's not exactly like that, Grandma. I'm a mutual arbitrator—I don't defend either side. I investigate the sexual harassment claims assigned to me from the Employee Assistance Line. After I review the case, I refer it for disciplinary action, if needed." He'd explained this many times before, but Grandma Dixon always put her own grandiose spin on things.

"That's what I said."

"You swamped over there?" Butch asked.

"The sexual harassment cases are down slightly, so they have me picking up lawsuits for wrongful dismissal." Roman described the caseload he currently juggled. The conversation became too technical for Grandma Dixon, who only wanted the juicy details; she went into the living room to watch television.

Roman gave Butch the details he had gathered surrounding Akira Reed's case.

"Any idea where you're going with it?" Butch rinsed his dishes at the kitchen sink. Roman recognized the new suit he wore from an ad in this month's *Upscale Magazine*.

"I've been doing job history research on Johnson and Reed. I'll start digging into the grit of the interviews tomorrow. I've got to wrap it up quickly. I'm really behind on filing my reports." Besides, the more time he spent thinking about Akira, the more inappropriate his thoughts became.

"Too bad the law can't be about the client instead of the report. Come on over to my firm, and you'll have a paralegal and a secretary to take care of the paper shuffling. We just hired a fulltime law librarian. You'd have the opportunity to focus on what you went to school for."

Roman might want more out of his position at Greico, but he would never rely on his best friend to find him work. He avoided the old argument by swiftly changing the subject.

Acquisitions

"After I finish this case, I want to take a vacation. I need to concentrate on something other than work for a change."

Butch came back to the table. "Yeah, let me know about that. I'll have to clear my schedule."

Roman looked pointedly at his friend and asked the question buzzing through his mind since he walked into his grandmother's kitchen. "Have you talked to Sherry?"

Butch hid an expression of aggravation and pity.

"Have you?" Roman asked again.

"No."

"Would you tell me if you had?"

"No. And you need to stop sending her e-mails."

"You have talked to her."

Butch pulled his chair in closer and lowered his voice, keeping their conversation private. "Let it go. Walk away. It's been too long. If Sherry wanted to be here, she'd be here. If she wanted to talk to you, she would. Let her go, and stop working your behind off at a job you know you hate to get her back."

"My job and Sherry are two separate issues."

"Getting a promotion at Greico, if it happens, won't win her back. Personally, I think you'll be as old as the geezer partners are now before you're even offered a partnership. They're stringing you along."

Roman's appetite soured. "I disagree." He moved to the sink to rinse his own dishes.

"Answer me this then: are you happy? Happy with your work? Your personal life? And if you're not, why aren't you doing something about it?"

Butch's words settled deep in the pit of Roman's stomach. He counterattacked by outlining Butch's shortcomings. "Your problem is that as soon as the situation gets tough and requires work, you leave."

"That's not true."

"When's the last time you had a woman in your life for more than a weekend?"

"But I'm happy with my lifestyle. Are you happy with yours? Have you done anything that makes you happy since Sherry left?"

Grandma Dixon interrupted. "You boys stop arguing in there."

"We're two sides of the same coin." Butch muttered.

The conversation being over for this night, Roman went into the living room to kiss his grandmother goodbye.

Being in Grandma Dixon's strong presence when life kicked him in the butt always made him feel better. His parents left him and his older sister, Gayle,, with Grandma Dixon right after his tenth birthday. Their marriage was strained, they said, and they needed to be alone to work things out. After they had worked things out, they needed to be alone to keep it working. They never came back to claim their children.

Strictly old school, Grandma Dixon believed it was her obligation to give her daughter a chance to live her life to the fullest. Raising her daughter's children helped accomplish this. Roman and his sister never felt abandoned because Grandma Dixon smothered them with love. It wasn't until Roman became a teenager that he had accepted his parents were lazy and selfish and had given up their children because they were an inconvenience.

Roman sat outside his grandmother's condo while his car's engine grumbled to a purr.

Butch had hit a nerve Roman believed long ago healed. If honest with himself, he couldn't deny that Sherry still occupied a corner of his mind. Lately, that area began to shrink.

His thoughts weren't on Sherry, but on Akira. The vulnerability behind her eyes called for him to pull her into his arms and protect her from the evils of the world. His mind wandered from depositions to the imagined feel of her full curves pressing against his body. He pictured evenings sipping wine and debating the latest political issues. When in her presence, he felt like a nervous boy about to ask for his first date. His desires were entirely inappropriate—his job was to inves-

Acquisitions

tigate her claim, not fall for her—and he wrestled daily to control his urges.

Butch's knuckles rapped against the window. He shrank into the warmth of his coat, shifting from foot to foot, waiting for Roman to respond.

"You've been sitting out here for a long time, everything alright?"

Roman nodded, still distracted by his yearning for Akira's company.

"Everything alright with us?"

"Of course," Roman answered, snapping out of his daydream.

"As long as we've been friends, well, tough love is sometimes called for."

"I understand. Believe me, worrying about Sherry is not occupying as much of my time as you assume. I have something else on my mind."

"Like?"

He thought of wrapping his fingers in Akira's auburn locks, pulling her to him and pressing his lips against hers.

"Do you want to go get a drink and talk?"

Roman rubbed his eyes to remove from his mind the image of his body tangled with Akira's in front of the fireplace in his den. "No. It's not serious. I need to get home."

"Alright, but if you need to talk…"

"I'll catch up with you later in the week."

Butch stood in the snow-covered driveway, blowing into his fist and watching Roman back away. Roman could read Butch as well as Butch could read him. Both knew that there was something bristling beneath Roman's skin and he needed to talk about it.

Roman's sudden, unprovoked attraction to Akira stirred warm and fuzzy emotions he had long ago buried. Emotions that he didn't want to ever feel if it meant being hurt again. Along with the attraction to the new came memories of the old.

Sherry and Akira were not comparable, but he did it all the

time. Sherry would have told off Latice for her overt flirting, called the owner and demanded that she be fired. Akira grinned and bared Latice's snub with dignity, refusing to get down on her level. Akira, vulnerable; Sherry, domineering. Akira curvy, voluptuous and gorgeous; Sherry lean, waiflike and beautiful.

He had to stop this. He laughed at himself—he had been out of the dating scene too long. Akira was a client of sorts. In a sexual harassment case no less. Whatever connection he felt growing between them was a hazardous figment of his imagi-,nation.

***

Roman made his way through a maze of cubicles to Mr. Johnson's office. He hadn't seen Akira since their lunch meeting. He didn't like the way her eyes glazed over when she told him about the encounter with Mr. Johnson in the storage room. He wanted to check on her, he told himself; make sure that everything was going okay at work.

Roman stepped through the chaos virtually unnoticed. It always amazed him the amount of hustle and bustle that went on around the sales office. Telephones rang constantly. Telemarketers wore headphones to quickly handle the volume of calls they made. Dispatchers arranged delivery schedules to clinics and hospitals.

The sales teams' offices lined the walls to the left and right of the elevator. The cubicles stood sandwiched in between. Roman dodged several workers hurrying around the maze on his way to Akira's office.

He knocked.

"She's not there," a nearby secretary announced. "I saw her go into the lounge about five minutes ago."

He waved his thanks before heading in the direction she pointed out.

Roman heard the high-pitched voices before he reached the door.

"Everybody knows you're only doing this because you

Acquisitions

want Barry."

Akira answered, "I'm doing it because what Mr. Johnson did to me is wrong."

As Roman neared the threshold, he could see three woman circling Akira. The tall, leggy blonde led the pack.

"No matter what you do," the blonde's finger jabbed at Akira's nose, "you won't have Barry. Get a grip. He doesn't want a pork chop like you."

Roman stepped into the room loudly announcing his presence. "What's going on here?"

The two of the three shrank back. The blonde placed her hand on her hips as if having a perfect figure granted her certain rights.

Akira stood silent. Her honey-dipped complexion, drained. She held her head high, maintaining the outward appearance of indestructible strength, but Roman could read the trepidation in her eyes.

He moved next to her. "Are you alright?"

She nodded her answer.

"Why don't you ladies go back to work? I need to speak to Ms. Reed."

The tall blonde snapped around, flipping her hair in a halo around her head. The other two women silently followed.

"Who are they?" Roman asked once they were alone.

"That was Candace and her girl groupies."

Roman remembered the name but couldn't connect it to the investigation.

"Giving you a hard time?"

Still distracted by whatever transpired between her and the three women, Akira didn't hear his question.

"Let's go back to your office." Roman placed his hand in the small of her back and nudged her in the right direction.

Once inside her office, he closed the door. "Who is Candace, and what did she say to make you upset?"

Akira snatched the top drawer of her file cabinet open and began leafing through it. Her fingers trembled as she fumbled for the file she needed. "It doesn't matter." She yanked the file bringing up several more with it. The files flew out, spilling their contents to the floor. He watched as she dropped to her knees and groped at the papers creating a heap of crumpled documents.

He tentatively stepped forward. "Akira?"

"What?" she snapped.

"It does matter," he replied softly as he watched her disintegrate before his eyes.

"It doesn't matter because everyone around here is treating me the same way." She dropped back on her haunches. "They're all acting like I'm the one who's wrong." She took a swipe at the paper mound before falling forward with her face in her hands.

Muffled sounds of distress wafted up to Roman. Seeing a tear roll down her cheek made him crumble. Without weighing consequences, his emotions leading the way, he dropped to his knees and pulled Akira's face into his chest. She fit perfectly—as if she belonged there and nowhere else. He stroked her hair and hushed her sobs.

Being in the position of power—being the pillar—was a new experience for Roman. His upbringing made him mild and passive. Since high school he dated domineering women that dictated the course of their relationship. Stroking Akira's hair, quieting her cries, made him feel every bit the Alpha male. His body tightened, as he grew hard against his thigh.

Akira dug deeper into his chest. "I'm not guilty. I didn't do anything wrong." Her arms grasped his waist as if she were drowning.

The fragmented pieces of their connection locked into jigsaw perfect placement. Forgetting his proper place in Akira's situation, Roman pressed his lips to the crown of her head.

Akira dragged in a long breath. Her head snapped up. She stared at him with narrowing eyes—unsure if what she had felt was real.

Roman released her abruptly, but reluctantly. At that fleet-

Acquisitions

ing moment, he didn't care about professional relationships or repercussions.

"I really lost it." Akira offered an apology as she scooted away from him.

"Understandably so." He stood, offering her his hand. She accepted, but released him quickly.

"I need to get out of here."

"I'll go with you," he blurted out. Seeing her eyes narrow in question again, he returned to business. "I have more questions for you."

"I can't now. Please."

Roman cleared his throat. There were other things he wanted to do with her right now. "I'd like to get this case wrapped up as soon as possible."

Akira appeared skeptical. She ignored the scattered papers and pulled her coat from the hook on the back of the door.

He watched her every movement with intimate interest. If he had met her in another place, another moment, they would already be lovers. After their first date of dinner and a movie he would have taken her home and ravished her. He would use the entire night to kiss, suckle, and lick every inch of her body. Slowly, meticulously, he would balance her breasts in his palms, pinching her nipples between his fingers. But before that—he would start slow, after all, they would have the entire night—he would devour her lips until she begged him to stop. He would make her scream his name through ragged breaths—

"Roman?"

He blinked, where had his mind taken him?

"I asked if we could meet another time?"

He rushed to help slip the coat over her shoulders. "The sooner we get it over with, the better."

Akira whirled around. She watched him questioningly. Feeling assured she had misinterpreted the closeness of his body to hers, she agreed. "I'll call your secretary in the morning and ask her to schedule the appointment."

Chapter 5

"I keep asking, who in the world believes that Barry would want a pork chop like her when he has me?" Candace whispered loud enough for Akira to overhear.

The small group of women gathered around Candace's chair moaned their agreement. Akira retained her dignity as she moved to the only vacant seat at the table.

She'd been stressed over attending the monthly sales meeting since the scene in the lounge. Candace and her cronies ambushed her, spouting off about how jealousy over Mr. Johnson was the reason she had filed the complaint. If not for Roman rescuing her, the exchange would have gotten ugly. She could only take so much of Candace before she snapped.

If she hadn't snapped already. She could have sworn that Roman Miller kissed her as she sat in a heap on her office floor sniffling. She smelled his winter freshness when he bundled her into his chest. She could have stayed there forever. His hard arms had pulled her into his protective circle, and a second later she felt him lean in and kiss her. Or she wanted that closeness so badly she had imagined it. The stoic Mr. Miller would never kiss a woman who filed a sexual harassment

Acquisitions

claim he was investigating.

With every interview Roman conducted, the intensity of the whispering grew. People—who invited Akira to lunch in the past—avoided her. Those who never cared for her substantiated their opinions by pointing out what she was trying to do to "poor Mr. Johnson". The more time that passed, the more Akira wished she could recant her complaint.

Danisha acknowledged Akira by making room for her to sit down.

"Are they making all the telemarketers attend the sales meetings now?" Akira asked Danisha in an attempt to drown out Candace's vicious whispering.

"Yes." Danisha flicked a stray eyelash from her cheek. "Mr. Johnson says it'll help to make us more proficient if we observe all the different roles here at Greico."

Akira took a silent survey of the people filling the room: Danisha was the only telemarketer. *No,* she tucked her suspicions away. *Mr. Johnson wouldn't be that blatant and Danisha couldn't be that naive.*

Akira ignored the stares as Candace pointed in her direction. Her anger was no surprise; she'd surely take Mr. Johnson's side in this. The sales team knew that Candace and Mr. Johnson were seeing each other. Candace—a leggy, strawberry blond that stood inches above his head—could have had almost any man in the company she desired. It didn't take much to understand her attraction. Mr. Johnson's power and bank account made him "tolerable" Candace often snickered in the lunchroom.

While Mr. Johnson tried to keep their relationship a secret, Candace bragged about it often. Where they went and what piece of jewelry he bought her—their private life became common knowledge over ham and cheese sandwiches during the lunch hour.

Akira should have predicted the response of the crowd gathered around Candace, too. No one advanced on Mr. Johnson's team without his endorsement. No one could apply for a promotion within Greico without a supervisor's recommendation. Candace being his girlfriend, the crowd needed to side with her to protect the future of their own employment.

Akira wondered what would happen if Mr. Johnson's superiors learned about his exploits with Candace. As the manager of the sales team, fraternizing with his charges would be frowned upon. The company feared it would open them up to litigations citing favoritism in assigning lucrative accounts.

Akira doubted that anyone would believe her if she told what she knew about Candace and Mr. Johnson. Candace sure wouldn't corroborate her story. Mr. Johnson would call her jealous. Looking around the room, she couldn't see anyone who would back her up.

At this point, Akira wanted out and away from the cliques at this branch office. She doubted that things would get better when Roman substantiated her charges against Mr. Johnson. She had been working the western suburbs of Detroit for over a year and had made considerable progress there. When the branch manager announced his retirement, she immediately put in her request for consideration for the promotion. Transferring there would be the solution to all her newfound problems.

Until that night in Mr. Johnson's office, Akira believed she had a good chance of getting it.

On cue, Mr. Johnson slithered into the room. "I hate these monthly meetings as much as all of you do, so I'll be brief."

Everyone took their seats as Mr. Johnson slapped packets on the table and jotted numbers on the white-erase board.

"The numbers on the board reflect a slight drop in sales this month. Check your individual accounts as listed in the packet and act accordingly. It has come down from above that if you show another month of decreased sales, you will be in my office explaining. Then I'll be in New York by the end of the month explaining to the managers in corporate." He faced his subordinates with a grin that shifted his thick beard. "People, I hate New York this time of year."

Acquisitions

The group erupted in a dignified laugh, the kind required when being polite about your unfunny host's jokes.

As Mr. Johnson went on to give the history of a new account contract, people asked questions to clarify their understanding. How could everyone go on as if nothing was wrong? Didn't they see that Akira could hardly look up from her paper because the sight of Mr. Johnson made her sick? They considered him charming—one of the best supervisors to work under at Greico. There was another side to Mr. Johnson that Akira encountered out of the sight of others.

In order to maintain her composure, Akira focused her eyes on the report. She used her fingertip to scan the page for any new accounts that might have fallen in her territory. None. More commission if there had been one, less work to do since there wasn't. She drowned out Mr. Johnson's voice as she flipped to the next page of the packet. Buried in Candace's list of accounts was Community Resource Clinic, a new account inside of Akira's geographic territory. She grumbled. Danisha looked over at her.

A brazen move on Mr. Johnson's part: assigning her account to Candace's listing. How should she handle this?

Mr. Johnson dismissed his group, re-energized to sell to the world. "If there are no questions, I'm done."

Akira spoke up, "Mr. Johnson—"

"Barry." Mr. Lawton, the regional manager, breezed into the room interrupting her. He shook hands with Mr. Johnson while they went on about the predicted contenders at the next PGA tour. They laughed together, speaking in a code no one could understand.

Akira became furious at this intimidating display of friendship. They had to know that discussing their social lives in front of Mr. Johnson's subordinates made everyone uncomfortable.

The door swung open again. This time, Roman stepped into the room. He pressed a legal pad against his broad chest and carried his reading glasses in his hand. The expression on his face said he wanted to be any place other than the conference room—until he noticed her sitting at the far end of the table. Akira saw the hiccup in his posture and the flutter of his long lashes. They broke eye contact quickly—as if looking at each other was wrong. With this gesture, with the guilt that bubbled in her stomach, Akira knew that their earlier meetings had crossed the line of professionalism.

"Come on in, Roman." Mr. Lawton patted his shoulder. "Have a seat."

Akira didn't need to look up to know that Roman was watching her. She could feel his heat radiating in her direction. Heat thick enough to melt metal caressed her cheek. The same heat she felt when he embraced her; the heat that made her believe he had pressed his lips to the top of her head to comfort her as she cried over the scene in the lounge.

Akira glanced at Danisha. Danisha dragged her eyes from Akira to Roman. She had noticed it, too.

Akira kept her eyes down. If rumor spread that she was after the attorney investigating her sexual harassment case, she'd be ruined. Wait. She isn't after Roman Miller. They had spent time together when she was at her lowest and built a positive rapport with each other. Nothing more.

The happiness Mr. Lawton greeted Mr. Johnson with quickly disappeared as he disclosed the reason for his presence. "Greico Enterprises has developed a drug formula that would put the company on the forefront of pharmaceutical research."

Mr. Johnson sat forward in his seat, riveted to Mr. Lawton's every word. Candace appeared captivated by the disclosure. If these two didn't know about Mr. Lawton's announcement beforehand, it must be big. Akira cleared images of Roman's perfect body from her mind and focused on Mr. Lawton's speech.

"This discovery could propel the company into the big leagues. We would be able to compete with the pharmaceutical companies that have entertainment budgets the size of our

Acquisitions

entire company's payroll."

Roman stopped scribbling on his legal pad. Their eyes met. Akira snapped her head away, catching Candace's perplexed glare.

Dignified and worldly, Mr. Lawton paced the length of the conference table, capturing the attention of the entire room. "Greico's scientists have developed a vaccine against HIV, the virus that causes AIDS. They were prepared to present it for testing within the next six months." He stopped pacing and examined each person at the table. "That formula has been stolen."

The sales group expressed their shock and disbelief. A vaccine against HIV? A cure for AIDS would not be far behind. This was big.

Akira didn't understand why Mr. Lawton wasted time giving them this information. He needed to scold security, hire investigators, and search high and low. This wasn't the first formula stolen between drug companies, but it was probably the biggest discovery made by a drug manufacturer since the polio vaccine.

Mr. Lawton wiped his forehead. "Unknown to most, the formula was being housed at this branch office."

Roman removed his reading glasses. Akira didn't like the apprehension that wrinkled his brow.

Mr. Lawton answered the obvious question everyone wanted to ask. "With the sensitivity surrounding the contents of the formula, corporate believed that it would be safer here. Separate from where we normally keep such information. This isn't an uncommon practice—tucking sensitive information away in the least likely place to be discovered."

Roman's attention had returned to Akira. He batted away his embarrassment and resumed scribbling on his pad. Candace's eyes were glued on her.

"Anyway," Mr. Lawton continued, "under the circumstances, security will be tighter. The police will question each and every one of you. Anything that you've witnessed out of the ordinary over the past several weeks should be reported, no matter how insignificant you may feel it is."

Mr. Johnson stepped up to Mr. Lawton. "Our sales staff is hardly ever in the office. We could narrow the list of people security needs to question if you know when the formula was stolen."

Lawton nodded. "November ninth."

All the blood drained from Akira's face. Her fingertips became icy cold. Mr. Lawton continued to ramble, but his words were lost on her.

As she recalled the night Mr. Johnson dropped to the floor and slathered his tongue across her pantyhose, she remembered the noises in the outer office, which had never been explained. She had assumed she heard Mr. Johnson searching the cubicles to make sure they were alone before he made his move. Now she couldn't be sure. Mr. Johnson wouldn't steal from the company. Would he? Before that night, though, she wouldn't have believed he would try to force her to sleep with him.

An ominous feeling of dread cloaked Akira's shoulders. She looked from suspect to suspect, searching for those who had an opportunity to steal the formula other than Mr. Johnson. She could find only one. Herself. Her heart raced. She couldn't breathe. Her desperate gaze fell on Roman Miller. She needed his assurance that he would be her all. He wore a scrunched expression, inhaling the same rotten stench of foul play that filled her nostrils.

***

Roman joined Mr. Lawton in Johnson's office. He should have taken action right away. With the announcement of the stolen formula, he had to move now before this became a spider web of accusations. He didn't like the way Akira's eyes glazed over at the sales meeting. She could see it too—she made the perfect scapegoat.

Roman closed the door behind him, shutting out the noise of the outer office. He rarely had interaction with the regional

Acquisitions

vice president, and when he did, it usually involved the disciplinary action of an employee. He took a seat next to Mr. Lawton, eyeing him as he talked about the number of hours he spent playing golf with Johnson. The unprofessional nature of their relationship made it easy to see how Akira believed in a conspiracy to cover up her complaint.

Mr. Johnson rambled on about putting irons. As Roman listened to the Tiger Woods of Greico Enterprises brag about his golfing accomplishments, he surveyed the room. Akira had described it in her complaint with vivid detail. A vision of the greasy-looking Mr. Johnson on the floor between Akira's legs rattled Roman. The uneasiness made him want to get out of the office as quickly as his business would allow.

Lawton's tone made an abrupt change. "Corporate is asking how something like this happened on my watch."

Johnson pulled up close to his desk. A short man, he looked like a boy at his father's place of work. "Maybe if corporate had told me the formula was here, I could have put special security measures in place."

"I didn't even know." Lawton tugged at his tie. "I knew it was at one of my branch offices, that's all. If I had known, I would have told you. Roman, I want you on top of this. And Barry, the police and security have full run of this office until that formula is found."

"Of course."

Roman noticed Mr. Lawton had eliminated Johnson as a suspect. The theft happened November ninth—the evening of the sexual harassment incident. Logically, Johnson should be a suspect.

"Mr. Lawton," Roman said, "my area of expertise is sexual harassment." *How did the stolen formula become his problem?*

"This is unprecedented. I want everyone on this. You handle any touchy legal aspects that come up with questioning the employees. The last thing I need is another discriminatory complaint on my hands in the middle of this."

Mr. Johnson's eyes darted away from Mr. Lawton.

Roman silently questioned Mr. Lawton's reasoning. Including all the corporate attorneys, Greico employed a fleet of lawyers in all areas of specialty. The investigation would consume Roman's already crowded days. What made Lawton feel *he* could best handle the case?

Mr. Lawton's posture slackened. "Roman, there is something else you needed to talk about."

"Mr. Johnson, I'll need to interview you regarding Ms. Reed's complaint."

"Of course," Johnson readily agreed. "How about we do this over lunch today?"

"I'd rather conduct the interview in my office."

Johnson looked across his desk to Mr. Lawton, soliciting his help.

Roman noted the body language between Johnson and Lawton before he continued. "Also, we need to make changes with your team."

"I don't understand." Mr. Johnson's fingers massaged his bearded chin.

"Until a determination is made, you shouldn't have supervisory authority over Ms. Reed. We must transfer you to another team, or place you on a non-disciplinary leave—with pay, of course."

"Wait one minute," Johnson bolted out of his chair. "I haven't done anything wrong. Your investigation will show that. Why am I being punished?"

"This is all standard procedure."

Johnson looked to Mr. Lawton, who picked up the wordless cue perfectly. "Roman, there's no need to make this a hostile situation."

"No, sir, you're right. I only want everything done by the book. There can be no questioning the integrity of my investigation. I'm sure you both appreciate that."

He felt like a hypocrite when he remembered his encounters with Akira thus far. But that was different. Right? She

Acquisitions

had been upset and he had to calm her down. Right? He struggled with his conscience and his desire to seek Akira out at that moment. The earlier sales meeting probably had her reeling.

Mr. Lawton made a hand motion that told Johnson to sit down.

"Why can't Akira be placed on leave or transferred?" Johnson demanded as he returned to his chair.

Roman explained. "Transferring the complainant is viewed as unlawful retaliation. The EEOC—Equal Employment Opportunity Commission—suggests moving the alleged violator. In this case, that's you."

"This never happened before," Mr. Johnson grumbled.

Lawton shot him a look, and Roman didn't miss a beat.

"Roman," Mr. Lawton took over, "moving Barry will also be unfair. To place him on another team directly affects his earning potential since a large part of his salary is based on commission. I have another solution. Akira Reed will report directly to me with any concerns until this is over. The sales associates work independently; the only guidance she may need will be with mandatory sales reports."

"Ms. Reed has applied for a promotion—"

"No promotions will be considered until this case is put to rest." Mr. Lawton assured Roman.

"That sounds agreeable. However, if Ms. Reed feels intimidated by this decision, we'll have to reconsider."

"Fair enough." Mr. Lawton smiled in a way Roman could not interpret.

Why did Roman get the feeling that they were trying to hide something? He could understand how Lawton and Johnson may have formed a friendship—they traveled together to sales meetings and went out on joint calls all the time. The question became, were they close enough that Lawton would cover up Johnson's alleged unethical behavior?

The suave Mr. Lawton continued since Johnson seemed to be at a loss for words. "We want this matter cleared up as quickly as possible, too—in a manner that leaves no lingering questions."

Johnson placed a finger inside his shirt collar and tugged. A guilty signal if ever Roman had seen one.

Chapter 6

"What does this whole HIV formula mess have to do with you?" Lara placed the Scrabble board in front of Akira on the dining room table.

Akira needed the support of her best friend now more than ever. "Nothing, yet, but I can see the wheels turning in Mr. Johnson's head. The formula disappeared the same night he propositioned me. He'll try to connect me to it somehow to keep the suspicion off of him."

"Do you think he did it?" Lara left the rest of the preparation of the game to Akira while she poured two glasses of white wine.

Absentmindedly, Akira flipped the wooden tiles. "I can't see it. Then again, I didn't see him coming on to me either."

"What kind of business are they running down there at Greico?"

Four rounds of play had passed before Akira broached another sensitive subject. "I have my interview with Roman in two days."

"Who's Roman?" Lara jotted down her score.

"Mr. Miller. The lawyer investigating my sexual harassment case."

Lara scratched her pudgy cheek. Slim and trim before her break up with Clifton, she gained over fifty pounds after their split. They rarely discussed the sticky details. Only recently had Lara voiced the obvious and shared the root of her sudden weight gain. She now realized the impact on her self-esteem and the potential health dangers and began treatment with a physician. Two months into treatment, Akira noticed a positive change in her friend's eating habits.

"Roman, huh?" Lara peered across the table. "Since when did you get on a first name basis?"

"Don't even start down that road."

"Yeah, how dare me? I forgot you don't date anymore since Eric called you an embarrassment."

"That stings."

"I've been called cruel. I like to think of myself as brutally honest. As much as I'd love to hear you give me the steamy details of how Mr. Miller became Roman, I'm not worried because I know you don't have any interest in dating anymore."

Akira placed her tiles horizontally on the board and calculated her points.

Lara laughed. "Or maybe I should be. What's going on? No rebuttal? Do you have something going on with this attorney?" Lara slapped the table causing it to vibrate. "You do! Isn't that unethical? He's investigating your complaint."

"Relax. I don't have anything going on with him."

"Liar! You're pinking up. Spill."

Akira rubbed the warmth of her cheeks. "It's not like that."

"Like what?" Lara leaned forward, waiting for the details.

Akira twisted a stray strand of auburn hair around her pinky. "Okay, he's fine. Fine-fine. And compassionate. And intelligent."

"Uh-huh."

"Nothing's going on." Akira sipped from her wine glass.

Acquisitions

"I don't think."

"You better give me the details. I'll help you sort it out."

Akira laughed with her friend. "Dr. Lara."

"Tell me your troubles."

Akira fell into a dreamy trance as she recited the memories of her encounters with Roman. Her body tingled in intimate places as she relived the experience. A new type of vulnerability swept over her. She felt open, desperate for his touch. She needed to be alone with him, in a dark room, to give him the chance to extinguish the fire he had built in her cold fireplace. As much as she denied it, she connected with him over lunch, and they kept clicking every time they were in the same room. Ending her story with the questionable kiss, she looked up to see Lara staring blankly across the table.

"Akira, the attorney investigating your *sexual harassment* complaint kissed you?"

Lara's expression of incredulity made Akira feel stupid. "Maybe. I mean it seemed like it at the time. I had a total mental breakdown, and he was there. He gave me a friendly hug to console me."

"And you enjoyed it? Him holding you? Giving you a little comfort?"

"Yes—no. Of course not." *She wanted more.* "It's not the end of the world, Lara."

"You did enjoy it, and you do have a thing for him. If you didn't, you'd see it's the end of the world. How can he be impartial if he's hugging the woman who filed the charges? Dawg, he's investigating an incident of *sexual harassment*— how could he hug you?"

"You're making it sound like he molested me. In the heat of the moment I can understand his mistake."

"Not me."

"You weren't there." Akira pulled replacement tiles and set them in front of her. "Roman was trying to calm me down. We connected, and he comforted me."

"Girlfriend, both of our past relationships ended badly.

We were both hurt. Neither of us handled it very well—I overeat, you don't date anymore—but we have to be smart the next time around. Otherwise the pain of the past taught us nothing and we'll repeat the same mistakes."

"Relationships?" Akira laughed. Her attempt to be non-chalant was unconvincing.

"This guy, Roman, how do you feel about him?"

"He's nice."

Lara shook her head. "That's not what I asked. Honestly, how do you feel about him? Listening to you, watching your eyes light up when you talk about him—I'm beginning to wonder if he's the problem. Or are you coming on to him?"

"I'm not coming on to him."

Lara watched her friend with brutally honest doubt.

"Okay, I'm attracted to him. But I know the implications. I know that I can't get involved with him. Falling for the lawyer looking into my sexual harassment complaint could severely damage my credibility. Besides, it sends the wrong signal. Maybe in another place or time, I could pursue it, but under the circumstances, I'll have to be content with admiring him from afar."

"The problem with matters of the heart, Akira, is that the heart wants what it wants, and it always finds a way to get it. Right or wrong, emotions are powerful and many kingdoms have been destroyed because of love, lust and jealousy."

"Tell me more, Plato," she said sarcastically.

"How many times have we sat up watching talk shows astounded by the women professing a great devotion to some jerk? What about people involved in affairs? They know it's wrong, but their hearts won't allow them to walk away. Like picking a scab, the pain ain't all that bad if it brings you a little bit of pleasure."

"I don't know if I like you comparing my situation to picking a scab."

Lara took her turn at the game.

"You have one thing right, though," Akira admitted. "No

Acquisitions

matter how wrong my brain tells me it is, I am attracted to Roman. The temptation is there."

"You've stepped close to the line, but you haven't crossed it. If the case had been settled, I'd think differently; but it's not. I don't know how you're going to do it, but you should stay as far away from Roman Miller as possible."

Akira denied the sensation moving through her heart. "It's only business between Roman and me. He'll finish his investigation and that'll be it."

And she would die if she couldn't see him again.

Chapter 7

For the record, Roman announced his name, the date and the time into the tape recorder that sat on his desk squarely between him and Johnson. For voice identification, Roman asked Johnson to do the same.

Johnson opened the buttons of his brown suit, tugged at his tie, and recited the requested information.

Roman pressed back against his chair, studying Mr. Johnson's mannerisms. "You've had the chance to read Ms. Reed's complaint; tell me what occurred the night of November ninth in your own words."

Johnson cleared his throat and sat forward, wanting the recorder to capture every word. "I stepped off the elevator onto the sixth floor, and Ms. Reed bumped into me. I asked her what she was doing in the office that late at night. She said she had to finish up a project. I hadn't assigned any projects. I questioned her about the details of what she was working on. She became unglued, rattled. That's when she pushed up close to me, pressing her breasts against my chest, and asked me if she could have a drink in my office. I'm a man, and Ms. Reed is attractive." Johnson paused. "I went against my better judg-

Acquisitions

ment and invited her into my office. We both had a drink. When I started asking her about the project again, she started flirting with me. Finally, my guilt kicked in and I confessed to her that I was involved with Candace. She got made because I shunned her and huffed off. I thought she would be too embarrassed to say anything about it. I didn't mention it either. I'm her supervisor, and I wanted her to be comfortable in the workplace."

Johnson patted his shiny forehead. Roman offered a drink of water.

Johnson sipped from the glass under Roman's intense scrutiny. "You don't know how surprised I was to learn she had filed a complaint against me."

What a crock of bull, Roman thought. Obviously, Johnson had been rehearsing. His entire statement sounded canned.

"Why were *you* in the office at that time of night, Mr. Johnson?"

He ran a hand over his beard. "I returned to pick up the figures I needed to prepare a sales projection report for Mr. Lawton due the following Monday."

"You said Ms. Reed seemed 'rattled'. Why do you think that was?"

"I can only guess, but after learning about the missing formula, I have to wonder if the two are linked."

Roman's head shot up in astonishment. He surveyed Johnson over the top of a twisted metal piece of art his grandmother had given him at his law school graduation. Johnson's eyes darted around the office, studying any artifact in the room to avoid Roman's stare. Could Johnson really believe what he accused Akira of? Or was he trying to save himself by throwing suspicion onto her about an unrelated matter? That would be too low for anyone to do. Falsely accusing Akira of stealing could lead to serious criminal charges.

Roman inquired further, "Did Ms. Reed say anything to you about hearing an intruder on the floor?"

"Never."

Roman scribbled Johnson's one-word reply and also noted the bead of perspiration that trickled down his left temple. "Why would Ms. Reed lie about all of this?"

Johnson released a subtle breath, his body relaxed slightly. "You know how women are when they want a man. She asked if I would like to go out with her. I told her no—I reminded her about Candace." Completely comfortable, he sat back as he continued. "She asked me to take her out of town for a long weekend, away from Candace."

Roman wished he could draw a picture of the smug smile revealing itself as Johnson's overbearing self-confidence came shining through.

"There's one more unusual thing," Johnson offered. "She clutched a purse to her the entire time we were talking."

"A purse? Why is that unusual?"

"She never let it go. Normally, a woman might put her purse down in the chair next to her or on top of the desk, but she never let it go. In light of what happened that night, it seems strange to me when I think back on it."

Behind Johnson's eyes, Roman could see the hopeful glimmer of a man who thought he had outsmarted his opponent.

Roman took down a list of other employees that Johnson felt might have relevant information about the harassment and the stolen formula. "I think I have everything that I need. I'll be speaking with Ms. Reed this afternoon. Is there anything else you'd like to add?"

"I have to reiterate that I have no idea why Ms. Reed is doing this. If it's a fatal attraction, I hope she gets the help she needs. I hold no grudge against her. I want this whole thing to end and my name to be cleared."

Canned. Rehearsed. Well prepared to deceive.

Roman stood behind his desk. He didn't shut off the recorder. From what he had observed, he thought it wiser to keep it running. He stretched out his hand, "Thank you for coming. I should have this resolved quickly."

Acquisitions

Johnson accepted his hand and hurried out of the office.

Roman checked the time—he had a few minutes before the next witness interview. He dialed the security office. "This is Mr. Miller in the legal department."

"Yes, sir?" The man's voice snapped to attention, displaying an attitude of hard work and attentiveness.

"I'd like to have the surveillance video from November ninth sent to my office as soon as possible."

"November ninth?"

Roman heard the pages of a book flipping rapidly.

"Here it is," the voice on the other end of the line said. "I thought that date sounded familiar to me. That tape has already been signed out."

"By who?" Roman's mind conjured up images of an elaborate scheme to clear Mr. Johnson's name.

"The management team from the corporate office. That's the night the formula was stolen. I don't expect to ever see it until after the thief is caught, and then it'll probably be used as evidence."

Roman hummed sounds of understanding while his mind raced to find another means to gain access to the video. Seeing the tape might uncover what really happened the night of Akira's incident.

"Don't you have a back-up in case the original tape gets lost or destroyed?"

"I've never been involved in anything like this before. I'll ask. Hold on." The security policeman pushed the button that started the easy-listening music.

This case had become more complicated than Roman had ever imagined it would. All the witnesses he had spoken to were vague at best, champions of Johnson at worst. Suspicion by Johnson now connected Akira to the stolen formula. He also couldn't ignore the fact that every minute he spent working on the case, his head filled with images of Akira that easily transitioned into sensuous daydreams.

The security officer returned to the line. "Mr. Miller, I

spoke to my supervisor and you're right. The tapes are backed up on disk in the main computer system. He says that if you want to view the film, you need to come down here. He says ask for him and he'll help you out."

Finally, the break he needed.

***

"I'm sorry, Mr. Miller." Danisha Marshall apologized as she stood and walked toward the door. "I haven't worked at Greico that long."

Roman looked up, exhausted and disappointed by the lack of information Danisha could supply. Although she was far from being unattractive, what caught Roman's attention was the tantalizing features of her frame. Thick curves and full breasts seemed to be the common denominator of the women Johnson hired. If Danisha were his daughter, he would never let her out of his sight. Men of all ages dreamt of taking advantage of a woman like her.

"If you think of anything that might be relevant, give me a call."

"I will." She stepped lightly through the door, closing it behind her.

Roman straightened up his desk. One last interview and his long, tedious day would end. Danisha's interview had gone smoother than the others over the past couple of days; she, at least, hadn't trashed Akira's name.

As he packed his briefcase and mentally reviewed the statements, he reminded himself to stay neutral. Look at the facts objectively. Emotion could only be used to make a determination on credibility issues. In a case like this, he needed to be cautious. With every witness that appeared in his office came the prayer that they would have testimony to support Akira's claim.

"Candace—" Columbia jumped aside as the tall blond brushed past her.

"Thank you," Roman said before Columbia had a chance to give Candace a piece of her mind.

Acquisitions

Candace strolled to the sofa. She positioned her buttocks toward the edge of the sofa and reclined, placing her arms out along the back, her breasts jutting forward. She crossed her long legs and wet her pink lips.

Roman knew where this was going, and he planned to put a stop to it immediately. "Candace, I called you here hoping you might have information in the Reed versus Johnson case."

"How lucky for you."

Candace spent her first twenty minutes in Roman's office blatantly trying to get him to notice how open she would be to his advances while trashing Akira's work and personal reputation. She then spent the next ten minutes, until Roman decided to put an end to her madness, praising the saint-like qualities of Mr. Barry Johnson.

He knew from the encounter in the lounge, and Johnson's own admission of a relationship, where Candace's alliances were rooted. The loyalty of Johnson's employees had become a charade around the time he finished with the fourth witness, but he was obligated to see it through. Worker after worker came into his office and repeated almost to the letter what the previous worker had said. "Akira is loose and brags about all the men she's seeing." Or, "Everybody knows she has a crush on Mr. Johnson." No one could give any direct evidence to substantiate these claims; they had heard it from someone who heard it from someone over lunch.

Mr. Johnson, on the other hand, was described as the best boss in the world: loyal and kind to his employees. Patient and understanding with complaining clients. One after another, witnesses related incidences of Johnson taking the chance of bending a rule to make their lives easier.

Roman had no doubt these things had occurred. It accounted for their loyalty to him now. Even women who filed complaints in the past recited the dribble. He imagined the women would be embarrassed and their jobs jeopardized if they admitted to succumbing to Johnson's advances.

And if Johnson ended up being punished with suspension,

or let go by the company, what type of boss would the sales team have then? Akira would be responsible for any negative fall-out. Cushy sales positions with large expense accounts and flexible hours were hard to come by in this competitive market. What would they do if Johnson decided to increase their quotas?

"Candace," Roman interrupted her tale of saving an emotionally crippled employee. "Have you ever noticed any unusual behavior directed to Ms. Reed from Mr. Johnson? Ever seen or heard anything inappropriate transpire between them?"

"Of course not. Don't be ridiculous."

"Do you have anything else you'd like to offer?"

Candace uncrossed her long legs and leaned forward as if to share a secret. "It's simple; she has a thing for him. Barry is a handsome, wealthy and powerful man."

"I see." Roman put his pen down, lining it up with the upper edge of his legal pad. "There couldn't be any truth to what she has said?"

"None."

"No other employees have suggested that Mr. Johnson may have said or done something they found offensive?" He asked the same question to every employee that worked on the sixth floor, and they all had the same answer.

"No. Barry is a good man. I've never seen him do or say anything that wasn't supportive of us all."

Chapter 8

For the record, Roman announced his name, the date and the time into the tape recorder that sat on his desk squarely between him and Akira. For voice identification, Roman asked her to do the same.

He'd reviewed who, what, when, where and how of the night in question. Not wanting to upset Akira, he had started with the easy questions. He listened intently while studying her body gestures, which proved to be much more of a pleasure than the examination of Johnson's squirming and sweating.

A picture of sophistication, Akira's straight-back posture hoisted her breasts, displaying a tantalizing hint of cleavage. She wore a touch of make-up that highlighted her cheeks and made her lips glisten. The auburn tips of her hair were curled under. She crossed her thick thighs and rested her hands, one on top of the other, in her lap.

Roman fought to concentrate on Akira's testimony, but his mind kept wandering to the curves of her legs.

Akira stopped abruptly. "This is very personal...is there someone else I could talk to?"

"If you intend to pursue this matter to its fullest, you

should become accustomed to telling your version of the events. It may become necessary for you to repeat this story several times to many of my colleagues." His face displayed understanding, his voice tenderness. He sat forward and poured her a glass of water from the pitcher sitting at the corner of his desk. "Please, take your time."

Akira searched his face. She wouldn't find the sarcasm or facetious attitude that had been there before.

Akira thanked him for the water. Hurrying to get past the embarrassing encounter with Mr. Johnson, she completed her story at a rapid pace.

"A few more questions." Roman removed his square reading glasses and placed them atop the desk.

She lifted her lips in a smile that was supposed to be friendly, but failed miserably.

"Did you say or do anything that might lead Mr. Johnson to believe that you're attracted to him?"

"No, nothing." She spat out, offended. As if her tone counted against her, she tried to relax the tension in her voice. "You have to investigate that possibility, right?"

"Right." Avoiding the innocence of her eyes, he checked his notes. The words "fatal attraction" jumped up from the notepad. "Have you ever asked Mr. Johnson out for personal reasons?"

Her face contorted with a look of disgust. "No."

"Other than on November ninth, has he ever asked you out for personal reasons?"

Her dark eyes dropped. She clutched her purse to her chest obstructing his view of her cleavage. "No."

Roman interlocked his fingers, watching her. What did she do to get a man's attention? Was she involved with anyone? If not, what kind of relationship was she looking for? In bed, was she timid or did she tell her man what she wants? Where to touch? How to touch?

Akira watched him, waiting.

Checking the inappropriateness of his thoughts, Roman

Acquisitions

resumed his questioning. "Tell me about the relationship you have with Mr. Johnson."

"The only relationship we have is a working relationship. He's my immediate supervisor, and I show him the respect that accompanies the position."

He planted his feet firmly on the floor. "What I'm trying to figure out is why Mr. Johnson approached you so strongly that night. Have there been any other incidents that led up to this?"

Akira's eyes moved around the room before resting on his. "There have been comments in the lounge. Remarks when I'm standing at the coffee island in the morning."

He picked up his pen and twisted it between his fingers. Jealous anger fluttered in his abdomen. "What kind of things did he say?"

She paused a moment. "Are you sure that there's not a woman I can talk to?"

Roman relaxed into the plush softness of his chair. "Take your time, Akira." He risked losing her to embarrassment. "Mr. Johnson had no trouble in describing his side of the story." *That should light her fire.*

She started slowly. "He's made several comments about the size of my breasts, other areas of my body."

"Such as?" Roman assured himself that he needed the information to complete his investigation.

"Once, when I was sitting on a stool helping a new tele-marketer learn the phones, he came up to me and whispered in my ear something about women sitting on stools and how it displayed—" she hesitated, "it gave him a view of certain 'juicy' female body parts."

She went on to repeat, with great difficulty, the many suggestive comments Mr. Johnson had made to her when they were alone.

Roman held up his hand to end her struggling. "I understand. Why didn't you report any of this to the EAL?"

"I thought I might be overly sensitive. I didn't want to

60

overreact."

Rubbing his weary eyes, "Did you tell *anyone* about these incidents?"

"Who would I tell?"

Exactly. Who would she tell? Mr. Johnson's superior and golf buddy, Mr. Lawton? Not if she wanted to be taken seriously.

Roman pushed away his personal disgust with what he had heard and regained his professional air. "Mr. Johnson stated in his testimony that you were upset when he found you in the office that evening. Were you?"

"Yes. I thought I heard someone moving around the outer office. And a light was on that I didn't remember being on when I came in. I was startled when I ran into Mr. Johnson."

Roman picked up his reading glasses and put them across the bridge of his nose. He noted her reply to his question.

Akira went on, adding an afterthought. "It's funny, I was actually glad to see him because I was scared. I never imagined he would..."

Roman looked up as her voice trailed off. She stared out the window.

"You had your purse with you that night?"

She looked puzzled by the question. "Yes."

"Did you take any work home with you?"

She paused to think. "I don't remember. After what happened, I ran out of Mr. Johnson's office as fast as I could."

Roman nodded his understanding. "Is there anyone else who might have relevant information about what happened that night?"

Akira shook her head.

"Please answer for the tape recorder."

Akira sat forward. "I don't think so."

Roman's eyes scanned the list of witnesses Johnson provided. "To your knowledge, has Mr. Johnson harassed anyone else?"

"I only know what I told you he said. That others in the

Acquisitions

company were going out with him in order to move up at Greico."

When asked, she denied having any physical evidence to back her claim.

Roman sat back in his chair, assessing Akira's demeanor. He was quickly tempted into assessing every curve of her body. His gaze lingered on her captivating eyes. "How would you like to see this situation resolved?"

Akira blinked, clearly surprised to be asked such a question. She smoothed her skirt, outlining her plush thighs. "Mr. Johnson can't get away with harassing anyone else. Whatever needs to be done to accomplish that will be fine with me."

Her answer showed the goodness of her nature.

Roman asked, "Is there anything else you would like to add?"

Akira shook her head. Their eyes met, and Roman could read her unspoken words. She wanted all this to be over. Like most victims, she only wanted vindication.

"That's all I need right now. Do you have any questions?"

"No." Akira shook her head, again trying to smile.

Roman recited the date and time into the recorder again before hitting the stop button.

Akira deflated. "I'm glad that's over. It is over, right?"

Roman removed his glasses. "I don't think I'll have to question you again."

"It's funny how you do that. When you're wearing your glasses, you're the picture of professionalism. When you remove them, you're a regular guy."

Roman grinned. "I'd like to think I'm a regular guy all the time."

"I didn't mean to insult you."

"I know." He stood and began packing away his desk. "It's late, I'll walk with you down to the garage."

Akira rose. "I'll be fine."

"I know you will," he flashed his dimples, "because I'll walk with you."

She slipped the strap of her purse onto her shoulder and patiently waited for him to finish up. Could she have stuffed the formula inside her purse, and when Mr. Johnson stumbled onto her theft, seduced him? And when that failed, could she have devised the sexual harassment plot to throw suspicion away from her?

Could this be the same woman who fell in a heap at his feet and cried under the pressure of her coworkers snub? Her innocence and need for protection seducing him to the point of merciless torture?

Could all these women be the same one that kept him awake—hard as steel—all through the night?

He glanced up to see Akira reading the plaques lining his wall. She stopped in front of his law degree.

Roman took in the thick thighs and plump backside from behind. No one was around to obstruct his view or hinder him taking an eyeful. Her attention was focused elsewhere. No one could judge him or his sensual thoughts but himself. Akira flipped her hair and a current ran through his gut. He felt his manhood snake down his thigh. Embarrassed by his adolescent thoughts, he grabbed his suit jacket and buttoned it over the tent in his pants. Lifting his briefcase, he joined her at the wall.

Near Akira, Roman could smell the heady fragrance of her perfume. "You smell good." He dipped his head closer. "What is that?"

"It's—" Akira turned around, pinning herself between the wall and his chest.

He didn't step back. He tried to get his feet to take one step backward, but he couldn't move. Common sense was no match for his healthy male libido. A silence blanketed the room, and Roman could hear the beat of his racing heart. The tick of the clock on his desk tocked as loud as Big Ben.

Akira parted her shiny red lips.

Kissable.

She could not be a thief, a liar, or a seductress.

63

Acquisitions

She was what he needed her to be: sweet, innocent, and in need—of him.

Akira moved sideways—out of his reach. "What was that?"

"What?"

"I heard a noise at the door."

Roman sat his briefcase at his feet and went to check it out. Columbia had left the door ajar. He pulled it completely open—a second too late—missing Candace step into the stairwell.

Chapter 9

Weeks after the start of Roman's investigation, dressed in a black full-length skirt with a deep split up the center back, matching hipster jacket and gray silk blouse, Akira felt certain she would accept the verdict humbly. She and Lara had spent most of the prior day finding her going-to-her-hearing suit.

Sheik but businesslike, confident but respectful, she entered the conference room. She chose to sit in the chair furthest from the door. Directly across from her sat Mr. Johnson. Mr. Lawton took the seat at Johnson's right flank. Columbia, Roman's secretary, sat to his left.

Roman entered the room last. Akira dropped her eyes from the dark brown suited body. The walnut shirt with its crisp collar accentuated the glow of his skin. From this distance, she felt only a breath away.

Roman apologized for an unrelated interview running long and took the only vacant seat, sandwiched between Columbia and Akira. Here the sweet-woodsy scent Akira had come to associate with Roman assaulted her, making her wish she could turn back the clock to the moment before she heard the noise outside his office door.

Acquisitions

The room remained silent as Roman opened his file folder. The hum of the heating unit whizzed on dutifully keeping the building warm. Mr. Johnson's face was shining under the sheen of perspiration. Cologne mixed with his body odor, making the fragrance all the more pungent. The scent sparked a vision of him kneeling on the floor pretending to retrieve a pen while his tongue assaulted her thigh.

"Columbia," Roman said, "please give everyone one of the packets."

She nodded and began to distribute a stack of legal documents. The picture of efficiency, she had had everyone sign a statement of attendance when they entered. The tape recorder was already running. More tapes were piled next to her in case she needed to make a change.

Akira's mind drifted to what she would do after the hearing. How would she celebrate? Lara had promised that they would have a low-calorie victory dinner at her place. After everything she had gone through to make Mr. Johnson accountable for his actions, she planned to celebrate. Wouldn't it be nice to be sitting in a darkened theatre watching a stage play with Roman Miller? *Way out of line*, Akira scolded herself. But maybe not. After his decision today, there would be no reason not to act on the building flames between them. She wanted to caress the fabric of his suit, explore what was hidden inside it. Her eyes drifted beyond the edge of the table and she received assurance that they were connecting with the puckering of his zipper.

Roman acknowledged everyone at the meeting. Looking directly at Akira he said, "This is an internal investigation. It has no bearing on charges either party choose to pursue outside of this investigation."

He followed all formalities as he outlined the procedures used during his investigation. Next, he gave an overview of what he had learned from the witnesses and job performance analyses.

Mr. Johnson smiled smugly at Mr. Lawton.

Lawton acknowledged him with a nod.

With all the formalities out of the way, Roman rendered his findings, not allowing a hint of emotion to seep into his voice. "I do not believe that Ms. Reed's allegations are without merit, but at this time, I find no independent evidence that any inappropriate behavior has taken place on Mr. Johnson's part."

Akira was sucked into a dark vacuum. She could hear Roman's words and Mr. Johnson's audible sigh of relief, but they didn't make sense to her. The hum of the heating system buzzed like a bee filling her ear canal. Her hands gripped the side of her chair. The repugnant taste of bile coated her tongue when Mr. Johnson's cologne came across the table in fresh waves. Her toes curled at the sight of his superior grin. She tried to regain focus as Roman raced on with the rest of his rehearsed speech.

"I had to judge the complaint based on the account of events by the parties involved, and the character assessments of their coworkers. There is no substantial evidence that will allow me to recommend punishment for Mr. Johnson. By the same token, as I have stated, I do not believe the allegations are completely false, and therefore, Ms. Reed should suffer no repercussions for filing the complaint."

Mr. Lawton suppressed his joy with the verdict and assumed a leadership stance. "Mr. Johnson, in the future you would be well served to conduct all of your business with your employees during regular business hours. Also, refer employees to the Employee Assistance Line if they are in need of counsel." He shifted toward Akira. "Ms. Reed, I would like to make you aware that we do have counseling services, free of charge, if you should desire to utilize them."

With that final assault to Akira's pride and self-respect, everyone began to gather their belongings. She snatched up the report, leaving as quickly as she could, careful not to reveal her devastation. She hurried to her office to retrieve her purse

Acquisitions

and briefcase. She had to get out of the office before curious coworkers questioned her about the outcome of the hearing. Her first thought was to flee the building, but she refused to act guilty or ashamed. She had done nothing wrong; she wouldn't run away in disgrace.

Akira grabbed her briefcase, and as she escaped to the elevator, heard a collective cheer rise from the employee lounge. When she hurried past the doorway, she saw Mr. Johnson standing at the front of the room making an announcement to his loyal employees. He bowed his head humbly and rocked back on the balls of his feet.

Danisha, who she considered her comrade, stood at the edge of the crowd.

Candace stood near the door snickering with her cronies. "Did you see that suit Akira wore today? Where did she think she was going?"

Appalled, Akira tucked her purse under her arm as she hurried past the lounge and stepped onto the elevator. The elevator had become her safe haven over the past weeks. She wanted to drop all pretenses and shed a tear of frustration once safely inside, but several people waited impatiently for her to step on and make her selection of a floor. In her haste, she didn't notice that the elevator was traveling up and not down to the lobby. When the doors opened at the floor of Roman Miller's office, Akira stepped off and marched down the corridor.

The floor appeared deserted except for a few lawyers trying to complete their work and start their Thanksgiving holiday. Akira ignored the attorneys, and they didn't notice her. She gripped the doorknob of Roman's office and pushed the door open with enough force for it to swing back against the wall.

"I'm sorry, Mr. Miller." Columbia stood helpless behind her.

Roman stood tall behind his desk completing the ritual: getting ready for the break. It angered Akira that everyone could go on with their lives and enjoy their holiday, ignoring the fact that her life and career were crumbling.

"It's okay, Columbia." Roman stepped from behind his desk and approached Akira. She stood holding her angry stance in the middle of his office. "Have a nice holiday," he dismissed Columbia without taking his eyes off Akira.

"How dare you?" Akira kept her voice low and her tone even. "You befriended me." *Flirted and made me feel something for you.* "All the while, you were in cahoots with Mr. Johnson and Mr. Lawton."

Roman threw his hands up in defense. "Wait a minute. I explained my findings. I conducted a fair investigation. There wasn't enough evidence to find that Mr. Johnson had done anything wrong."

"I told the truth. Isn't that enough evidence?" She had remained civil throughout the entire investigative process, although everyone else had shunned her and prejudged her to be the guilty party. Now she was angry, and someone would have to take the wrath of her perceived betrayal.

She stepped closer and buried the blunt tip of her finger in Roman's massive chest with every word. "Mr. Johnson lied, and you know it. What's worse is that you let him get away with it."

"I understand you're angry," he matched the volume of her voice, "but I had to be as fair to him as I was with you. I resent the fact that you're accusing me of anything otherwise."

Akira's anger dissipated, but resurfaced as defeat. She dropped her arms to her side. Mental exhaustion relaxed her body unwillingly. Mr. Johnson had won again, controlling another area of her life. Her voice dragged with sadness. "You know what? I give up. I tried to do the right thing, but it only came back to kick me in the face. Maybe I shouldn't have said anything in the first place. Maybe I should have let him continue with the sexist remarks, the accidental bumping and the insulting references to my body. At least then I would be able to work without everyone sneering at me."

Acquisitions

She lifted her head and straightened her back for one last show of confidence before turning to walk away.

Roman watched as a confusing mixture of emotions washed over her face. The thought that he may be responsible for her pain made him shudder. He had made the victim a victim a second time while the guilty party celebrated his unjust triumph.

Akira wouldn't recover from this assault. No matter how strong she pretended to be, he could see all of the misery filing the complaint had caused. He wanted to pull her body into his and protect her. Her eyes searched his face for an answer—as if he could recall the meeting, deem it a mistake and recommend that Mr. Johnson be fired on the spot. He couldn't.

But there was something he could do to ease her pain, relieve the burden she had been carrying, show his support. There was something he could do to ease his own guilt, relieve his burden. Wanting her, but knowing it's wrong to have her. Remaining professional, but feeling desperate he might miss the opportunity of a lifetime.

Roman boldly grasped the sides of Akira's face and lifted her head up to him. He stepped in and bent slightly at the knees. Too important to him, too risky to mess up—he wanted perfection. Akira looked up at him with a glimmer of longing. The shiny red lips screamed, "kissable." Moving his face to hers, he pressed their lips together—gently, barely making contact.

The kiss tasted sweet. Her lips were slippery with cherry flavoring. He wanted to lick up the sweet zest, savor it the entire day. He had been anticipating what her mouth would feel like for too long. His lashes dipped as his thumbs caressed the softness of her skin.

Eyes wide, Akira stepped back.

He hadn't prepared himself with what to say in that moment of awkwardness, but as an attorney, thinking fast on his feet was his livelihood. "Akira—"

She raised her hand and swept it across his jaw with such force that his head snapped to the left. "I see how it works now. You think I came on to Mr. Johnson, and if he can have some why not you?"

"No!" *No,* she was completely off track. This had been a long time coming. Didn't she feel it at the café or in her office or in his office?

"Akira—"

"You were supposed to help me." She turned and fled the office, ignoring Roman's voice as he called after her.

Chapter 10

"Tell me what Mr. Johnson's face looked like when he got the boot," Lara closed Akira's door behind her. "I've been trying your number for the last hour." The phone rang. "Why aren't you answering?" Lara scrunched her face together at the incessant ringing of the phone. "You want me to pick that up?"

"No!"

Akira led Lara into the dining room where sat at the table. The lights were dimmed in the apartment, and the only other light came from the muted television.

Lara lowered her voice, matching the solemn mood of the apartment. "What are you doing?"

Akira crossed her forearms on the table and rested her head. She stared at the neatly lined documents on the wood grain table. She drew in a long, jagged breath as she explained. "Roman Miller found that my claim could not be substantiated, *however*, he does believe I had cause to file the complaint."

Lara shook her head in disbelief. "What does that mean? Mr. Johnson walks away without any punishment?"

"Now you're with me," Akira answered with disdain.

"What are you going to do?"

"That brings me to the documents on this table." Arching her back, Akira sat up straight in the chair. She pointed out each document as she explained its significance. "This document is a record of Roman Miller's findings." She pushed it away with the tip of one finger as if it were a test tube of contagious material. "This is my diploma, a bachelor's degree in business. What exactly can I do with it? All of my professional work experience is at Greico."

She paused to suppress the sob building in her throat. Not the time to break down. "That brings me to this little innocent looking sheet of paper. It's the non-compete agreement I signed when I was promoted into the sales executive position."

"Non-compete agreement?"

Akira's voice took on a false lilt. "A rather standard contractual agreement in the pharmaceutical sales industry. Basically, it states that if I'm terminated or quit Greico, I won't seek work in the same field, in this state, for a year. If I do, Greico can sue me and the company that hires me."

Lara's mouth dropped open.

Akira continued before she could interrupt. "Let's see what's behind door number three, Johnny." The sad reality of her situation pushed up into her throat occupying a space the size of a walnut. She swallowed it away and continued. "The list on this piece of paper outlines all of my debts and all of my assets." She lifted the paper at the corner and waved it in the air. "It ain't pretty."

"How ugly?" Lara asked.

"I won't be barging into the office to quit my job Monday morning."

Akira's eyes held on to Lara's for dear life. Sensing Lara's helplessness in finding a solution to her problems, she burst into tears.

Lara moved behind Akira's chair and rubbed her shoulders. "There's something else we can do. We need to regroup."

Acquisitions

The thought brought forth more sobs. "That isn't all."

"What else is there?"

"I went to see Roman after the hearing. I didn't plan to. I got so mad that I pushed my way into his office."

"Good. I hope you told him off."

"I did. I started to. And then he-he propositioned me."

"Wait. What do you mean he propositioned you?"

"He kissed me."

Lara looked horrified.

Akira wanted to confess, *I kissed him back. I liked the way his mouth felt pressed against mine. I wanted him to do it again.*

Lara read her clearly. "What happened next?"

"Nothing. I slapped him and ran out of his office."

"That's all?"

"That's all."

"Why do I get the feeling you're not telling me everything? This isn't going to turn into Eric all over again, is it?"

"Oh, God, no. Roman Miller is nothing like Eric."

"Yeah? What makes him so special? From where I'm sitting, he sounds like an opportunist."

Akira took a calming breath before she continued. "Whenever Roman comes near, we connect. Have you ever met a man that makes you…?" She braced for Lara's reaction. "I want him. I admit it. No matter how wrong it might be, I'm attracted to him. When he comes into the room, I see myself lying in his arms, wanting him to take whatever he needs. Have you ever felt that for a man? Felt willing to give him all you had—everything—emotionally and physically? One look from him, and I want to surrender, forget about professionalism and ethics. Give him all I have. And I try to tell him what's in my heart every time I look into his eyes."

Lara's pudgy hands worked the kinks out of Akira's neck. Her touch never faltered, even with Akira's candid confession. "This is going to be alright. Your emotions are heightened—you're more sensitive than usual with everything that's been going on."

No "I told you so" from her friend.

"You go ahead and cry now because come Monday morning, you're not going to be able to show any weakness. Monday, you'll go into the office and hold your head high."

***

Akira threw back the quilt she had wrapped herself in and grudgingly released the comfort and safety of her favorite recliner. She dabbed at the tears underneath her eyes, hoping to remove any makeup that may have been smudged. Tugging at the bottom of her camisole, she moved to answer the knock at her door. After Lara left, she took two aspirins and sank into her favorite chair, still searching for a solution to her problems.

"Ms. Reed?" The short man in the cheap suit addressed her in a no-nonsense tone.

Akira looked between the short man and his partner, a white man with wavy black hair.

The short man pulled his badge from his breast pocket. His partner silently copied the gesture. "I'm Detective Casser. This is Detective Downs. We need to ask you some questions."

"What's this about?"

"We're investigating a report of stolen property—a drug formula—from Greico Enterprises."

"Can we come in?" Detective Downs asked, his eyes softer. Not hardened by his work, he looked as if he regretted having to ask about her involvement.

Akira stepped aside, allowing the officers to enter. They took inventory of her surroundings. She had watched enough police shows on television to know that they were assessing her means and comparing them to her salary level.

After dispensing with the details of the reason for their visit, the officers questioned Akira about the intruder she had reported hearing in her harassment complaint. She answered honestly. "I really can't tell you much. I heard someone in the outer office, but I never really saw anyone. No one was in the

Acquisitions

cubicles when I went into my office. I thought it best for me not to hang around, so I got my things and started to leave."

Detective Downs looked up from his notepad. "Started to leave? Did something stop you?"

Akira shifted in her seat. They didn't seem to know the intimate details of her harassment claim, and she didn't want to relive it. She had decided while she cried over Roman's findings that she would put the incident behind her and start to consider new career options.

"Well," she hesitated, "that's when I bumped into Mr. Johnson."

Officer Casser directed a raised eyebrow to his partner. "Mr. Johnson was in the outer office as you prepared to leave?"

"Yes."

The officers shared a look of doubt. Casser turned his no-nonsense tone up a notch and added the bass of an overworked policeman. "Ms. Reed, the surveillance tapes show when Mr. Johnson entered the sixth floor and when he left the area. It doesn't show when you entered your office."

"Although—" Downs started, but was interrupted by his partner.

"Although, we do see you moving near the secured area acting very suspiciously. Nervous. Shaky. Scared. Caught?"

Akira looked to the dark-haired officer who showed her a measure of kindness earlier in their conversation. His face was now accusatory. He broke their stare and glanced over at his partner.

"Are you implying that I had something to do with stealing the formula?"

"It did occur to me." Casser made up for his lack of height with monumental attitude. Akira wanted to make him stand up so she could punch him on the top of the head like Fred did to Barney on *The Flintstones*.

"That's ridiculous."

"Tell us why?" Downs almost pleaded.

"I wouldn't do something like that. I don't have a reason to steal."

"Actually, you do." Casser leafed through his notepad. All of the men ruining her life did so with the help of a notepad. "We did a little checking. A salesperson's salary fluctuates. If you received a few late notices and a couple of irate phone calls from collection agencies you might get pretty upset." He flipped forward in the pad. "We also talked with your coworkers. Maybe you were jealous of working hard and watching Mr. Johnson gross more profits from your sales."

"I don't think I should talk to you anymore." Akira jumped up. She would not be able to remain composed for much longer.

The two detectives stood together at a leisurely pace. They were in no hurry to go. They made it clear that they were leaving only because they were ready.

Casser dropped his business card on the coffee table. "Give us a call if you think of anything. Otherwise, stay close to home. We'll be in touch soon."

Chapter 11

Roman sat on his sofa in the semi-darkness, still wearing his coat and boots. "What could I have been thinking?" he asked himself aloud.

After living through the turmoil Sherry inflicted upon his life when she waltzed off to New York, ending their engagement, how could he upset Akira's life this way?

There were so many loose ends with him and Sherry. No closure. Emotions lingered that made Sherry come to mind at the worst times. What those emotions were Roman couldn't readily identify.

The feelings he had for Akira, though, were crystal clear.

Roman threw back his head and chugged from the bottle. Would being with Akira be worth the risk of losing his job? Officially, the sexual harassment case was closed. What was the worse that could happen if Grieco knew they were dating? Roman was kidding himself. If anyone ever found out, he would be suspended at the least, terminated most likely. He had crossed professional boundaries when he kissed her. Actually, he had crossed that border when he took her in his arms in her office.

He might escape with a stern reprimand.

Did Akira feel strongly enough about him to jeopardize her career and her already damaged reputation to pursue a relationship with him?

"What do I do to fix this?" He considered calling Butch and asking his advice. But he knew what Butch would say. And he would be right. That's why he wouldn't call, because he couldn't do what his mind told him he should.

His heart would win this battle.

***

Roman didn't notice how cold his feet were inside his insulated boots until he stood outside Akira's apartment door poised to ring the bell. Having copied her address from her complaint form, he easily found his way to her apartment. He hit the heels of his feet, one at a time, against the floor mat to remove the snow from the soles. He removed his leather gloves and stuffed them into his pocket. He fingered his cell phone. If it would ring, the interruption would stop him before crossing over into forbidden territory.

No ring. He pressed the buzzer.

Akira swung the door open, annoyed with the intrusion. She appeared disheveled. Her eyes were red, puffy. Black streaks magnified the path of her tears.

Roman had never seen a woman more beautiful.

She wore the same power suit from earlier. The one that made her look like a brutal businesswoman waiting to be stripped naked and made love to by her voracious lover.

"What are *you* doing here?" Akira asked.

"I came to check on you. I wanted to make sure you were okay."

"You've done enough." She moved to shut the door.

Roman had come too far to let her slam the door in his face. He stood primed to topple over the edge of a cliff. He couldn't step back now.

He stretched out his massive hand and stopped the door. "I didn't *do* anything to you. I conducted a fair investigation.

Acquisitions

There wasn't enough evidence to prove that Mr. Johnson acted inappropriately. What did you want me to do? Lie?"

His hand slid slowly down the wood grain of the door. "You made it clear the first day I met you that you wanted a fair investigation. You wouldn't have wanted me to shade my findings, even if it was to help you prove your case."

"I can't argue with that. I want Mr. Johnson exposed, but if by unethical means, it makes me no better than he is."

Roman's anxiety began to diminish. She would be righteous about the situation.

"Why did you have to go to the police and implicate me in the theft of the formula? Is that fair too?"

"I never went to the police about anything. My investigation was conducted internally for Greico Enterprises. I didn't share that information with anyone."

Akira searched his face. "You may have honorable intentions, but you're still partially responsible for ruining my reputation at work, and now with the police. I won't accept your apology. The fact that you came here to ask for it doesn't impress me. Neither does the way you're staring at me."

Roman grinned down at Akira, hope alive in his eyes.

"Why are you here?"

Her unwavering harshness made him lose the smile. "I didn't want to let things between us hang in the air until after the holiday. I wanted to explain what I did. It—the kiss—isn't what you think."

"I don't want to hear anymore. My life is spinning out of control. I have no time to deal with an oversexed lawyer who thinks he can take advantage of me while I'm in the middle of a crisis. You probably do this sort of thing all the time."

In a nervous gesture, Roman pulled the collar of his full-length brown wool overcoat up against his neck. "Akira, I have never approached anyone I deal with professionally in that way. I wanted to come here and apologize. Explain, somehow, why I-I—"

Always eloquent with words, Roman began to stammer,

not able to clearly make his point. His attraction to Akira's soft curves and tough armor jumbled his thoughts and mashed his words together in a gumbo of indistinguishable emotions.

"It wasn't necessary for you to come here for that." She attempted to close the door, but its progress was again stopped by the force of Roman's hand.

"Can I come inside and talk?" He looked down the hallway hoping that he hadn't drawn the attention of her neighbors.

"What do you *want?*" she shouted.

Roman looked down at the defeated, but determined, face of the woman he could not keep off his mind since meeting her. He began to freefall over the side of the cliff. The best thing, the right thing, the only thing to do was to excuse his intrusion and walk away. His behavior violated several of his personal codes of ethics. His coming to her home was wrong on so many levels he couldn't list them all. But, his job aside, he was entitled to be a man, right?

Akira interrupted his thoughts. "I have no reason to stand in this cold drafty doorway waiting for you to explain yourself. I'm on my own time. The investigation is over. I never have to see you again. Whatever this is will fade with time. Good bye, Mr. Miller."

Whatever this is will fade. If Roman lost this chance, he wouldn't have another.

He stepped inside before she could close the door.

Despite the fact that his actions would bring a waterfall of trouble pouring down upon him, he decided to surge forward. What words were appropriate? He was out of touch with the latest slang he needed to use to sound aloof, cool. A snappy line from Butch's arsenal would be helpful. A line from the many poetry books he read would come in handy, but he couldn't remember a single word that would adequately describe what he wanted Akira to understand.

Her shoulders slumped in defeat. "I'm in my own home, and Greico Enterprises continues to violate me. First by send-

Acquisitions

ing the police, and now the lawyer that has condemned me to being the office's freakish outcast." Her eyes glazed over with a clear sheen. "Alright," her voice dropped, losing its feisty defiance, "you win. I can't deal with this pressure."

She fought to hold back the tears.

Despite all of her efforts, Roman watched tears pour from her eyes.

The tears told Roman that he had to open himself up to Akira, or leave her to her grief. If he couldn't make her situation better, he would only make it worse.

He continued to stammer over the words he needed to express his raw emotions. "I want— I want—"

"What?"

"I want—"

Akira's voice quivered. "Can't you see how you're making this worse for me? There's nothing you can do to help me now. What is it with you that you can't let this case go? I don't understand what you hoped to accomplish by coming here. Mr. Miller, what do you want from me?"

Roman stepped toward Akira.

She stepped back.

This could be your last chance, are you willing to walk away from this woman?

The words began to flow for Roman. "I want to sit in my den knowing that you're in the living room. I want to walk into the kitchen and watch you cooking."

He placed his thumb near her tear duct and captured the next drop that fell. "I want to beat up anyone who makes you cry."

He gave her a faint smile. Confusion washed over her face; she was unsure of his motives. The intensity of his eyes made her believe he could view her thoughts and discern the difference between truth and lies. He already knew her tears were coming more from frustration than anger.

Roman kicked the front door closed with the heel of his boot.

82

His voice dipped lower with every seductive sentence. "I want to hold you in my arms and wrap myself in you. I want you to call me in the middle of the night and wake me up when you aren't able to sleep. I want you to massage my back."

Roman stepped closer, his voice dropped lower. "I want to make love to you so thoroughly that afterwards you beg me for more."

This time when Roman stepped up to Akira, she did not move away. Her body joined her oppressors in its betrayal. As she tried to call forth vile words that would push him away, her head filled with visions of straddling his back and kneading his muscles with only the sound of his moans filling the room.

Roman's vise-like arms coiled around Akira and pulled her soft, into his body.

Akira raised a hand against him, but was distracted by his rock solid chest. "What are you doing?"

He shrugged one arm and then the other out of his coat, never completely surrendering his hold on her.

"Back off—" Akira lost her train of thought when his overcoat fell to the floor. The sound of it landing on the carpet resounded loudly in the hushed stillness of the room. She looked down at the pile of brown wool crumpled at his boots. When she looked up into Roman's eyes, he was already descending toward her mouth with his lips slightly parted. Spiraling emotions made her raise her hand.

Roman's head snapped to the left. He froze, his jaw tight and shifting slightly back and forth.

Akira regretted slapping him the moment her palm connected with his baby soft skin. She regretted her actions being opposed to what her heart wanted to do.

Roman relaxed his jaw muscles before facing her. "I came here to say I'm sorry for the way things worked out. I truly tried to find the evidence I needed..." He lifted his hand and massaged the area she had just struck. "I could lose my job for coming here. I felt something. I thought you did too. I know we made a connection."

Acquisitions

He waited for her to confirm in words what her eyes were saying. Her silence urged him to continue. "You have to be aware of the implications of me coming here—of me kissing you." He softened, pressing his hand to his chest. "I know you feel it, Akira."

Roman dropped his hand and stood back slightly.

"Do you now understand why I'm here?" Roman asked, his lashes flipping upward.

Her 'no' was barely audible.

"I'm here because I can only think of one or two more reasons to come down to the sixth floor to see you. After that, I won't have any excuses. After that, I can't see you again. And that's unacceptable.

"I want to kiss you, Akira, but I have to know you want it too. Slapping me doesn't say that. Making the wrong move right now could end my career and land me in jail, so if you want me to kiss you, ask me to."

Akira stood frozen into silence. She didn't hear correctly, did she? Roman felt the attraction too? He wanted to kiss her as badly as she wanted to be kissed by him. But the sexual harassment case... The stolen formula...her job...his job...would she ever have a chance as wonderful as this again in her life?

"I'm waiting." Roman felt a surge of power in having control in this situation, a surge that raced to his groin and awoke his manhood. Fighting, clamoring to have a shot with Akira.

"I—I—"

Roman brought his hand to her cheek, a breath away, teasing her with his touch. He raised his thumb and gestured over her lips, a breath away, teasing her with his caress. "You won't get it unless you ask for it."

"I can't just say..."

"How you feel?"

Akira looked away, the whole episode too intense. What was she doing even *thinking* about kissing the man who had

84

found her claim unsubstantiated?

"Akira?"

Shadowing her. Watching her behind long lashes with smoky eyes and tempting lips, how could she say anything but the truth?

"Akira?"

"I want you to kiss me."

"Say, please."

Before Akira could utter a word or register her contempt with his game, Roman embraced her and pulled her in to rest against him.

"*This* is exactly what I want." Eyes closed, Roman bent his knees and found the path to her lips strictly by memory of their earlier kiss. He wanted to absorb her into him. He felt her lips part. *Cherries.* He pressed his tongue next to her teeth until they separated, allowing him passage to explore. His tongue moved longingly into this separation and searched her mouth for proof that she too felt something developing between them. He hoped that the skillful movements of his tongue conveyed his feelings more artistically than he had been able to do with words. He moved his tongue inside her mouth, consuming all her insecurities.

Roman's body hadn't felt so electric, so stimulated, so excited since before he lost his virginity. He wanted Akira's body against his, every inch of her next to every inch of him. His inches were growing longer and stronger with every thrust of her tongue. He wanted her to feel her effect on him, take responsibility, and rectify the situation. His arms wrapped around Akira's torso with the grip of a python. Like a python, he crushed her and pulled her into him for his consumption.

Akira melted into his touch, letting her lips go where they pleased. They left his mouth and moved to his cheeks, chin and neck. Letting her guard down was exhilarating. Her hands moved across his back. For a little while, she could have this dream. She flicked her tongue against the hollow of his neck. She'd savor the taste forever.

Acquisitions

Roman removed his suit jacket—he needed to soak her up into his being. He took her earlobe between his teeth, and her nipples hardened and pressed into his chest. She wanted a little pain with her pleasure. He cupped her the nape of her neck and pulled her closer, his tongue slipping inside. Deeper.

"Akira…"

"Roman?"

"Deeper…"

The double ring stopped his request.

Roman ignored the ring coming from the pocket of his coat, which still lay on the living room floor; his voicemail would pick up.

It stopped, then rang again.

Roman pulled himself away from Akira and fished for his phone. He moved too hurriedly, making finding the annoying cellular more difficult than it should have been. He sat on the floor with his back against a chair until he found the phone.

"Roman Miller."

"What took you so long to pick up?" Butch asked.

"Let me call you later."

A horn honked in the background. "I'll see you at Grandma Dixon's for dinner tomorrow?"

"I'll be there."

"Okay. Peace."

"Peace." Roman flipped the phone closed and immediately turned his body to Akira who had moved to the recliner. Her face clearly displayed doubt and suspicion. Her mind was battling with whether or not he could be trusted.

The heat of her fire seeped through during their kiss: she couldn't deny the truth. Taking no chance of losing her, Roman reached out from his spot on the floor. "Come here."

"No." Akira pulled at her shirt and ran her palms over the crease of her skirt.

"Come here, *please*?" He gave her a faint smile.

"No." Not as strong as the first—she was wavering.

"Akira?" His kept his voice low, pleading.

"No." Weaker still.

"My arms are getting tired."

Akira hesitated, tucking her legs beneath her. "I don't understand what's going on here."

Roman moved next to her on the edge of the sofa. "I'm attracted to you. I've struggled with this for weeks. Since the day I met you, I felt something. I tried to ignore it; I understand my actions are questionable. But today, when I looked into your eyes in my office, I saw my last chance. Believe me, it would have been easier on both of us if I had let you storm out of my life, but I couldn't do it."

Akira's body relaxed, just a little.

He locked his eyes with hers—she would see and interpret his sincerity. "I thought I sensed something coming from you, too. I know that my being here, under these circumstances, can cause a lot of trouble for us both. I'm here because my feelings for you won't allow me to be anyplace else. If you don't feel the same, tell me, and I'll walk away."

When a torturous minute passed and she hadn't answered, Roman moved to his coat pooled in the middle of the floor.

Akira stood up slowly, cautiously.

"Do you want me to leave?"

She shook her head. No. Her eyes still harbored skepticism.

Roman held his arms open for her. "My arms."

Akira didn't move.

"If this is what we both want, it'll work. We'll make it work."

Frozen in place, she licked her lips.

"Save some of the cherries for me."

The mistrust marring her face cracked into pieces, replaced by a gorgeous smile that lit her eyes.

She took a guarded step forward.

Roman met her, pulling her into his arms. "Ask me, Akira."

Chapter 12

Butch opened the door of Grandma Dixon's condo.

"Man, why are you always here?" Roman asked, shrugging out of his coat.

"Move." Butch playfully shoved him aside. "Where is she?"

Grandma Dixon came fluttering around the corner squawking the same question. "Where is she?"

Roman stepped inside and let his older sister, Gayle, be smothered in love. His big sister, also a foot shorter, Gayle looked the splitting image of their mother—the last time Roman had seen her. He brought in Gayle's bags, the airline luggage tags still swinging from the handles. He had taken it hard when Gayle announced she was moving out to California to pursue a career in fashion design. After their parents abandoned them, she was the only original memory he had of what a real family should be.

Butch joined Roman in the spare bedroom. "What are you doing in here?"

"Gayle looks good, doesn't she? Tanned and—"

"—That Angela Bassett hard body."

"Watch it. That's my sister."

Butch held up his hands in surrender, a diamond-studded watch catching the light. "So why are you hiding out in here instead of spending time with Gayle before she has to go back?"

Roman hesitated to discuss his dilemma with Butch because he knew what the advice would be. Maybe he needed someone to talk sense into him. He started out slowly, telling Butch the whole story about his attraction to Akira from the beginning.

"Well, you were right about one thing," Butch said sarcastically. "You did do something stupid. Did you sleep with her?"

"No."

Butch raised an eyebrow. His gold link bracelet glimmered under the lights as he scratched his premature balding head.

"I didn't." Both of their honors were still intact. They'd kissed, and he held her while they discussed the implications of their relationship, but he hadn't gone too far over the line.

"We may still be able to salvage this disaster. As your lawyer, I'm going to tell you to never see her again. Avoid her at the office. Don't call her at home. Walk away before this gets out of hand. You'll lose your job if this gets out at the office."

"Will I, really? The sexual harassment investigation is closed."

"That doesn't matter when your reputation is at stake. Besides, you don't know this woman. Maybe she did steal the formula. What if she made up the whole sexual harassment claim and you're next? Did you think about that?"

"I—"

"Wait a minute." Butch threw up his hand exposing a new diamond sprinkled ring on his forefinger. "As your *friend*, I'm saying leave her alone. You aren't ready to get involved with another woman. If she's as special as you say, you'll only end

Acquisitions

up hurting her."

"I don't like any of the advice you're giving me."

"You didn't think, you acted on an impulse. That's your defense—explanation—to give to her. You were sitting at home feeling guilty about the outcome of her complaint, and you were sucked in."

If Butch weren't closer to Roman than his own parents, he'd never let him get away with scolding him like a child. Butch had supported him through many rough times. And he'd done the same for Butch. The hard times were what made their bond strong and their friendship based on brutal honesty.

Butch continued. "We'll go up to the cabin. Hit the slopes. Do a little ice fishing. Gayle will love it, and it'll clear your mind."

Roman nodded.

Butch clasped his shoulder. "We can still do damage control."

Roman pulled away from Butch and found solace in his grandmother's bedroom. He needed a minute to clear his head. He dropped down on the edge of the bed, head hung. He didn't want to think about the consequences of his attraction to Akira. Being with her felt good, and he wanted to preserve that warmth. Until meeting Akira, he'd forgotten the rewards of having a special someone. Work kept him busy, but not fulfilled. Having met Akira, he couldn't imagine walking away from the unexplored possibilities of having a relationship with her.

Butch was right on all accounts, as usual.

Roman wasn't ready to enter into another relationship. Akira could be setting him up. They could both be fired. His hormones got away from him—it had been a long, long time since he held a woman against him.

Roman entered the dining room and took the seat between Grandma Dixon and Gayle, across from Butch. After dinner, he would go home and forget that he ever met Akira Reed. He'd do what was painfully right for the both of them.

The makeshift family joined hands encircling the Thanksgiving feast Grandma had slaved two days to prepare. Roman recited the traditional grace. As they passed dishes and raved over the food, his mind wandered back to Akira.

After the kiss, Roman's world had brightened. His hazy, distorted view of life became crisp, like the restoration of an analog film to digital.

For over thirty years he had been walking in darkness. When he had listened to the taped statement of Akira's coworkers, his mind dreamed of kissing her. Late in the night, when his hardened shaft woke him, it was Akira's face that helped him find his release.

He admitted to taking a leap from his fantasies to kissing Akira without thinking it through. But his emotions ruled him. He knew what he wanted and needed. He didn't ask permission or ponder the consequences. He felt he had one fleeting moment to win her, and he had seized it.

The cherries jubilee Grandma Dixon heaped in a bowl reminded him of burgundy-lined lips with shiny sweet gloss. When he kissed Akira, his soul opened wide, the beating of his heart slowed to a melodious tempo, the tension in his body mellowed to mimic the rhythm of his heart. All of the negative energy gripping his heart floated away. He felt refreshed, ready to face any obstacle tossed in his way.

Roman's spirit had been fortified.

At the expense of Akira's well-being. He cursed himself for even considering walking away from her.

"Sherry walked away without giving our future together a chance."

All eyes turned to Roman.

"What did you say, boy?" Grandma Dixon asked.

"Sherry up and walked out on me without even discussing our problem and what we could do to fix it."

Grandma Dixon turned up her nose as if she caught a whiff of skunk. "Why you wanna bring that gal's name up on Thanksgiving? Unless it's to thank God she isn't here."

Acquisitions

"Amen," Gayle mumbled.

Roman ignored the snide comments.

"Forget about it," Butch whispered across the table.

"How?"

Gayle piped in, "What are you two going on about?" Her question went ignored.

Butch tossed his napkin next to his plate. "Roman, I'm telling you—as your friend and as your attorney—forget about pursuing this."

"I can't." Roman pushed his chair back. "Grandma, I need to leave for a little while."

Grandma Dixon and Gayle looked at each other, at Butch, at Roman, clearly confused about what was going on. Before anything could be said, Roman left the table and rushed from his grandmother's house.

Inside his car, Roman grinned at the giddiness of it all. Thirty minutes later, he pulled up to Akira's apartment after fighting the thick blanket of snow covering the roads.

This time when he rang the bell, Akira would open her door to him.

"Roman!" A huge smile brightened her face. Every man should be greeted this way by the woman in his life. He'd made the right decision.

"What are you doing?" he asked, peering into the darkened apartment.

Akira shrugged. "Catching up on work."

"It's Thanksgiving. Are you spending it alone?"

"My little brother is over in Italy—he plays basketball. My parents are spending the holiday with him there. I could have spent the day with my friend Lara and her family." She glanced away. "I didn't think I'd be very good company. I have a lot on my mind."

Roman wanted to explore her family lineage, but became sidetracked by her luscious lips. "You'll spend the day with my family and me."

"I can't barge in on your family."

"No, what you can't do is sit in this apartment alone without your family or friends. My grandmother would drag you to dinner herself if she knew you were alone for the holidays. You'll have a good time. We're nice people."

"I don't know."

"You don't know?"

"Having dinner with your family is a big step and we've just started dating."

Roman understood Akira not wanting to take their relationship too fast. Sharing a holiday dinner was what you did with friends. When they were committed he would introduce her to his parents. For several reasons, he wondered if that would ever happen. Before he plunged into that sea of pain, he tried to persuade Akira to have dinner with him. "No one should spend the holidays alone. It'll give us more time to get to know each other." He pulled her into his arms to persuade her with the art of his tongue. He withdrew, leaving Akira with dazed longing. "I won't take no for an answer." He pulled her closer. She molded around him, enveloping him in her warmth.

***

Akira watched Roman wearing an eager smile as he stepped into the foyer of his grandmother's home. "Come in." He took her hand and pulled her along.

Eric never acknowledged her in public.

"Grandma," he called out while he helped Akira out of her coat.

Akira felt the familiar smoldering of her insides that occurred whenever Roman branded her with his touch.

"Grandma, I have company."

The announcement brought a group of people scurrying, all whispering in anticipation. Akira braced for their reaction. Dread slithered down her spine. What if their mouths dropped open at Roman's choice of a Thanksgiving date? Would he banish her to videos and take-out at home where no one could run into him?

Acquisitions

"Everybody, this is Akira."

Roman grabbed her hand and pulled her next to him, "Come here."

She almost melted.

"Akira, this is my sister, Gayle."

Gayle nodded and let her eyes wander to Roman in question. Akira saw no negativity there—only curiosity as to what her presence at the holiday dinner meant.

"This is my Grandma Dixon."

Grandma Dixon's eyes glittered with delight as she welcomed her with a hug.

"The diamond-clad stud over there is my best friend, Butch."

Butch stepped forward and offered his hand. Without speaking one word, Akira knew he had to be a lawyer. The way he masked any emotion—approval or disapproval—of her presence.

Roman dipped down near her face. "Are you hungry? Would you like something to eat? Grandma, Akira hasn't eaten dinner."

Gayle lifted an eyebrow then smiled at Butch.

"Well, let me make you a plate." Grandma Dixon took Akira from Roman's safe embrace and coaxed her to the dining room. Akira looked back with a smile as Grandma Dixon pulled her away from the comfort of his touch.

Minutes later, Akira sat wide-eyed in front of a plate piled high with food. "Mrs. Dixon, I can't possibly eat all this."

Eric would have prepared her food, giving her tiny portions while telling her she should join a weight loss clinic. Every minute she spent with Roman was confirmation that only Eric had a problem with her body image—other men appreciated her round curves and full breasts. Roman's family didn't look at her like she would single-handedly destroy his career if she showed up with him at social gatherings. Akira sat up straighter, comfortable in herself and with Roman's family.

"Everybody calls me Grandma Dixon and of course you can eat this little bit of food. And then you'll try my cherries jubilee and tell me what you think. I wanted apple pie, but that grandson of mine didn't get the apples I asked for."

"I'll get to it, Grandma," Roman answered from the living room. "I've been busy at work."

Akira cringed. She looked up to see Roman craning his neck from the sofa to read her reaction. He mouthed the words, "I'm sorry."

Akira smiled, accepting the apology for the slip of his tongue.

Grandma Dixon slipped into a chair and watched Akira dig into her food. She felt obliged to taste everything on her plate, but once she swallowed that first bite, obligation no longer played a part in her consumption. She missed not living near her parents and being able to drop by for home-cooked meals.

Gayle joined them at the table, picking at her cherries jubilee and vanilla ice cream while she told Akira about her life in California. The sounds of a football game came from the living room where Roman and Butch heartily debated whose team had more talent.

Akira started in on the dish when Roman pulled a chair up next to her. His finger smoothed her hair and tucked a strand behind her ear. Akira glanced up at Grandma Dixon and Gayle. They grinned. She blushed.

"Are you okay?"

Akira nodded.

Roman leaned over and kissed her cheek, which filled her face with the color of embarrassment. He kissed her in front of his family! After being thought of as an embarrassment, an obstacle between Eric and his career goals, that small gesture meant so much to her. He leaned near her ear, totally aware that Grandma Dixon and Gayle were pretending to hold a conversation. "The cherries remind me of your kisses."

"Roman." She twisted her spoon around the bowl.

Acquisitions

He kissed her cheek, her temple.

The wall of stone surrounding Akira's heart crumbled with the touch of his lips.

She placed her hand tenderly on his knee.

Roman's hand covered hers. "Give me a taste."

***

Hours later, Roman drove Akira home through the snow and slush that covered the streets. Her heart leapt with joy when she recalled the events of the night.

Meeting Eric's family wasn't even a consideration. As she talked, laughed and played games with Roman's family, she questioned her sanity when dating Eric. Why had she settled for his cunning words and slick moves? He had made it clear that he cared for her—but she didn't fit the mold. She didn't have the pizzazz he needed to fill the role of his wife. He had ambitions, he would tell her. Corporate leaders had to have a certain *type* of wife and she wasn't it. After the initial shock of his words, she ingested them and told herself that what they had was too good to throw away. Eric would come around, she tried to convince herself. He never did, and her self-confidence had suffered because of it. Once she came to her senses and walked away from that toxic relationship, Akira realized exactly who it was that had a problem, and it certainly was not her.

"What are you thinking about?" Roman asked when he opened Akira's door, helping her from his Infiniti.

Traveling down memory lane, she hadn't noticed when he pulled into her apartment complex. "Nothing." Nothing would ruin this night for her. "I had a really good time with your family. I'm glad you made me go."

They walked in silence to her apartment. Roman stood back as she slipped her key into the door and went inside. She turned to him, sank into the depth of his twin dimples and couldn't let him leave. "I know it's late, but maybe you could come in for a glass of wine?" There. She held her breath, waiting for his answer.

Very coolly, as if the invitation were expected and so was his response, he said, "I'd like that."

Once inside and all the winter gear had been removed, Akira and Roman settled together comfortably on the sofa. Never in her dreams did Akira ever think she'd be sitting on her sofa holding Roman's head in her lap while they discussed their hopes and fears.

"I like that you've already begun to spoil me." He ran his fingers down her arm and back up again, leaving a fire blazing in the wake of his touch.

"Tell me about the rest of your family."

"Well, my grandma is tough, but sweet. She raised me and Gayle."

"Did your parents—"

"My parents didn't have time to care for us. They decided that other things in life were more important. Such as moving away, starting another life, and partying without the need of babysitters."

"You sound like you're still bitter about it." Akira could not resist the urge to run her fingers over the waves of his hair. When she did, he nuzzled into her lap, coming dangerously close to starting another more dangerous fire in the V of her sensual soul.

"I'm *very* bitter about it. When I have kids, they will always feel loved and wanted. I would never even consider marrying a woman who didn't have the qualities of a good mother."

"Maybe you should talk to your parents. Try to work it out."

He shook his head, his eyes glued to the ceiling. "Gayle went that route. I spent many nights on the phone trying to console her afterwards. She dropped a fortune on shrinks.

"There's something unnatural about not wanting your kids. They made us. They did this not once—where they could claim it was an accident—but twice. We come from them. We are them. How could they not love us enough to

Acquisitions

have us in their lives?" He searched Akira's eyes for the answer.

"I don't know. It's awful you had to go through that."

Roman laced his fingers in her hair and pulled her down to him for a kiss. She closed her eyes and floated away. His mouth, hot and greedy. She pulled away, breathless and seeing stars. He had to feel the heat searing the back of her neck.

"What about your family?" Roman asked. "Your brother is a basketball player?"

Akira smiled with pride. "My little brother is seven feet tall with arms the size of treasure chests. He's mean on the court, sweet as can be off the court. I miss him a lot, but he's doing what he loves. He's been playing overseas for two years now. There are too many talented players for the limited positions available in the league here in the States. He says the American scouts have been showing up more frequently at the games. Maybe they're looking at him. We're hoping."

"Your parents are visiting him for the holidays?"

"Yeah, they miss him, too. They live in Seattle. They saved a long time to go over there. My brother was willing to send for them, but they wouldn't have it. My parents are very supportive of us. They don't interfere unless we ask for help. And then they're right there."

Stroking Roman's hair eased her tension as much as it rid him of the pain of his childhood.

"Why did you become a lawyer?" she asked.

"I don't look like I should be a lawyer?"

"Only when you wear your glasses."

"I hate wearing glasses. They're only for reading—a sure sign that I'm getting old. What do I look like I should be doing?"

Akira smiled down at him trying to decide. "Let's see. No hard labor for you. Maybe a scientist."

"I'm terrible in math and science. I'm a great orator." He puffed out his chest. "How'd you end up at Greico Enterprises selling drugs? Is there some secret desire hidden there?"

Akira laughed with him. "It's a good job. Good pay, nice hours. I'm happy being part of the regular work force. I'm an ordinary person, doing ordinary things."

"You're not ordinary." He twisted a lock of her hair. "Whatever brought you to Greico, I'm glad, because I wouldn't be here now."

The obvious sincerity behind his sweet words made Akira's cheeks warm.

After a long silence, Akira ventured to the subject they were both struggling to avoid all evening. "What do you think will happen when I go back to work on Monday?"

"I'm not sure. Hopefully, the gossip will have died down."

Akira knew better. "What about Mr. Johnson?"

"Go about your work. He'd be stupid to try something again."

"Again? Do you believe me?"

Roman sat up. "I thought I made that clear. I believe every word of what you said. I just couldn't gather enough independent evidence to prove it."

A giant anvil was lifted from Akira's chest. She needed to know he believed her. If he did, she could let her guard down and believe that he really did have a romantic interest in her. Although, at this point, she was too far-gone with her own sentiments to pull back from him. She separated herself from the thick emotions by moving to the living room window. The snow showed no sign of slowing. The roads were covered. A few brave drivers had ventured out, leaving behind brownish-black slush in the gutters. She glanced at Roman. "The snow is still coming down."

He joined her at the window. "Do you think it'll stop soon?"

"I hope not."

***

"Good morning. Are you ready?" Roman greeted Akira the next morning with a kiss.

Acquisitions

"You were serious!" she squealed with delight. "You really are going to the orchard to pick apples at the end of November?"

"You doubted me?"

"There aren't any apples on the trees this late in the season."

"The orchard sells apples at their country store. You've met my grandmother—if she says the apples have to come from the orchard, then the apples have to come from the orchard." He eased up to her and wrapped his arms around her waist. "I'll take you on a hayride. Want to come?"

"That sounds…"

Roman pressed his lips to hers while she searched for the right word.

Sizzling from his kiss, she nodded.

"You better put on an extra sweater."

Slowly recovering, Akira found her voice. "Come in and have breakfast before we leave."

Roman brought the chill from outside in with him. Akira watched as he pulled away the skullcap and unzipped his jacket. Her fingertips longed to caress the cashmere sweater clinging to his chest. She glanced at the curve of his behind on display in his jeans as she hung his jacket in the hall closet. Sensitive and sexy, Roman presented the complete package. All for the taking.

They moved to the kitchen and Akira scrambled eggs while Roman assessed the contents of her refrigerator. "You don't have anything decent in here."

She cringed. *Here it comes.*

"Do you ever shop?"

"Well, it's only me, and I'm on the road working until late…"

"There's only you, huh?" He closed the refrigerator door. "We'll take care of that."

Did he mean her lack of food in the refrigerator or something else?

"Can you cook?" Akira asked after a considerable amount of time had passed with Roman still trying to make the toast.

"Not a bit." He squinted to keep the smoke from the toaster out of his eyes.

Akira vibrated with laughter. "What are you doing?"

"Making toast."

No, he could not cook. The toast was hard, but still white with partially melted butter. A cloud of wicked smelling smoke streamed up from the toaster making them both cough. If the toast was sitting on the counter, what was burning? Akira gave him a sideways glance. He wore the apologetic grin of a choirboy. She tossed the toast and started anew. "I'll talk you through it."

"What's your story?" Akira asked, busying herself at the stove.

"My story?" Roman searched the cabinets for the plates.

"Is there someone waiting for you to come home?"

"My grandma." He tossed a grin over his shoulder.

"You know that's not what I meant."

His face took on a look of innocence of a sweet little boy. She was learning that Roman wore many faces. The thought both thrilled and worried her. The poisonous thoughts crept into her mind again—was his interest in her a sick game? Or, as her heart wished, did he really see her true loving nature that no other man had taken the time to notice?

"There's no woman in my life if that's what you mean. How about you?"

Akira wasn't sure she believed him. He was too handsome and too successful not to be snagged by a very lucky woman.

"Akira?" Roman placed the plates down on the table. "Who's looking for you about now?"

She shook her head.

"Good, then there won't be anybody for me to beat up."

"What is it with you and beating people up?"

Roman's face shifted, turned hard and serious. The stoic

Acquisitions

attorney's expression Akira had become familiar with over the past weeks. "I couldn't protect you once. It won't happen again."

If she weren't careful, his words would make her fall too hard and too fast.

Roman finished setting the table and Akira dished out their breakfast. They fell into an easy routine like they had spent many breakfasts together.

Roman ate each bite like he had been shipwrecked on a deserted island for years. Each morsel met his appreciative lips with the flash of his tongue. Starving, but restraining his pace. He would go about all his tasks this way. Being thorough, eager, but controlled. Akira's body heated in anticipation of his kisses—his touch—his lips devouring her warm wet place. He smiled, and as if he could read her mind, he slipped a finger between his lips and licked away the grape jelly.

After several minutes of eating in silence, Akira picked up the conversation again. "I don't understand why you're here."

Roman's head tilted, he studied her face and then dropped his eyes. His long fingers twirled his juice glass around in quick circles. "I'm not sure I understand the question. Not sure I want to understand."

To cure the sudden dryness of her mouth, Akira took a long gulp of juice. "I suppose I'm asking—"

Roman pushed his chair away from the table in one continuous motion. He turned his back to her at the sink while he cleaned his plate.

Suspicion would not allow Akira to end the conversation, although Roman obviously did not want to talk about. "I'm asking why you'd risk your job to go out with me."

Roman dried his hands before he turned to her, leaning against the sink, his thighs taunt against the fabric of his pants. "We discussed this, and I thought we had come to an understanding." His expressionless face and stony voice were those of a seasoned attorney.

Akira looked up into his eyes. Never would she be

ashamed of who she was, but doubts now clouded her head. Roman being tall, bronze, intelligent, and gorgeous—her coming to him with a load of baggage. She couldn't help but wonder if the outcome of her complaint was entangled with his reason for being in her kitchen after a night of sharing their successes and failures.

Roman continued, "I'm unclear about what you're trying to say. I don't know if you're insulting me or questioning yourself. From what I've learned about you over the past several weeks, it's probably a shot at me and my integrity."

"I didn't mean it that way."

Roman interrupted. "You had to. You had to be referring to me because there's no way you could ever see yourself as anything other than a beautiful woman who has everything going for her. Let's get something clear. I'm here because I'm attracted to you and want to see where this can go between us."

These were the words she dreamt of hearing since her first reading of *Cinderella*. To have them come from a man as dynamic as Roman, well, it left her speechless.

"Akira," Roman's voice softened in unspoken understanding, "this is a conversation I'd rather not have again."

***

The hour drive to the apple orchard gave Akira more time to get to know Roman. They discussed everything from politics to religion. They debated the two taboo subjects heartily and ended the discussion with an understanding of the other's viewpoint. They ventured into hobbies and current events, steering clear of Greico Enterprises and the sexual harassment case.

Akira realized that they couldn't avoid the subject forever, but for this brief moment, she wanted to live in fantasyland. She wanted to open herself to Roman and his sweet talk and gentle nature. She would believe that the glimmer in his eye was meant only for her to see.

Lara would warn her that she was playing her old games again. Just like with Eric, when she pretended that his prob-

Acquisitions

lem with her "imperfect" body would go away when he fell in love with her.

Akira hadn't been with a man since Eric. She deserved this and she would enjoy every second until they returned to work—and harsh reality—on Monday morning.

Akira watched as Roman answered his cell. Her fingers gripped the handle of the shopping cart. He laughed, "No, I don't need bail money." He listened intently. "I'm with Akira. What did my grandmother want?" A pause. Roman held the phone up to Akira's ear. "Say hello to Butch."

"Hi, Butch."

Roman said his goodbyes and tucked the phone into his jacket pocket. "He's worried about me."

"Does he think I'll hurt you?"

A strange shadow covered his face. "Or that I'll hurt you."

"Do you have a track record of doing wrong?"

Roman playfully rolled his eyes before answering. "When I was ten, I told my girlfriend that I loved her, and then I told her sister I loved her."

"Get out of here. You know that's not what I meant."

Roman took the shopping cart and wheeled it to the checkout. "I know."

"Well?"

"I've never hurt a woman in my life, and I never will. I think it has a lot to do with the way my grandmother raised me—and seeing my sister stumble through her teen dating years. It's made me more aware of how sensitive women can be about things that hardly faze men."

"Truth?"

"I promise."

They inched forward in the checkout line.

"I see a little sadness." He brushed the slope of her nose. "Did someone hurt you?"

"I've never been in a serious enough relationship for that to be a problem." She refused to let Eric invade this moment.

"Would you like that to be a problem?"

"The pain? No, but—"

"But?"

"Living the romance would be nice. I've never had that."

"I have to confess I'm a little handicapped in that department. Poor baby." He pulled her to him by the collar of her coat. "Come here and let Roman make it better."

Public displays of affection. Akira tossed the phrase around as she rocked in the hay wagon. That's what Eric called it. He said they were unnecessary and tasteless. "Who cares what other people think about our relationship?" he asked when she questioned him about it. But he cared. That was the source of all their problems. Akira put too much emphasis on whether a man held her hand or kissed her cheek in public, Eric had said. And she knew why. Because Eric had been adamant about portraying her as a friend when they went out together.

Roman's hand-holding and caressing meant the world to her. It showed that he felt proud to be out with her. He melted all her defenses when he showed up on Thanksgiving and took her to meet his family. Grandma Dixon had to shoo him away, telling him to leave the women alone to get to know each other. Even then Akira looked up several times and found him watching her from the living room.

Roman wrapped his arm around her shoulder. "You're cold."

Akira nodded.

They sat in the corner of the wagon behind the driver bumping down the dirt path with two other couples.

"This was a crazy idea. A hayride in the middle of winter." Roman grabbed a wool blanket from the stack near the hay bundles. He spread it across Akira's legs and tucked it at her hips. "This will help." His arm wrapped her shoulders again.

Darkness enveloped them as the horses clip-clopped deeper into the orchard. The other couples in the back of the wagon

Acquisitions

whispered, giggled and smooched. The horses made a U-turn signaling that they were on the way back to the country store where the ride had begun.

Roman rested his head on Akira's shoulder, stable as they bumped along the path. She memorized his posture during the ride. Every detail—his breathing pattern, the weight of his head on her shoulder—thrilled her. Sexy without effort, he sent a current through her body. She stroked his cheek. His skin, a pretty summertime golden brown, the color of the leaves in the fall after the red, but before the brown. She ran her finger across the wavy pattern of his dark hair. Everything about his body was too perfect: tall and thin, but with arms that could pull her to him and secure her with the strength of ten men. His chest solid and well-defined. Could his build be natural? Or did he spend hours in the gym working out to maintain his stature? No one could have thighs this hard and well-defined without working to maintain their shapely ridges. She hoped that they were smooth, not covered with mounds of dark hair.

Roman sat up abruptly, the intensity of his gaze halting her breath. He grabbed her in a bear hug before dipping to devour her lips. The crisp night air couldn't cool her body. He kissed her slowly at first, nibbling her bottom lip. His tongue slid into her mouth and moved slowly from corner to corner, consuming every heated pant she emitted.

His kisses changed, became more aggressive. The rhythm sped up to full throttle as he breached the blanket and rested his palm on her thigh.

He withdrew his tongue and pulled away.

Now she was cold and lonely, longing.

He nibbled her lips, watching her as his hand blazed forward, branding his symbol in a trail from her outer thigh. Her eyes drifted closed, her lips parted in sync with her tongue. Roman delved into her mouth, defining what made her a woman. His kiss deepened to smother her moan. Akira felt a burning that intensified with his every rotation. Conscious that there were other couples near the wagon gate, she struggled to keep her hips on the hay-covered floor and her moans low. She grabbed two fistfuls of his jacket and held on, less she catapult from the wagon.

Roman tugged at her ear, whispered, "Ask me."

Akira inhaled deeply, her head falling back.

Roman chased her mouth. "Ask me, Akira."

She felt her body preparing itself—becoming wet and pliable—in anticipation of him touching her, loving her. Frustration over the fact that they could only go so far in this dark wagon on a deserted trail made her body more determined.

She knew what he wanted to hear, but ecstasy kept her from speaking.

Roman began to withdraw.

Akira's arms went around his neck, locking him to her. "Kiss me."

Roman assaulted her lips.

Akira wrapped her arms around his shoulders and held on tightly through the ride of her life.

Acquisitions

Chapter 13

Talk about your public displays of affection! Akira still couldn't believe how brazen Roman had been and how willing she had received his touches. This next morning, she pulled a cart of groceries behind her while carrying another bag in her free hand, still grinning.

The make-out session in his car hadn't been any more respectable. But when Roman came near, her basic and natural needs controlled her behavior. They had run from the wagon to his car, giggling all the way. As soon as they were both inside, he kissed her with raw hunger. Every one was filled with desire. Desire that only she could fill. As he covered her body with his, meshing their concave and convex parts, he whispered secrets in her ears. She shivered, imagining the intensity of his touch.

"Need help?" Luke, Akira's neighbor from across the hall, grabbed the cart handle and the bag in her hand allowing her to unlock the door.

"Thanks—don't let your pants fall down."

"Now I'm being a gentleman, why you gotta front on me 'bout my pants."

"I don't understand why you'd want to walk around show-ing everybody your goods." Akira tugged at the waistband of his jogging pants until they were positioned properly.

"I'll let you get away with that since my hands are full." Luke's bad boy image worked well for him. He placed her groceries in the kitchen and returned to the living room all smiles.

"You're a sweetie." She dropped her purse and keys on the closest table.

"I stopped by to deliver a package. I saw it sitting outside your door. I thought I should take it inside. Be right back."

Akira stood in her doorway and waited for him to return. "Wow, it's big." She pointed to the sofa. "Probably a Christmas gift from my parents."

"It's not heavy, just awkward 'cause it's big. There's a card, too." He produced a canary yellow envelope from the back pocket of his jogging pants.

"Thanks, Luke."

"See ya."

"Have you finished shopping for those kids of yours?"

"Not yet," he called over his shoulder. "Maybe we can hook up and hit the mall together."

"Any time."

After Luke let himself out, Akira began the tedious task of putting away groceries. She hated trying to make room for cans and boxes almost as much as cooking for herself. She grocery shopped only when absolutely necessary. Roman's remarks about her lack of sustenance urged her to make this shopping trip.

Time passed too quickly when she was with Roman. All of her troubles at work and with the police crowded in on her with him not there. Without Roman as a diversion, her tribu-lations gained her full attention.

She wondered where he spent his day. Who did he spend it with? Could he be somewhere questioning his sanity? Guilt attracted him to her. Now that they had spent time together, he

Acquisitions

could assure himself that he had paid his penance and she would never hear from him again.

What about his passion on the hayride?

Their personalities meshed, and they interacted like long-time friends. Romantic dinners, family outings—they had only scratched the surface. Her mind explored the possibilities; her heart lived out her every fantasy with Roman in the leading role.

She wanted to live with this illusion, no matter how surreal, for a little longer. With him near, she told herself, she could believe the things he said and cherish the moments he touched her. When they returned to work, she feared it would all disappear in a dark cloud of smoke.

A man like Roman didn't come around often, and when they did, they didn't look twice at a female the opposite of society's ideal woman. Eric drummed that into her head over and over again. Instead of a size two, she wore a size sixteen. She was proud of her looks and did her best with what she had to offer, but she would only be hurt if she considered herself Roman's prize catch. No, for this time they were together, she would live the dream, but as soon as they returned to work, she would release the fantasy like a child losing a helium balloon to the sky.

When she finished putting away the groceries, Akira let her curiosity get the best of her and she opened the card.

A lone red heart covered the outside. The neatly hand-written note inside read "Open." Excitement took over as she tore away the tape along the seam of the box. Only Roman would place a box outside her door.

Inside were two numbered envelopes. She opened envelope number one. This message read, "Answer the phone." She swung around, peering into the darkness of her bedroom. Hadn't she watched a horror movie that began like this? She moved through the house, awaiting the ring of the telephone while shedding light in her bedroom. A few minutes passed. Nothing happened. She checked the phone for a dial tone. She dialed Roman's house—no answer.

She suspended playing the game and made a chef salad, took a long bath, and curled up to the dogged-eared copy of *Friends and Lovers* Lara swore she had to read. An avid Eric Jerome Dickey fan, Lara used his books as her own personal self-help system. Akira had grown tired of being left out of conversations during their outings with other friends and finally gave in to starting the novel. In the middle of chapter three, when the plot pulled her in, the telephone rang.

"Hi."

"Roman, did you send the box?"

"Yes. Did you open the first envelope?"

"Yes."

"Did you open the second?"

"No."

"Good. Don't. Did you like your gift?"

"There wasn't anything inside."

"Of course there is. Take another look."

"Hold on."

"Take me with you."

Akira rushed to the living room, carrying Roman along on the cordless while turning on the lights as she went. She checked the box again. "It's empty except for the second card. What did you put inside?"

"Why don't you open the door and let me help you find it?"

"What?"

"Open your door."

She opened the door to find Roman leaning against the frame. The seductive heat of his body warmed the cold air that rode in on his heels. Full of mischief, he stood with his overnight bag slung over his shoulder. She tore her eyes away from the bag and all it implied. Looped over his hand he held a brown paper bag with handles made of rope. The logo across the front showed two lovers entwined in a fiery lip-lock. Her eyes skipped up the terrain of his body, crashing into his hood-

Acquisitions

ed eyes.

He scorched the space between them with his one word greeting, "Hi."

"Hi."

"Can I come in?" Roman disconnected the cell phone.

Akira stepped back. Disconnected.

"Where's the box?"

She pointed in the direction of the beautifully wrapped, empty box.

Roman peered into the darkness. "There it is. Come here." The serious tone disappeared, replaced with mischief.

"Roman, there's nothing inside."

"All the affection and passion you'll ever need is in this box. It's so magnificent, you can't see it with the naked eye."

Akira stood speechless. Her heart flipped. A wave passed through her stomach.

"I never want you to be without what you need to be happy, so I'm going to give you something you've never had."

"And that is?" Her throat tightened with desire as she looked up into the dancing flames of his eyes.

"Romance. You told me you've never had a whirlwind relationship. I have everything I could think of to make this a romantic evening for you."

"You didn't have to do that." Akira lowered her eyes as they began to cloud over. This man had her sprung, and it overpowered her with emotion to look into his eyes.

"I wouldn't do it if it were *mandatory*. I'm doing it because it should have been done a long time ago. Tonight, I'm righting the wrong of a brother before me. Because I know we won't get past that bump in our relationship until I do."

Roman dropped his bags down on the sofa and began to remove his winter gear. "I'm sorry I couldn't get here until late. Butch tied me up this morning, and then I had to take my sister to the airport."

Akira took his coat and gloves and went to hang them in

the outer closet.

"Do you want to unpack these?"

She gave him a questioning glance but tore into the bags. "What is this?"

"They match." He pulled out the pajama bottoms that matched the gown for her. "Go change."

"Roman."

"Take your time. I've got things to do out here."

She stalled. "What about the other card?"

"You'll open it later."

"But—"

"But you're stalling. Why?"

"It's that...we've just started dating and..."

"And with all that we're risking just to go out to dinner together, you're going to put limits on what might or might not happen between us tonight? Instead of forgetting the rules and letting your feelings take control, you're going to play by the rules."

She ran her tongue over her lips.

"Akira," he stepped forward and blazed her mouth with one of his heart-stopping kisses. "I want to give you this gift. Go change." He turned her by the shoulders and gave her a swat on the behind, sending her in the right direction.

Obediently, Akira entered her bathroom and examined the gown that felt like silky pearls. Anticipating what Roman's brawny thighs would look like in the matching bottoms weakened her. She sank down on the side of the tub. "What am I doing?" she mumbled to herself as she listened to Roman move around outside the door.

She wanted this. A romantic evening dressed in a sexy gown, talking and laughing and kissing. All with Roman. Yes, she wanted this to go as far as it would go.

But she hesitated. She made excuses. She questioned Roman's integrity, hoping to avoid the true roots of her uncertainty.

Being self conscious about her body image rattled her.

Acquisitions

She never cared how people judged her before—before Eric planted this seed of doubt in her head. As long as she treated people well and was a good person, being a size two never mattered. She used what she had. Not everybody could be stick thin. God bless those who were, but no blessings were denied to those who weren't.

She twisted in the mirror. The women in fashion magazines had stomachs as flat as ironing boards. She held the gown to her chest. Would it fall in a way to hide her love handles? She searched her thighs for signs of cellulite. Why couldn't she have thighs as firm as Roman's were muscular? She twisted to study her butt. Roman had to know when he purchased the gown that she wouldn't look the same in it as the women in the magazines would.

She slipped the gown over her head and checked her body in the full-length mirror. The gown flattered her curvy figure. The stretchy lace lifted and rounded her full breasts. The tapered waist and flared skirt accentuated her hips. Roman never stopped amazing her.

"Akira?" Roman thumped the door. "What's taking you so long?"

She shook the doubts. Shrugged them away. This would not be ruined by an endless analysis of their relationship. She took in a long breath and walked out the door. What she saw made her rock unsteadily on her bare feet.

Roman stood next to the bed, dressed in smoke-colored pajama bottoms. Her eyes glimpsed the cement slabs that were his thighs. His arms folded over his smooth caramel chest. His nipples stood on point. After taking it all in—the dimpled smile, the square shoulders, and the flat navel—her eyes roamed the course of dark hair that provided directions to the bulge in his pants.

"Do you like it?"

"What?" Akira's eyes snapped upward to his waiting grin.

"The gown? The room? I was going to write you a poem or sing a song, but I have no artistic talent."

114

Akira noticed the elaborate decorating that had occurred while she mused in the bathroom mirror. Candles smelling of vanilla, peaches and tangerines made the room glow. Roses—red, yellow, and white—covered the bed. Confetti matching the colors of the flowers covered the carpet. On the floor next to the bed was a huge bowl of ice cream covered with strawberries. Sprinkled over the pillows were tiny chocolates. Soft jazzy music flowed through the room.

"You don't like it?" Roman's dimples faded as quickly as he dropped his arms to his side.

"It's wonderful," she whispered, blinking wildly to keep the tears from falling. "I'm usually not this emotional. It must be everything at work—"

A grin moved his lips upward. "Would you like ice cream?"

"Yeah," the only word that escaped the thick build up of emotion constricting her throat.

Roman guided her by the waist to sit on the red body pillow he had thrown on the floor. He hadn't missed one detail. He joined her with the bowl of ice cream in hand.

"I think you were supposed to use the petals from the roses." She blew confetti into the air.

"My own twist."

Roman slipped a spoonful of ice cream into her mouth. He followed by lifting a strawberry to her lips. When she bit down, sweet whipped cream flowed over her tongue. He pulled another plump strawberry from the bowl, twirled it in the ice cream and popped it in his mouth. He rumbled with laughter when he caught her watching him.

"What about the second card?"

He fed her another spoonful of ice cream, "Later." He didn't take his eyes off the task of scooping up another strawberry. "Being here like this is nice."

"This is a dream."

Near the head of the bed, Roman retrieved a bottle of chilled wine. Two long-stem glasses were next. With a dim-

Acquisitions

pled smile, Roman served her whipped creamed stuffed straw-berries dripping with white wine.

They ate in a silence interrupted only by their laughs or Akira's soft humming. She filled her lungs with his sweet-woodsy scent, hoping to store a little piece of his essence inside to recall when he left her alone. He moved with delib-erate purpose, dipping the strawberries, careful not to spill a drop of wine. She nibbled at the fruit, sharing her sexy side as he openly displayed his.

If arousal was his intent, he had her on the brink of wan-ton. If she were brave, she would have pulled him to the car-pet and become the aggressor in this intimate game. All the pulse points of her body throbbed. Moisture pooled in the val-ley of her breasts. She crossed her legs to keep the aroma of her wet, steamy sex from escaping.

Roman bit the tip away from one of the strawberries. His finger went deep inside to scoop out the whip cream. He used it to paint her lips before lapping up every drop. Lost in his motion, she parted her lips and invited him inside. He took her as hungrily as he had on the hayride, behaving as if this were their first kiss.

He reluctantly pulled away and cleared the chocolates and the roses from the bed. He turned down the blankets and invit-ed her into her bed. "Join me, Akira."

The realization that her fantasy may come true made her eager, but shy. She wanted him to settle between her legs and teach her the rhythm of his movements. She had dreamed of his thighs trapping her long before their first kiss. The wicked gloom of doubt over his motives ebbed. The depth of his dim-ples chased it away.

Roman moved to take Akira in his arms the moment she swung her feet into bed.

"Something wrong?" he asked.

"This is a big step."

Roman nodded. His intense gaze revealed his determina-tion to understand the reason for her reluctance.

116

She tensed. Could she be all that Roman built her up to be? She had learned that Eric was wrong and she was satisfied with her body before the perfect stud of a man—Roman—walked into her life and started kissing her like she was the object of his desire. Now look at her. She had worked herself up into a state of personal crisis.

"I really enjoyed touching you last night." Roman's husky voice caressed her in the flickering vanilla and peach and tangerine darkness.

"Me too."

"Look at me."

She turned to face him, her heart jumping at his raw handsomeness.

He moved his head onto the pillow. His breath tickled her nose when he spoke. "I thought about you all day. I don't know what you've done to me." With that profound statement, he seized her lips. His tongue moved into her mouth and his passion flowed freely into her system. His hand gripped her waist.

She withdrew from his kiss.

"What's wrong?" His hand moved through her auburn curls and clasped the back of her head massaging her scalp. "You can talk to me. Whatever it is."

She stalled, "This is soon."

"Do you want me?"

She couldn't lie. "Yes."

"Then it's not too soon. You tensed up when I touched you. Why?"

Akira didn't answer, too embarrassed to verbalize her fears and bring attention to her deficiencies.

"Akira," he beamed. "C'mon."

She dropped her eyes to his bare, smooth chest. *Smooth legs, please.*

"Tell me."

"I wonder how I compare to the women in your past."

"You don't compare to them. You're completely different

117

Acquisitions

from anyone I've dated in the past."

"I know, but—"

"You're gorgeous." Roman moved to the foot of the bed where he produced a bottle of pink oil with the aroma of exotic flowers. He placed her bare foot in his lap, drizzled several warm drops onto the top of it, and began to knead the sole. He kneeled up to let his fingers dance in her hair. "And smart, and funny, and challenging, and adorable." He ended with a kiss to her forehead before settling down with her foot again in his lap.

"I don't have a perfect hourglass figure." She sat up to see his reaction.

"Oh, I get it now. Do you think I haven't noticed how your body's made? Do you think I'm blind, knucklehead?"

Akira dropped back as his fingers vigorously massaged her arch.

"You're a beautiful woman, and I can't wait to experience every inch of you." He lifted her other foot and placed it in his lap, repeating the pattern of his massage. "Do you like the smell of this?"

The scent of the oil mixed with the roses gave her visions of sitting English garden. "It's nice."

His palms roamed together up the length of her calves. "I won't push you if you're not ready." His thumbs stroked the underside of her knees making her wiggle from the tickle.

The synchronized beat of a snare drum monopolized the conversation. Roman silently concentrated his path of exploration up the inside of her thighs. His strong fingers worked magic, making desire radiate through her body. She laid back enjoying his full service of her. Silently willing him to travel higher and higher.

"Don't you know I wonder about your opinion of my body?"

"No," she answered. He had to be kidding. His body was perfect. Flat with ridged muscles that rippled when he walked. And the way his body carried a suit—obscene.

"I do. I wonder, 'Does Akira like guys taller than me or shorter? Does she think I'm too skinny? Is my nose too big?' And I know what women say about the size of a man's hands and feet." His hand enveloped her entire foot. "I don't want you to have any doubts about how attracted I am to you. Mind and body." He kissed the arch of her foot, sending shock waves to the triangle between her thighs.

He continued. "I'm under tremendous pressure to perform. Women say 'Don't do it right, then don't come back.'"

Akira tried to protest, but Roman's fingers began pulsating against her upper thigh. She moaned and twisted. *Higher, higher.*

"Are you alright?" A seductive lilt warmed his voice. A sly grin lit his eyes.

"I'm a little nervous."

"Then lay back." His tongue lazily caressed her inner thigh. "Close your eyes," a tender kiss absorbed her wetness, "and concentrate on relaxing while I take over. Remember, this is my gift to you."

Akira dropped back against the pillow, and the darkness engulfed her. She thought of the erotic hayride and how his kisses made her convulse. She had daydreamed about this pleasure many times. With every vision, her fantasy advanced. She wanted to place her lips on his abdomen directly below his navel and kiss him as gently as possible. While she did this, she wanted his body to respond by becoming hard, rising toward her, and waiting for its reward.

Roman left the bed, and a gust of cold air passed over Akira, hardening her swollen nipples to painful peaks. He stood near the head of the bed, his legs slightly parted. "Sit up," a gentle command.

Akira did.

"I want you to look at me." He tugged at the drawstring of his pajama bottoms.

Akira's mouth formed an O. The bottoms hit the floor with a loud wisp that reverberated through her body. She

Acquisitions

could not speak. He stood before her, completely naked with his hands held out. He turned in a slow circle, his back facing her. "Are you looking?"

"Y-yes."

Oh, gawd. His haunches stood high and firm, twin dimples leaving their indentions much like the dimples on either side of his face. His shoulders were square and straight. Golden brown skin covered every mouth-watering inch of his back and legs.

Akira's body responded as if he were stroking her. She turned to mush. She dripped with wetness.

Roman glanced over his shoulder, grinned with mischief, and turned to face her.

Thick neck, broad shoulders, wide smooth chest, narrow waist, round inverted navel, straight line of curly black hair, dense brush of curls between his thighs, and in the middle...standing at full attention, pointing at her accusingly...identifying her thirst for passion...

Akira swallowed. The dynamics immediately changed. She studied the rings of skin circling the upturned shaft, ending at the bulbous dark peak that glistened in the candlelight. Thick, rigid and ready with a sparkling pearl-drop... the issue became, could she take all that he had to offer.

"You can touch me."

She clamped her mouth closed.

He laughed. "Why do I feel like I'm seducing a virgin?"

She couldn't move. She had no words.

He came to her in one swift move, pushing her down on the bed, his lips meeting her with a fury. "Now I get to look at you."

His hand pressed into her thigh, his tongue circled her abdomen. His fingers gathered the gown, exposing her abdomen. He pushed it up, up, up, over her breasts, off and away. It landed silently next to his pajama bottoms.

Roman pressed his body to hers. His flesh burned, leaving a brand that no other man would ever be able to remove.

The blunt tip of his erection jabbed into her stomach. He ruined her—no man's touch would be acceptable when compared to his. Their skin meshed, his lips seared her neck, and his whispered words melted her. The burning throb at the top of her thighs made her spring up, groping his lips.

"Will you offer to let me touch you?"

"Touch me," she panted.

Roman sprung to his knees. His fingertips danced over her skin. Starting at her shoulders, over her breasts and squeezing her nipples, down her abdomen. He avoided the wetness soaking her triangle even though she arched her hips for him. Teasing the tender skin inside her thighs and tickling the back of her calves.

Liking the writhing effect his touch had on her, Roman leaned in until their lips almost met. "You like my touch." It wasn't a question. It was a prelude—a warning—of how he would violate her sanity next.

One long finger traced the triangle of her middle. Three times he made the rotation, never filling the space.

"Roman," Akira pleaded. All doubt of his attraction was long gone. She felt desperate for him to fulfill the promise, and she would beg if she had to.

Roman ignored her moans and pleas. He had a plan and he would move at his own pace. No matter if she thought she would go crazy if he didn't climb between her legs and fill her.

Roman sat back on his haunches. He parted her thighs.

Akira bent her knees, welcoming him, wishing he would hurry.

He used his thumbs to burrow through her tangled, wet hair.

A sharp intake of air. Hers or his? Too far gone, Akira couldn't distinguish. She panted in anticipation of the first electric shock that would accompany his caress.

Roman held the folds apart—wide. He showed her the finger he would use. Traced the slope of her nose and her cher-

Acquisitions

ry lips with it.

He started at the top of the fold and moved downward, agonizingly slow. Akira's thighs fell apart when she thought he would caress the bulging nub that screamed for his attention. He swerved around it, extremely careful to do just the opposite.

She whimpered in protest.

He stopped his journey at the opening that needed to be filled. With a twisting motion, he leisurely entered the cavity.

She whimpered for more.

She rocked her hips as he advanced deeper and deeper into the silky moisture dripping past his finger. He joined her moans with another sharp intake of air as he plunged another finger into the cavern.

He knew, as did she, that the fit would be tight. He added another finger to test the elasticity.

"Roman, please." Akira bucked at the sensation of being speared, but still not quite full. Not full enough to make her teeter over the edge. She wanted the emotional closeness of having him inside her with their bodies pressed together as one.

"Any doubt that I want you?" His voice sounded too cool, too controlled when Akira felt she was losing her mind.

"No, none." And there wasn't. "Please…" Akira felt erotic frustration welling in her eyes.

"Open the second card."

How could he be controlled in the mist of the frenzy consuming her mind and body?

"Open the second card." His fingers twisted and drove into her, emphasizing his message. "Open…the…second…card."

She groped near the pillow and found the card. With impatience and a touch of anger at his erotic torture, she ripped the card open. Inside, two words, "Ask me."

Her head snapped up.

Roman's thumb grazed her pulsating nub and all anger

disappeared. Tiny currents, burning her limbs.

"I want you. Roman, please." Akira writhed, pulling him to her.

His breath came in hot moist puffs next to her cheek as he removed his long fingers one by one. "I want you too, Akira."

Her hands cupped his behind. His hard thighs pushed hers aside and he laid in her warm wetness.

Roman's eyes were closed, his moans interrupted only by the faint sound of him calling her name. His sticky fingers enveloped her face while he guided himself inside her. She stretched to take in the shaft. He devoured her lips as he advanced further. While her body complied with his width, he whispered reassurances in her ear, kissing her shoulders.

After the initial shock of adjusting to him, Akira moved her body along with his rocking and grinding. He impaled her, stretching and stretching until their curly hairs kissed. She felt full, cocooned with him. He begged her to withstand the size and allow him to go deeper. He needed to touch that place in her that made them both surrender to their emotions. She wrapped her thighs around the inward curve of his waist, and he surged forward with an endless groan.

As passion-filled as their foreplay had been, their intimacy made Akira soar even higher. She floated above the earth with Roman as her safety net. As they sailed to the ground, her heart refused to land. She closed her eyes and buried her face in the safe haven of his chest.

Hang gliding turned into a roller coaster car ride, whipping her around sharp corners, uphill, and plummeting down steep curves. She relinquished her body to his control. Her heart and mind merged, bursting with magnificent color. She surrendered all her emotions to Roman.

"You are beautiful." He kissed her neck, helping her to regain her sanity.

Akira wrapped her arms around his back and pulled him in deeper toward his reward.

Acquisitions

Roman whispered, "I can never be deep enough." His breath came faster and hotter against the side of her face. He pumped and jabbed, losing the cocky control he had earlier. With a growl, he burrowed into her, releasing hot lava that burned like acid down her thigh.

"This—being with you—is what I've been needing," Roman confessed before he collapsed on top of her.

"Me, too." She held him for dear life.

They pulsed, him submerged in her wetness, and she bathed in his lava.

In the afterglow, they laid side by side in the darkness. Each with their own thoughts about the magnitude of what they'd shared.

Roman's cottony voice stirred Akira away from her private thoughts. "We need to talk."

She knew the time would come. She had known that all weekend. She thought she had mentally prepared herself, but she was not ready. Not after they had shared this level of closeness.

"What happens now?" Roman asked.

"Not yet." Her voice quivered, her chest shook.

"What?" He rested his head on his forearm.

"You don't need to say anything. I'm a grown woman. I know what happens from here."

"Meaning?"

"Meaning no strings attached."

"Are you saying this for my benefit or yours?"

"Both," she said.

Roman paused in contemplation. "Am I being dismissed?"

"I'm not in the habit of making anyone stay with me who doesn't want to be here."

"Is that what you think? That I don't want to be with you? What kind of person do you think I am?"

Akira remained silent.

"Is it *you* that wants to reconsider you and me becoming

us?"

"No." *God, no.*

"This whole weekend has been about me confessing my feelings for you. Maybe it's time you tell me what you feel and what you want."

"I don't know."

"That's not true. You know exactly what you want."

Akira confessed. "What I want and what is realistically possible are two different things."

"How do you know? You haven't discussed it with me."

Silence.

"Akira, you are the key to the only happiness I have felt in a very long time. I don't want to walk away from this." He reached over in the darkness and placed his palm against her cheek. "What do you want to happen now?"

"I don't want you to ever leave me."

Roman kissed her lips and pulled her to him. "Then I won't go."

Chapter 14

Roman expected Akira to say she wanted lavish dinners and expensive Christmas gifts. Or a serious relationship that led to marriage. Or a tall, dark and handsome rich man to spoil her rotten.

Instead, Akira wanted him to stay.

I don't want you to ever leave me.

Simple, yet profound.

Roman greeted morning with Akira's head on his chest. He brushed back the curly auburn mane tickling his chin.

The sun sliced through the Venetian blinds, striping the walls. Even though Akira's bedroom was warm, and they were cozy together, there could be no mistaking the cold, crisp wind whipping around outside. As a gusty breeze rattled the storm windows, Roman inched closer to her warmth.

The cellular phone rang in the other room. Roman ignored it and kissed the top of Akira's head instead. He didn't want to enter the outside world any sooner than necessary.

Akira drifted into semi-unconsciousness soon after Roman made her body shudder and shake. He had made the right decision. Butch had his best interests at heart, but he was wrong about this. He couldn't walk away from an attraction this strong. Coming to her and confessing his feelings had been his only option.

Decisions would have to be made between them. They had much at stake—their jobs and reputations to name only the major issues. The weight of their relationship would have to be evaluated, but Roman knew he was where he should be. As Akira snuggled against him, all he wanted to do was preserve the intimacy they shared when she released her body to his care.

"What are you thinking about?" Akira pulled up next to him.

"Nothing."

"Your forehead is wrinkled."

"I'm thinking about how wild you were last night." He lifted his arm and brought her closer. "How'd you sleep?"

"Good. You?"

"Hard."

Akira traced each of his dimples. "You have gorgeous dimples."

She shivered and he wished he could change the seasons.

Akira burrowed deeper. "Definitely time to consider moving to a warmer climate. Michigan winters are for people who wish they could live in Alaska, but can't find work there."

"Come here." Roman tightened his arms around her. "How about I take you to breakfast?" He glanced at the bed-side clock. "Or lunch. We could catch a movie, and I'll still get you home before late. Work tomorrow."

"Work tomorrow," she murmured.

Roman felt the negative mood shift. "Get dressed. I need to go home and change."

Akira whimpered before leaving his arms and trudging into the bathroom to shower.

***

"Make yourself at home," Roman said when they arrived

Acquisitions

at his house. He dropped his keys on the beige marble table next to the door and moved directly to the thermostat.

Akira had no idea there was a trendy new neighborhood off the shore of the Detroit River in the downtown area that boasted homes like these. Several houses had been abandoned in the new neighborhood before the construction had been completed, probably because of the weather. The neighborhood was an entanglement of one-way streets and cul-de-sacs that projected an atmosphere of block meetings and friendly conversation out on the front lawn.

"How long have you lived here?" Akira moved across the tiled floors of the foyer onto the hardwood floors of the great room.

"Close to a year."

She found him by following his voice. "Do you like it here?"

"Yeah, I really do. My neighbors are nice. They've sorta adopted me since I seem to be the only single man in the cul-de-sac."

I bet. Akira found him standing in the walk-in closet of the guest bedroom. As she watched him flip through the rack of clothing, she had to remind herself several times that this holiday weekend would soon end and everything would go back to normal. She understood how Cinderella felt as the clock ticked down to midnight.

"Here it is." Roman pulled out hunter green wool and silk blend slacks. "Perfect match, huh?"

"Perfect."

"I can't cook, but I can spot a decent suit a mile away. No wise cracks."

Akira held up her hand in surrender. "I wouldn't dream of it."

He grabbed a matching pullover. "I'll be dressed in fifteen minutes."

Akira took the opportunity to wander around his house. The décor of the spacious ranch felt comfortable and cozy.

128

The dark, rich wood grain flooring flowed throughout. It was buffed and shined so well, she could see her reflection in it. As she steered through the house, she stayed her course on the scattered throw rugs. The rugs were of different designs but shared a dark blue color in their pattern. The black leather furniture in the living room was the mark of a classic young bachelor. The room looked as if no one ever used it. Everything remained in its place.

Akira waited in the den. She pictured him sitting next to the fireplace at night reading his paper, or going over legal documents at his desk. She sank into the overstuffed chair next to the hearth after clearing away the discarded newspapers. All she needed was a cozy comforter, and she would feel right at home. After fitting herself into the permanent grooves left by Roman's frame, she turned on the television and flipped channel after channel trying to calm her mind. It had raced forward years into the future, past the millennium, to the time when she would be bundled in her comforter made cocoon watching Roman work behind his reading glasses at his desk. She leaned her head back against the softness of the chair and wondered how long her dream could last.

"What a goofy grin." Roman leaned over the back of the chair and kissed her forehead. "Do you like Mickey Mouse that much?"

Akira blinked and focused in on the television screen. "Yeah, I do."

I do. I do. I'm crazy.

"Did you check the paper to see when the movie starts?"

"No." She had been too busy dreaming about a storybook future.

He gave her a sideways glance before stooping down and gathering the discarded newspapers.

"I need to freshen up."

Roman collapsed in the matching recliner. "Do you remember where the bathrooms are?" he asked absently, thumbing through the paper.

Acquisitions

"I'll find it."

Akira wove her way back through the house until she found Roman's bedroom. She had freshened her make-up and was leaving the master bathroom when she came face-to-face with his past.

Against her better judgment, Akira went to the corner of the room where the chest of drawers stood. The woman in the pictures was more gorgeous than she could have imagined. Her demeanor in the photos displayed intelligence, class, and strength.

Akira's heart sank as she took in a sharp breath. Her happy illusion disappeared into a puff of smoke. She counted the picture frames—twenty of different sizes, shapes, and textures, but they had two things in common. All the frames were laced with gold trim, and the same woman appeared in each photo.

One photo in particular caught her attention. Until she examined the way Roman enveloped the woman in his arms and smiled at the camera, dimples fully exposed, she had hoped that maybe the girl was a relative. Any lingering hopes sank when she found the photo album with page after page of pictures of them together in poses reserved only for lovers. Now that she knew the truth, questions flooded her mind. She should have never trusted him.

Why was Roman pretending to feel something for her? Who could this woman be? Where was she? Was this all a sick game? His ruling—the kiss—last night—none of it made sense.

"I've been calling you."

Akira whirled around to face Roman with the photo album still in her hands.

"I got worried when you didn't answer."

"What is this?" she asked.

"Maybe I should ask you that." He lifted the photo album from her hands and replaced it on top of the chest. "You're going through my things?"

"Who is she?"

"If you're ready, we should be going." He turned to walk from the room, leaving her unanswered question hanging in the air.

Akira questioned her use of common sense when it came to Roman. After all, she knew nothing about this man. How could she have been so stupid as to let him into her bed? Into her heart?

What did she think would happen? Her daydream of more hayrides quickly faded into the past. She knew it. She knew that there was a woman hidden in his life. She had asked him. He had lied.

Roman reappeared in the doorway. "Are you coming?"

"I think I should go home. This isn't a good idea."

"Why? Because you found pictures of me with a woman?"

"Partly."

"What are you thinking?"

"I'm wondering if you have a girlfriend that would be very upset if she knew I was here. I'm starting to question my own judgment, letting you stay the night with me—"

"We slept together," he corrected.

Another reason to question her common sense. "I'm starting to challenge my own sanity. With everything that has happened to me in the past few weeks, it wasn't a good idea for me to let you get close this soon."

"It's normal for you to be stressed with everything you've gone through."

That's it? "That's it? That's all you have to say?"

"You want me to explain pictures that were taken before I ever met you?"

Akira crossed her arms over her chest and waited.

"I *will* tell you that I'm not involved with anyone. If I were, I wouldn't have told you how I feel about you. But I won't apologize for what I did before I even knew you."

They stood across from each other in a stare down.

Acquisitions

After a moment, Roman reached out for her hand. "We should be going."

"I'm not going anywhere with you. Not until you explain what this is."

"Do you think you have the right to question my past because we spent a few days together?"

Akira matched his attitude. "I specifically asked you, Roman. I asked you and you told me that there is nobody in your life. You had no trouble coming up with the perfect thing to say yesterday when you wanted to crawl in my bed. Why won't you answer me now?"

"Crawl in your bed?" he repeated incredulously.

Akira held firm. "Why won't you tell me what this is about?"

"I don't want to discuss this with you yet."

"I'm supposed to accept that?"

"Yes, you are, Akira. You're supposed to trust me enough to let me come to you about this when I'm ready."

"This is unbelievable."

"It's unbelievable that I found you going through my things, and you're demanding explanations from me." Roman paused, easing his anger and softening his tone. "You're making a big deal out of nothing."

"Nothing?" Akira swept her arm wide to indicate the picture collection. "What kind of games are you playing?"

"Games?"

"You came to my door, uninvited, and made space for yourself in my life. I didn't approach you, you approached me. Now you want to back off? After we've slept together? What do we talk about, and what do we keep secret? If you wanted to treat me like this, you could have left me alone."

"She's my last girlfriend," Roman blurted out. "The one who left me. There, you wanted to know."

"Obviously you didn't want her to go."

"This is why I didn't want to talk about her. We're not ready. We're still getting to know each other. You're pushing me to discuss this, accusing me of lying to you, and it's not like that at all. I want to know about your past, but not right now. Right now I want to know about you. Trust me to talk to you about this when I'm ready."

Akira looked away.

"I guess I've identified the problem: trust. Look, I know you have reservations because of the way the sexual harassment case came out, but we have to work past that."

Akira studied the desperate sincerity filling Roman's eyes. Her reaction wasn't about his dating history. She suspected he'd had many women before meeting her. Her reaction was based on her dating history with Eric and how he dismissed her feelings because she didn't make the perfect trophy wife. Taking a calming breath, she admitted the root of her insecurity. "I'm nothing like her."

"I never said I wanted you to be like her. Why are you comparing yourself to my last girlfriend? Do you think I'm running around trying to replace her?"

"Roman, I don't play games."

"Meaning?"

"Meaning, I'll be real with you—good or bad—I'll always tell you the truth. I look at these pictures and question your interest in me. If you feel guilty about your finding in the sexual harassment case, don't. I understand you could only work with the evidence you had. If you think I'm a wild woman because of the sexual harassment case, I'm not."

"Do you really believe this is only about sex for me? After last night?" Roman moved closer. "We talked about this already." He lowered his voice, twisted a lock of her hair between his fingers. "You've always come across as a tough, take-no-mess woman. Now you have doubts in your judgment? You don't believe in your heart that I'm being real with you? You think I came to you out of guilt and not because I've wanted to kiss you since that first day in my office?"

"I think a woman like her might fit your specifications perfectly." Akira pointed an accusing finger at the photos.

Acquisitions

Animosity filled his words. "You don't know what kind of woman she is."

Glancing toward the gold-trimmed picture frames, "I have an idea."

"What kind of woman do you think *you* are?"

Akira lifted her head with pride. "I know what kind of woman I am."

"I don't think you do—or you'd know she can't compare with you." He shook his head. "You're complex." His finger traced the bone structure of her face. "Tough as nails, soft as a baby doll."

"I'm not soft." She turned her head away from his finger. She wouldn't fall for the sweet lines. He couldn't win her over with fluff.

"Then there's only one explanation."

"What?"

"I scare you."

"No, you don't."

"You're scared about the intensity of your attraction to me. You're scared about the depth of my feelings for you."

Akira remained stoic. "That doesn't make sense."

"Yes, it does. That's why you're questioning everything that has happened between us. Don't play mind games with yourself. I'm where I want to be."

"How am I supposed to believe that when I find all these pictures?"

Picture after picture after collage of pictures.

His back stiffened. "Akira, either trust me or don't, but I won't justify my past to you."

Chapter 15

Akira chose the latter.

Returning to work would end it all anyway. Why sweat over the whole scene? She would not compete with the woman in the photos.

What had she been thinking? Letting Roman into her bed. The gown, the roses, the confetti, the music—him standing at attention, allowing her to take in every inch of his naked body—it added up to a lethal combination.

Having Roman gaze at her with lust in his eyes and touch her with desire made her head spin. She had jumped into bed with a man two days into their relationship. She lived by the three-month rule. Three months of dating, and then she decided if she wanted to move to the next level. Most times she didn't. Most men would leave before three months had passed because she hadn't met their agenda.

Akira slung her portfolio across the seat of her car and checked her pager. It had gone off several times during her meeting, but she was unable to respond until closing the deal. The commission she would receive from this account would come in handy as Christmas approached. She wanted to visit

Acquisitions

her brother overseas, and now that wish could actually become a reality.

The first two numbers belonged to Lara. The next was Roman's line at work. She continued to scroll through the numbers. A frown crossed her lips when she recognized Mr. Johnson's number. With dread, she called in to retrieve the message from his secretary. He needed her to see him when she returned to the office. She dialed Lara.

"Where is he?" Lara asked after Akira gave her the sketchy details of her argument with Roman.

"At the office. Where I'm heading."

"What are you going to do?"

"I don't know." She started her engine. "Roman makes me feel good; sexy and important. I wasn't missing anything before he came, but now that I've spent time with him, I see how much more there is to life." She paused. "But I can't deal with Roman right now. I have to go into the office and meet with Mr. Johnson."

"Is it fallout from the case?"

"I don't know. He's probably going to tell me that I have to start reporting to him again—instead of Mr. Lawton. Or maybe he'll gloat about denying me the promotion and transfer. I'm determined not to let him get to me. I'm going to stick it out until another opportunity arises, and I can leave Greico. I know Mr. Johnson lied. I know I did nothing wrong."

"That's my girl. Have you had time to deal with all of this? I mean, Roman was there right after you got the news. You need time to mourn what happened with your complaint."

"I tried. There's nothing more I can do."

"I'm not sure if I believe that, but that's not what I meant. You need to get angry, tear out the pages of a book, cry."

"I've been angry."

"Have you cried?" Lara's concern touched an area inside Akira she wanted to keep buried.

"I can't cry right now. I have to get through this. I have

to work. I'm afraid that if I start crying again I won't be able to stop."

"Oh, Akira...."

"I'm fine. Don't worry about me."

"Why don't we get together for dinner?"

"We will. I'll call you."

***

The moment Akira stepped off the elevator onto the sixth floor, she knew something was amidst. Whispers filled the room, mimicking the music of a swarm of bugs on a summer evening. People looked up when she passed by, silencing their conversations. She didn't expect things to be back to normal immediately after the dismissal of her sexual harassment case, but the blatant stares worried her.

When Akira opened her office door, Detectives Casser and Downs were inside. Casser sat at her desk going through the contents of her desk. Downs stood talking with Mr. Lawton and Roman. Akira dropped her portfolio on her desk and scanned the room for evidence of how much of her privacy had been invaded.

"What's going on here?" Akira addressed Mr. Lawton.

"As you know, a valuable drug formula was stolen several weeks ago," he answered with a harsh tone of conviction.

Akira waited as he stated the obvious.

"Certain evidence has implicated you in the theft."

"What evidence?" She looked over at Roman, who remained silent and averted his eyes to Casser. The detective busied himself reading her papers.

Casser stood up, his full height barely bringing his waist over the top of the desk. "We have a few questions we need to ask you. We'd like to do that here. Or we can do it down at the station."

Roman moved to Akira. His face and voice pleaded with her. "Ms. Reed, you're entitled to counsel before you answer any questions. Don't feel pressured to do this now."

Acquisitions

Ms. Reed? She knew that their short-lived relationship could cause problems for them at Greico if anyone found out—they'd decided together not to openly advertise their involvement—but Roman was standing against her with her enemies.

"I don't have anything to hide," she spat at him.

What they had shared meant absolutely nothing to him. Akira turned off all emotions directed to Roman. She had made a huge mistake trusting him. It would not happen again. But right now she could not deal with Roman Miller and his empty promises.

"Great," Detective Casser said sarcastically. "Let's have a seat."

"Do all these people have to be here?" Akira asked, not taking her eyes from Roman.

"No, not at all." Detective Downs shook his head to move the stray clump of brownish-black hair that had fallen into his eyes.

Roman hesitated to leave.

"I'd like to speak to the detectives without a representative of Greico Enterprises present." Akira stated coldly, looking straight through him.

Mr. Lawton ushered Roman out of the office with him. "If *she* is responsible for this," Akira could hear Lawton saying, "I will personally see to it that she is punished to the full extent of the law. Akira Reed has caused more trouble around here lately than she's worth. I wish I could fire her and be done with it. I probably would have to, damn the consequences, but Barry pleaded her case. He's a good man. There's no way I would have defended her after the hell she put him through."

Roman reached behind him to close the door.

Akira used her height advantage over Detective Casser to intimidate him into stepping away from her desk. She took the seat he previously occupied and asked the obvious, "Who implicated me in taking the formula?"

Casser ran his hand over the contents of her interoffice

mailbox. "A witness puts you at the scene around the time the formula is believed to have been taken."

"I didn't have anything to do with it. Everyone knows that the night the formula was stolen I was being attacked by Mr. Johnson."

Casser shared a furtive look with Downs. Akira read the silent transmission as his way of calling her a liar.

Downs stopped fighting his unruly hair long enough to enter the conversation. "Ms. Reed, the theft of the formula is a criminal investigation. It has nothing to do with the internal politics of Greico Enterprises."

"In other words," Casser interrupted, "if you have anything to say, say it now."

"I don't know anything about the formula. I didn't have anything to do with it. Who else are you questioning?"

"That's not important." Casser dropped down in the chair directly in front of her desk. "Right now we're talking to you, and I think you know more about this than you're letting on."

Akira waited for him to go on.

"I believe you took that formula. Yes, I do. I think you were in the middle of making your escape when Mr. Johnson showed up and interfered. Now we've talked to Mr. Johnson, and he is a piece of scum, so it's possible he came on to you. I don't know about that, and frankly, I don't care. Whether you wanted it or not, it provided you with a way to keep attention away from what you had done. Filing a sexual harassment complaint was a nice touch."

"You believe this, too?" Akira asked Downs. She needed someone to be on her side. In their previous meeting, he had seemed to be the more compassionate of the two.

Downs stepped up to her desk. "It is a bit convenient."

***

The doorbell continued to chime disturbed intermittently by the ringing of Akira's phone.

The shrill ringing aggravated her into snatching the phone from the cradle. "You used me. Go away and leave me alone."

Acquisitions

She slammed the phone down and walked to the back of her apartment.

Akira did not want anything more to do with Roman. She had learned during her dating years that it was very valuable to be able to let go and walk away. That's what she had decided to do as the detectives accused her of stealing. She was in deep trouble, not only with her job, but also with the law. She considered quitting and finding other employment, but now she feared it would paint a guilty picture if she left the company while the investigation went on.

The cry Lara spoke of earlier would come as a comfort now as Akira's world began a counter rotation that threw all of her safe routines off kilter. She tried to embrace the fear and anger and turn it into a waterfall of tears, but it wouldn't come. Tears were equivalent to self-pity in her book. She had no time for pity or regrets. She was in deep trouble and could only rely on herself to get out of it.

The incessant ringing of the doorbell and phone tore at her nerves. She took a hot shower and dressed in her favorite gown. When she came out of the bathroom, the ringing bells had stopped. Roman had gotten the message—after being in the hallway for an hour—that she was finished with him. She went to the kitchen to begin cooking her dinner when the knocking started.

Couldn't he see that she didn't want to hear anything he had to say? She owed him nothing. She didn't have to hear him out. If he insisted on banging on her door all night, she'd call the police to remove him.

His knocking became an urgent pounding. "Akira! Open the door. I want to talk to you."

The door rocked on its hinges. Akira could hear her neighbors yelling at him to keep the noise down. She wouldn't have to call the police—one of them would.

"Akira, don't let him in. Hold your ground." The elderly woman down the hall shared words of solidarity.

Roman kept pounding. "Akira, open the door. Let me

explain."

Akira picked at her salad while Roman stood in the hall-way making a jerk out of himself. Her stomach twisted as she pretended not to hear his pleas.

"I'm making a fool out of myself, Akira. Please let me in."

Roman would have thought he had enough of making a fool out of himself with Sherry, but here he stood knocking on Akira's door begging her to let him inside. Memories of the surprise visit he paid to Sherry's hotel room in New York resurfaced.

Soon after she left town, Roman decided to prove that she was wrong. They *could* sustain a long-distance relationship. Even though Sherry told him not to follow her, he tried to save their relationship. He flew to New York and popped up at her hotel to surprise her. The desk clerk surprised him by telling him that Sherry had checked out after two days and moved into an uptown apartment. He wouldn't give Roman the address. No amount of money would loosen the desk clerk's lips. Roman returned home and never heard from her again.

He didn't know why Sherry easily walked away from what he believed to be their future. She had dreams of a part-nership at a Wall Street firm. Roman had dreams of being with her forever. Career came first with Sherry, Roman second. Her rejection of him fueled his desire to rise to partner at Greico Enterprises. Never once did he question his compla-cent attitude at Greico. His future was there. And when he made it to the top, he would show Sherry that he could be equally as ambitious.

To this day, he hadn't talked to her. Months after her dis-appearance from his life she resurfaced at Butch's firm. She flew into town unannounced, met with Butch regarding team-ing up on a case, and whipped out of town again before he knew she had come. The way she wanted it to happen. Butch showed up on his doorstep that evening with the news. The second rejection hurt far worse than the first.

Acquisitions

Akira came into his life, teaching him who he truly was inside. Career goals were important, but having her meant much more. Never once did she imply that he didn't try hard enough. She never hinted that he should network more often. They never discussed his work at all. Akira wanted to know about him, his past and his dreams.

Seeing her with the intimate pictures of his vulnerability rattled him. He reacted defensively. Akira and Sherry were two separate issues in his life. They could not occupy the same space. Like he told Akira, he wasn't ready to go there with her yet.

The pictures had lined his dresser for years. They became part of the decor. They were as permanent as the beige paint on the walls. They'd become so familiar, he didn't see them anymore. But if they were gone, he'd recognize the absence right away.

"Damn, man." A young man dressed only in blue jogging pants joined Roman at Akira's door. He raised his fist and pounded loudly. "Akira, I gots to get me some sleep. You know I work the midnight shift. Now either open the door up, or I'm gonna call the police." He gave one last thump on the door.

The women standing in the hallway watching the scene waited with stalled breath to see if the police would be making an arrest in their building. The older woman was ready to be a witness and tell everything she had observed.

The door opened a slither.

"You want me to call the cops for you, Akira?" His voice lost its angry edge. Tenderly, he asked through the opening of the door, "Is he bothering you?"

Roman watched the interaction of the twenty-something-year-old-boy taking care of his thirty-something-year-old-man business. He questioned why the boy felt enough at ease with Akira that he could not only get her to open the door, but knew how to make her feel safe.

Akira said something to him that Roman could not hear

from his vantage point.

"Alright then, but you have any trouble, you give me a call."

The boy turned and looked at Roman with tired disgust. "You need to learn how to handle your woman, dawg." With that he walked off and returned to his apartment.

The women in the hallway sensed that the show had ended and closed their doors.

Akira opened the door wide enough for Roman to enter.

"I did not betray you." He started in on his defense the second he stepped inside. "I paged you to tell you that the police were waiting for you." "What good would that have done? Did you think I would pack my stuff and go to a safe house?"

"I could have helped you. I told you not to talk to them without a lawyer present. If you would have refused I could have told you what to do next."

"I don't need anymore of your help. Look what it has gotten me so far."

"I told you that I wasn't going to let you down, and I meant it." Roman really did want to help her, he wasn't sure of the best way to go about it.

"You've gotten what you wanted, now why don't you go away and leave me to handle my own problems?" Roman raised an eyebrow, his face angry and confused. "Meaning?"

She turned her back to him.

"Are you implying that since we've slept together I've 'gotten what I wanted'?"

Akira locked her arms across her chest as defense against the emotions swirling freely around the room.

"Is that what you think I'm about, Akira?"

She remained silent.

"Okay, fine." Roman moved to the door. "If that's what you think it's all about, then fine. That's what it'll be about."

Roman swung the door open. A gush of cold air hit Akira

Acquisitions

in the face, sobering her too late. He stepped through the archway, pulling the door shut with a bang.

Chapter 16

An impromptu blizzard hit the city, and traveler's advisory warnings went into full effect by three. Anticipating that the rumors were flying around the office about her guilt in the theft of the drug formula, Akira decided she would not go to the office until the people on the sixth floor had gone for the day. All the employees were sent home with the announcement of the advisory, and Akira seized the opportunity to visit the office unnoticed.

"You're in quite a bit of trouble."

Akira whirled around to see that Mr. Johnson had slipped in her office. He closed the door with a soft click. "Do you understand that the only reason you still have a job is because I went to bat for you with Mr. Lawton?"

Should she thank him? Her life had been shattered because he refused to stand up and take responsibility for his actions. Saying this to him might not be the wisest move since they were alone on the sixth floor.

Mr. Johnson's stubby fingers moved over the thickness of his beard reminding Akira of how the texture felt against her thighs. She shuddered internally, refusing to allow him to see

Acquisitions

her nervousness. She spoke firmly, "You shouldn't be here."

"Why not? Because you might accuse me of assaulting you again?"

Akira pushed away from her desk to stand up.

Mr. Johnson impeded her progress by bolting around the desk and trapping her chair. "What are you going to do? Scream for help?"

"I will if I have to. You don't scare me." Once she spoke the words, she realized his menacing presence did scare her. "I'll file another sexual harassment suit against you—outside of Greico Enterprises—where you won't be able to have your friends cover for you."

"I don't think anyone would take you seriously, little girl who cried wolf. Everyone is fully aware of the fact that you're a spurned wannabe lover out for revenge at any cost. Including stealing from the company."

Akira's head whipped up and around. "Are you responsible for the police thinking I took the formula?"

Mr. Johnson, not Roman.

"No, not really. I might have planted the idea in that lawyer's head when I told my side of what happened, but I won't take full responsibility. You're to blame for most of it. If you hadn't filed that complaint, no one would've known you were here alone that night."

Mr. Johnson lied. He was responsible for implicating her to the police. Roman hadn't told the police anything about her—just as he tried to tell her. As Akira cursed for turning on Roman so easily, Mr. Johnson's hands began to slither down her shoulders. His fingers came to a stop when they found the impression of her bra strap.

The familiar fear of the night that started this whole mess crept up on Akira with the tiny legs of beetles. "I better leave."

"Where are you going? There's a blizzard outside." He pushed his lower body against the chair, keeping her from sliding away from the desk. "On the other hand, I have something in the office that will warm you." A sickening moan of sexual

146

need came from him as his thumbs outlined the length of her straps. "And then you can warm me, show me a little appreciation for what I've done to save your job. Prove that you're a team player. Now that you know the rules, we can put this whole incident behind us, and you can start to act appropriately toward your boss."

Before Akira could answer, Mr. Johnson's face was next to hers, planting kisses on her cheek. She struggled, fighting to get up and keep his lips away at the same time. His hands came around and grabbed her breasts. The violation gave her an adrenaline rush that enabled her to push the chair back into the knot of his groin. He stumbled, but recovered quickly. He lunged at her. She responded with a swift kick to the groin. He doubled over with an agonizing moan.

"Stay away from me," Akira yelled, grabbing her coat and racing to the elevator.

Cupping his groin, Mr. Johnson limped behind her.

"The surveillance cameras will see what you're trying to do. This time there'll be evidence to back me up."

The threat stopped Mr. Johnson cold. He watched her hurry onto the elevator, pushing the buttons frantically.

"It's the chase that makes it sweet." Struggling to stand upright, he put an arrogant smile on his face. "Remember, this is to stay between us. You're hardly in a position to make anymore waves around here."

Chapter 17

"And now she's not speaking to you?" Butch asked as he pulled the Christmas evergreen by the stump out of the back of his SUV.

Roman grabbed the top of the tree. His tight-lipped reply, "Nope."

They started across the compact yard toward Grandma Dixon's condo.

"Roman, Akira's nice—don't get me wrong—but what about her has gotten under your skin?"

"Did you see her eyes?"

"Yes, but this isn't about a pretty face. It can't be just a physical thing. I know you wouldn't get involved with a woman tangled up in a sexual harassment case because you like her eyes."

They maneuvered the tree to fit through the doorway.

"The day she walked into my office I looked up into her vulnerable eyes and something happened. I can't explain it."

"Try." Butch dropped his end of the tree and began to stabilize it in the stand.

Roman held the trunk in his gloved hand while Butch

worked. "Akira is incredible. Right away it felt like we've known each other for years. I can't stand to see her hurting. She's exposed, defenseless against Johnson. I know he's up to something."

"And you want to protect her?"

"Anything wrong with that?"

Butch stepped back to study the tree. He gave Roman hand signals until it stood straight. When the job was done he asked, "Since when have you started liking the I-need-a-big-strong-man-to-protect-me type? You're usually the vulnerable one in the relationship."

Roman cut him a harsh look.

"Sorry. You have to admit that you're usually the passive partner. You let Sherry run the show, and you loved every minute of it. Sherry decided your career path, social calendar—hell, she picked out what suits you would wear everyday."

Roman cringed at memories of his foolishness.

Comparing Sherry and Akira seemed foul.

Roman tried to explain. "I'm trying out a new role, and I'm finding that I like it much better. Akira needs me. I like that. I like being the man with her. I like that she wants me to be the man."

Always wise, Butch pointed out the obvious, "Except that she's not speaking to you right now."

"Roman! Butch!" Grandma Dixon's frantic voice sliced into their conversation.

Within a breath they were at her side in the doorway.

"My goodness, child. What are you doing out in this weather?" Grandma Dixon grabbed Akira's shoulder and pulled into the foyer.

"I'm looking for Roman. Is he here?"

Roman rushed up. "Akira. What's wrong?"

She glanced at his grandmother.

"Grandma, I can take it from here."

Grandma Dixon looked between them with a smidgeon of

Acquisitions

doubt. Butch helped take her away by asking her to check out the tree.

"What happened? Are you hurt or something?" Roman helped Akira remove her coat as he guided her into the living room. Tiny tremors moved across her shoulders. The dark, alluring eyes that attracted him to her were full of terror.

"I'm sorry for what I said to you. I didn't mean it. I was scared and didn't know what to do."

He knelt in front of her. "I know. Is that why you're upset?"

"The police made me crazy after questioning me about stealing from the company. I should have known you would never—"

"Akira." Roman cradled her face in his palms, focusing her. "Forget about yesterday."

Akira pressed her head against his palm and soaked in his forgiveness. "Mr. Johnson came on to me again. I ran out the office and went straight to your place. I couldn't find it. I got lost in the one-way streets. That made me more scared. I didn't know what to do. I came here hoping to find you."

"You did the right thing." Roman thanked his higher power that she made it to his grandmother's home in one piece. The roads were snow-covered and slick with ice. In her distraught condition, she could have wound up a statistic.

He moved next to Akira on the sofa, never releasing her hands. "Calm down. I'm here now. What did Johnson do?"

As Roman listened, he kissed Akira's temple and soothed away her jitters with a tender touch and soft words. Inside, he blazed with anger. He wanted to drive to the office and pummel Johnson into the ground. If Johnson wanted a fight, let him take on a man.

Grandma Dixon, who overheard with the help of her new hearing aid, eased into the room. "I don't understand what's going on in my own home. What are you going to do about this, boy?"

Akira interjected. "Grandma Dixon, this isn't Roman's

150

problem."

"Nonsense. He's your man ain't he? Then he's supposed to protect what's his. He can't let another man go around disrespecting his woman like that. Now, boy, what are you going to do about this?"

"I'm going to take care of it, Grandma." He gazed into the dark eyes that stole his heart and made the promise again. "I'm going to take care of it."

Grandma Dixon did what she does best and fed Akira a heaping plate of meatloaf, green bean casserole and mashed potatoes. Akira picked over the food while Grandma Dixon prodded her to eat up, and Butch kept careful watch over the entire scene. Sensing Akira's weariness, Roman took her back to his place.

In front of the fireplace in his den, Akira huddled on one end of the sofa and he on the other.

"Akira, what are you thinking?" She had been silent too long.

She placed her glass of wine on the end table. "You tell me you want me. Mr. Johnson says he wants me. I'm asking the same question with two very different men, why?"

And you don't trust either of us, Roman thought. He asked, "You compare me with Johnson?"

A shadow passed over her face.

Roman wanted to know, but couldn't stand to hear it. A man had tried to shake her self-esteem. Akira didn't let her passion flow freely. He had to advance her timid kisses. The reluctance of undressing—giving him full reign of her body to observe and titillate—had been the first sign. He knew men who were intimidated by strong women. Their ability to control the relationship related directly to the degree of guilt and self-doubt they could impose on the woman. He tried to right the wrong the other night, in her bed, by burying himself inside her and pushing the memories out with every thrust of his hips. As he watched the sadness and suspicion crowding her, he learned it hadn't been enough.

Acquisitions

His gut tightened. "You think what I feel for you is no different than Johnson's violation."

She stared into the fireplace. The crackling and aroma of hickory gave the illusion that the electric fireplace burned real wood. With splintering sentiment, Roman realized that having sex made the emotional bond of their relationship no more real than the manufactured authenticity of the fire.

"You can't see the difference?" he demanded.

She rubbed her temples. "I can't see anything clearly right now."

"Explain."

"I can't."

"You will." He dipped his head, seeking her gaze.

She couldn't explain because she couldn't acknowledge the pain attached to whatever was blocking her acceptance of their relationship. No bond of trust existed between them. That's why she so easily accused him of implicating her in the theft of the HIV vaccine.

"Roman—"

"The other night, in your bed, what do you think that was about?"

"I..."

"I told you—trust me or don't. It was too easy for you to believe that I called the police on you. How hard was it to come to me tonight when you were scared?"

Silence, too long, the artificial fire cried out with a sizzle and pop.

Roman pressed. "When I made your body feel good, when you let your guard down, you said you never wanted me to leave you. At Greico, you told me to go away. Tonight you say our connection is the same as Johnson violating your body." Roman turned her to face him, his anger building in proportion to his frustration. "Ask me. Right now, you ask me."

Confusion exploded with the brilliance of firecrackers. Trust, suspicion. Need, desire. Sex, making love.

Akira pressed her lips together.

Roman wanted to kiss away her fears.

He would.

If she would ask.

"Roman," Akira asked with a controlled tone, "did you have anything to do with the police questioning me?"

"Nothing."

Visible relief. "I will never accuse you again."

Roman waited.

"Tonight, when Mr. Johnson…" She shuddered at the memory of Johnson violating her. "The only thing I wanted to do was find you. The only thing I wanted was the safety of your arms."

"Ask me. Ask me for what you want and I *will* give it to you."

"I want to stay with you tonight."

"Done."

"I want you to save me."

Startled into silence, rocked into arousal, Roman leaned over and teased the cherry flavoring from her bottom lip. Physically, Akira provided the playground for his lust. Mentally, emotionally, she made him see his strength as her protector. He nibbled her lips, savoring the sensuality of it all—physically, mentally, emotionally—Akira was the whole package. His arousal was instantaneous, growing and hardening with each stoke of her tongue. As his kisses grew deeper, Akira fell into his arms. He nibbled on her top lip. When she moaned, he gave her his tongue. When she whimpered, he slipped his finger into the corner of her mouth.

Akira latched on to the length of his finger, suckling as if she would never let him go.

Roman dipped his head and returned the gesture to the peak of her nipple, penetrating her pink silk shirt, then her bra. He suckled until she fell backwards. Forcing the issue of trust, he took her hands and pinned them to the arm of the sofa.

He kissed his way across her chest, finding the bud of her

153

Acquisitions

right nipple. The one he soon learned was more sensitive than her left. He latched on to the peak through the layers of lace and silk. Akira thrashed beneath him, signaling for more. Her arms slipped. He tightened his grip on her wrists and continued to suckle.

Akira lifted her hips to meet him in a slow bump and grind. He felt the tightness in his groin, the wet pearl saturate his boxers. Her moans encouraged him to add more suction to her breast.

"Roman."

He looked up, falling into the depth of her dark eyes. He pressed his forehead to hers, nibbling at the corners of her mouth.

"Roman…" She found his lips and kissed him passionately.

Unable to harness his response to her passion, he matched the rhythm of her hips. Her motions grew faster until she exploded beneath him.

***

Roman tucked Akira into his bed and went into the den to place a phone call.

Butch brought their argument to a crescendo. "Only trouble will come from this. I know you feel for Akira, but I told you to let her go."

"But I didn't," Roman retorted through a locked jaw. "Now I need your help."

He had considered jumping in his car and chasing Mr. Johnson down like a dog. The depth of Akira's problems stopped him. A time would come when he would get the chance to take Johnson down. Right now his priorities were comforting Akira and determining the thief inside Greico's walls.

"What am I supposed to do," Butch asked, "when you won't listen to anything I say?"

"Akira can file another complaint."

"Which, by the way, her boyfriend will be in charge of

investigating. Do you see where I'm going here?"

Roman silently held on to his frustration.

"I ask again, what am I supposed to do when you won't listen to my good advice?"

"Are you going to help me or what?"

Butch sighed long and deep. "I like her, okay? I felt sorry for her tonight. I'll think on it." He made a shivering noise.

"What are you doing?" Roman asked, annoyed. He had a fair idea of what made his friend shiver on the other end of the phone. He wanted Butch to drop everything and help him solve Akira's problem.

"I have company. It's a cold night. Why don't you climb into bed and get warm?" Butch sucked in a jagged breath. "I'll think of an angle, make phone calls. I'll talk to you in the morning. Peace."

"Peace out." Roman hung up knowing that he did the right thing calling Butch. He would help. He'd never been in a jam that he couldn't count on Butch to get him out of.

"Who are you talking to? Butch?"

"What are you doing up?" He swiveled his chair around and held up his arms for Akira. She switched her hips across the room. His button down shirt strained to conceal her bare breasts. The space between the buttons provided a peek-a-boo pouch. Inside, the creamy smoothness of her honey-brown skin winked. Before she crossed the room and dropped into his lap her nipples were hard.

"I woke up, and you weren't there."

"I called Butch. He's going to help."

"I don't know what I would do without your support."

"Don't make it sound like I'm making a supreme sacrifice. Butch and I are going to take care of this. With him working from the outside and me inside, we'll find the person who stole the formula. When that's put to rest, we'll find a way to prove what Johnson did to you. In the meantime, stay away from the office as much as possible. Let me know if you need to go in. I'll find a way to be there. Keep working, remain focused and

Acquisitions

stay strong. This is going to be alright."

Akira embraced his neck with a force that told him not many had gone out of their way to protect her.

"Christmas is less than a month away. Put your effort into packing."

Her head shot up. "Packing?"

"Butch and I have a timeshare cabin up north. We spend a lot of time there skiing and ice fishing. Our schedules have been clashing, and we haven't made the trip this year. Anyway, we've planned to spend Christmas there, and I want you to come along. You need to get away, and I'm not leaving you alone on Christmas."

"I'd love to go but I promised Lara we'd do something together."

"Bring her along."

"I'll ask her."

"You're tense again."

She snuggled into his chest. "You left me."

"I know how to loosen you up. Put you to sleep but good."

Her dark eyes danced at his not so subtle seduction. "Race you."

She hopped off his lap and darted down the hall. Roman stayed an admirable distance behind. Where he could get the best view of her swaying bottom.

Chapter 18

Roman became obsessed with solving the mystery. He had two issues to resolve: the theft of the drug formula and proving the truth about Johnson's behavior. The second might be easier than the first. Roman started there.

Akira's strength and pride drew Roman to her initially, but they were starting to get in the way. She wanted to handle Johnson's continued advances on her own. Despite his promise to let her, he called Johnson first thing the morning after she ran to him. Roman told Johnson they needed to meet before he could officially close the sexual harassment file. Told him that he would be calling Akira for the same, a subtle warning that he was monitoring the situation.

Roman covertly reopened the sexual harassment case. He concentrated on finding evidence that would prove Johnson's guilt. His impartial viewpoint vanished. He no longer relied on credibility issues to determine who was telling the truth. As his grandmother kept needling him into doing, he let common sense guide him while he protected his woman.

One by one, Roman called the women of the sixth floor to his office for informal interviews. He focused on those not

Acquisitions

involved with his original investigation. He took a third look at the cases that were filed involving Johnson over the past few years. He worked with Columbia to review the recent raises and promotions of the women working under Johnson. Several had advanced quicker than the norm. Many pay scales were abnormally high for the number of years working in the company, including the pay rate of the newly hired Danisha, and Candace, Johnson's girlfriend.

There had to be one other woman in the company who had had the courage to tell her story, one woman who would come forward and substantiate Akira's charges. If one of the victims who filed charges in the past would trust him enough to tell him what made them recant, Roman would hopefully have the evidence he needed. Of course, if Johnson learned what Roman was up to, he would threaten their jobs, driving them deeper into silence.

Roman's mind rattled with the injustice of it all. He assured Akira every day that he was working on uncovering the truth. After several weeks, she began to give up hope of vindication, but he never stopped trying to protect her.

The elevator arrived quickly; most of the employees had gone for the day. Roman stepped on, its lone passenger, and pushed the button for the basement. The bright lights in the hallway burned his eyes. He maneuvered through the maze of unmarked offices, finding the security pods by sheer memory. To label the underground floor the basement was deceiving. The decor varied from the decor in the rest of the office building, but it didn't resemble the guts of an old building.

The lower level had recently been remodeled. The walls were painted, pictures hung, and new tan carpeting installed. Roman rang the buzzer for entrance into the security pods. He removed his badge from his suit jacket and ran it through the scanner when requested. The man behind the glass punched a series of numbers into a computer console.

Roman heard the lock release. "Enter." The door closed behind him with a solid thump, and the lock engaged.

158

The security pods were a new network of corners and rooms to learn. Roman was disoriented by the time he reached his destination. Television screens in every room displayed different areas in the building, the elevators, and the parking lot. The stark white rooms combined with the bright light of the screens to irritate his eyes. The pods had a sterile appearance. All the security police passing him were armed with black revolvers and handcuffs. He even passed a room where two officers sat watching television while they guarded an empty jail cell.

"This is some set up," Roman said, hoisting himself up in a chair to view the television monitor.

Mr. Tabrinsky, the security supervisor, loaded a diskette for Roman. "Yes, sir. We're responsible for guarding highly secretive information at Greico. This company provides security for all the branches of Greico Enterprises throughout the country. The incident with the missing formula is a disgrace on this department, and we're taking it personal, if you know what I mean. We're working closely with the police to solve this crime."

"You provide security for all the Greico offices? I thought you were a part of building security."

Mr. Tabrinsky proudly shook his head. "The security this building supplies is limited to patrolling the parking lot, validating parking, and watching the camera in the main lobby. We do the real work here."

Roman nodded. "Who was on duty the night the formula was stolen?"

"We scale down on personnel at night, which makes no sense to me, but it was Mr. Johnson's decision."

"Mr. Johnson wanted you to cut the staff at night? Why? When did this happen?"

Mr. Tabrinsky shrugged. "Several months ago. He told me it had to do with his budget; he needed to cut people across the board, 'It came from above,' he said. Personally, I think it's because the more money he saves in office expenses, the

Acquisitions

bigger his bonus at the end of the quarter. Or," he laughed, "because of what happened a couple of months ago."

"What happened?"

"He and that great looking woman, Candace, had a late night sales meeting in the lounge, if you know what I mean. One of my guys was making his rounds every half hour when he found them."

Roman nodded, silently contemplating how this all might influence Johnson's motivation to lie, or establish a pattern of sexual harassment in the office.

"Who knows about this?" Roman asked.

"Me and the security policeman that found them. Mr. Johnson *encouraged* me to keep it quiet. Stood in my office while I destroyed the disk."

"Did he threaten your job?"

"No. Johnson has this way of explaining things to you that make you feel like you're in the wrong. If you know what I mean."

Intimidation 101. Roman backed off not wanting to alienate a valuable source of information. "So, who was on duty November ninth?"

Mr. Tabrinsky blew a puff of air. "Diller. Off the record, not my best man. I've been trying to get him out of here for a long time. The union says he stays, he stays."

Roman made a mental note to research Diller's work history. "Have you viewed the tapes?"

"Yes, of course. Whoever broke into the safe where the formulas are kept is clever. I have no doubt in my mind it was an inside job. As you'll see, he knew where all the cameras were placed and was very careful not to be captured on tape. It looks as if they used something to black out the cameras outside the vault—that's where the formulas are kept. What they didn't know is that we have cameras installed in the ceilings. None of the general staff is aware of that. We do have pictures, but they aren't revealing enough to make any arrests at this time, if you know what I mean. But we are working on

160

enhancing them in the hope we can identify who is responsible."

"I'm sure you will." Roman knew exactly what he meant. The images hadn't been enough to prove Akira's sexual harassment case either. But today, Roman was looking at the tape for a different purpose.

Mr. Tabrinsky gave Roman basic instructions on how to view, enlarge, and reverse images. "I'll be across the hall in my office, give me a yell when you're done."

Roman spent the next hour viewing the surveillance tape. When he finished, he knew three things. One, someone had stolen the formula right before Akira bumped into Mr. Johnson. Two, from an overhead view he couldn't tell if it was a man or a woman. The thief had cleverly disguised his or herself in black oversized clothing from head to toe. And three, Akira or Johnson could have easily had time to slip out of the disguise before the encounter.

No, not Akira.

Roman tapped on the open door of Mr. Tabrinsky's office. He placed his phone call on hold.

"Only a few more questions, Mr. Tabrinsky. Do you know anything about the formula that was stolen?"

He stood up from his chair, his face displaying a look of suspicion. "Being from the legal department, I thought you would've been given all the details about that."

"I normally handle the sexual harassment cases. The missing formula may be tied into one of my cases, so Lawson gave it to me."

Mr. Tabrinsky sized up the situation before releasing any information. "All I know is that it had something to do with a HIV vaccine or cure."

Roman turned to leave the office, but stopped once more. "I didn't see any video of the closed offices on the sixth floor." He needed evidence about what occurred inside Mr. Johnson's office the night he propositioned Akira.

"No, sir, you wouldn't have. We used to have twenty-four

Acquisitions

hour surveillance cameras in all of those offices, but there was a lawsuit several years ago. One of the employees up there called it an invasion of his privacy. Greico pulled the cameras once the dollar amount for the legal bills hit six digits. Can you imagine someone having the nerve to say their employer was invading their privacy while they were at work?"

***

"You're sure Akira didn't have anything to do with this?" Butch asked.

Roman drummed his fingers across his desktop and pressed the phone receiver to his ear. "I'm positive."

"There's a lot of circumstantial evidence stacked up against her. This could be hard to fight. Any leads on who's on the security tape?"

Roman explained that Mr. Tabrinsky was in the process of enhancing the image and comparing it to the security photos taken for the employee files. He proved willing to help Roman with every area of his investigation. They hoped the two of them working from different angles would meet in the middle with the key to the whole mystery.

"Will you take her on as a client?" Roman asked.

Butch gave a halfhearted laugh. "Akira can't afford my firm to represent her, but I can refer you to someone."

Butch's firm dealt with criminal defense, and by nature, the clientele tended to be the shady type. To avoid potential problems and maintain a semblance of legitimacy, the firm charged a retainer of five thousand dollars and four hundred dollars an hour; six hundred dollars an hour and more for court appearances. Complicated or high profile cases were extra. This dramatically changed the client mix to rich men accused of embezzlement instead of petty drug dealers.

"Butch, Akira isn't just another client. She's special. I'm asking you as my best friend to help her. I'll cover the costs."

As a senior partner at his law firm, Butch could, and would, move a mountain or mountain lion to help his friend. He held the phone in silence, contemplating the offer. "I think

I can push it past the partners."

Finally, Butch understood Roman's relationship with Akira.

"One more thing," Roman added. "I only want *you* to represent her."

"If the partners agree to take the case, I'll represent her."

"Thanks, man."

"Yeah, you owe me. The police will add one and one and come up with four." Butch's dislike for the police was no secret. "Greico will push them to make arrests."

"Mr. Lawton will push for it. With prodding from Johnson."

"We have a plan. Tabrinsky is enhancing the tape. Snoop around on the sixth floor and see what you can find. If you tap into the right person, they'll spill everything they know."

"I will."

"I'll get started on my end and get back to you. Peace."

"Peace out."

"Oh yeah," Butch said, catching Roman before he put the phone down. "My date cancelled for Christmas at the cabin. Actually, I cancelled her; too much pressure for a commitment. You and Akira go alone."

Roman explained that he had invited Lara to join them. "You come and we'll all hang out together."

"Bet."

"Peace out."

Roman placed his square reading glasses in his top desk drawer and checked his watch. It was too late to take Akira to dinner. He needed to be alone with his thoughts. He'd call her once he settled in for the night. Wearily, he packed his briefcase with the work he had neglected while investigating Akira's case. With all his efforts, the probability Roman could not help Akira prove her innocence hung over him.

Chapter 19

The Christmas holiday didn't come soon enough. Akira needed to get away from Mr. Johnson, Greico and the missing formula. Initially hesitant about going on vacation with Roman because their relationship was still new, Akira sat in the back seat of Butch's white Suburban with Lara debating life philosophies with Butch and Roman in the front seat.

"I guess we're going to have to call this one a draw because we're here." Butch parked alongside a modern wood cabin surrounded by deep, freshly fallen, powdery snow. The closest neighbor was a family-owned general store half a mile away where they had stopped to pick up forgotten essentials.

Roman and Butch stood together, smiling as they waited for the women to climb out of the truck. "Butch and I have decided that since you ladies believe all things are equal between men and women, you and Lara get to carry in the luggage."

Akira locked eyes with her friend. "They're joking."

"My dear," Butch said, draping his arm around Akira's shoulder, "we are lawyers. We have no sense of humor. Haven't you learned that from hanging out with Roman?" He tweaked her nose, then headed for the cabin with Roman at his side. They ignored Akira and Lara's pleas as they pouted beside the truck waiting for the guys to call off their bluff.

"Lara, we're either going to have to carry all of these suitcases inside or go in and tell them that we concede—there are certain things men do better than women."

"I choose going in and groveling," Lara said, struggling with one of the oversized pieces of luggage. "Let's massage their egos and tell them to get out here and haul these bags."

"We'll have to live with those egos all weekend."

Lara gave up on the suitcase. "This stuff weighs a ton."

Roman and Butch were inside sprawled out on twin sofas when they entered.

"Give up?" Butch gloated.

Akira put her hands on her hips. "We give up."

Butch jumped up. "I'll get the bags. You two go choose your room."

"I'll start a fire." Roman kneeled at the fireplace. The muscles of his back—which Akira knew from experience, were strong and unyielding—flexed with each piece of lumber he lifted. He turned to her, capturing her gaze.

The entire cabin was nothing like what Akira pictured when she envisioned spending a week in the woods. Equipped with top-of-the-line appliances and plush new furniture, it resembled a five-star resort.

Lara tugged at Akira's coat, pulling her away to choose the room they would share over the Christmas break. They unpacked in the room with two twin-size beds. The space overlooked the woods at the back of the cabin. Roman took the room off the kitchen with its own bathroom. Butch settled between them in a spacious room with a picture window the length of one wall.

"I'm a morning person—I'll make breakfast." Lara selected her chore for the weekend.

Akira spoke up next, "I can make dinner."

"No, you'll be busy with me at dinnertime," Roman

Acquisitions

smiled as he placed another log into the fireplace. "Take lunch."

Butch dropped down on the sofa between Akira and Lara. "That leaves me with dinner."

Roman stood and faced the trio. "What about me?"

"You can't cook," Akira and Butch said together.

"I guess that leaves you with cleaning detail," Lara added.

Butch teased his friend. "With a dishwasher and four adults, cleaning detail would be easy. Roman, you should be able to work a dishwasher without too much trouble."

***

The raucous chatter made Roman slam his dresser drawer closed and march into the living room. He found Akira lying across the sofa, reading a magazine as if she couldn't hear Butch and Lara in the kitchen clanging dishes and debating the pros and cons of the justice system.

"What's going on in there?"

Akira closed the magazine. "They're cooking dinner together."

He turned, looking between Akira and the racket in the kitchen.

"They started going at it, and I left. I tried to intervene, but they shut me completely out of the conversation."

"I thought they would get along. Maybe we should think about heading back if they're going to be like this all weekend."

Akira giggled. "I think you have the wrong idea—they're having a good time. They're fighting like two wet cats, but if you try to interfere, they'll defend each other."

Butch raised his voice to make his final undisputed point about the evil of three-strikes rule. Lara boldly questioned his reasoning process and how it had led him from discussing affirmative action to the three-strikes rule. Butch answered, angrily. Lara fell silent.

Roman looked down at Akira. "I'll talk to them."

Lara and Butch broke out in uncontrolled laughter.

166

"They're crazy," Roman grumbled.

Butch had an unusual approach to his relationships with women. Even friendship could not be ordinary. If what Akira said was true, they were in for a long weekend of male versus female.

Roman remembered one particular woman Butch dated who never stood up to him. And Butch loved it. He ran around doing all the things he would never normally do when dating a woman. Whenever this woman found out, Butch would play with his words until he had her believing that she had driven him to commit his heinous acts. If, by some chance, she didn't fall for that, he would become sappy and have her crying because he loved her so much. It was a sight for every man who claimed to be a player to witness. Butch proved undisputedly that if he wanted to join that arena, all men would have to bow down to him. Forging a friendship with someone as lively and feisty as Lara would be good for Butch, teach him that women are more than playthings.

Roman couldn't wait for Lara and Butch to call it a night. Their endless debate during dinner kept Roman and Akira on the sidelines. They slipped away from the table, leaving Butch and Lara at the sink rinsing the dishes and debating their points. The cabin fell silent once they returned to the neutral corners of their bedrooms.

Akira giggled, "I didn't think they'd ever quit."

"Me either." Roman led her to the fireplace. He placed a pillow on the floor and sat with his back to the sofa. Stretching out his long legs, he invited Akira into his lap. He situated her over his thighs, facing him.

"Finally, time alone." He traced the slope of her nose.

"Thank you for this." Akira's palms pressed flat against his chest.

Roman swooped in and took her lips. He slipped his tongue past the remnants of cherry gloss into the heat he craved. Every time he kissed her, his body reacted the same—desperate for more. He massaged her back, her shoulders. He

167

Acquisitions

pressed her into him. Her nipples came to a peak quickly because she wanted him as badly as he wanted her.

"Roman," Akira pulled away, "they'll hear us."

"Don't scream."

"I don't scream."

"Oh, no?" he raised a questioning brow.

Akira hid the blush of her cheeks in the crook of his neck.

Roman placed his hands on her waist and rotated his hips until the peak of him pressed into the dip of her.

She moaned. Her arms came around his neck.

His hands slid down her hips to her thighs to the hem of her dress resting below her knee. He rewarded her lack of pantyhose with a fiery kiss. He swallowed her protest, swiped it away with his tongue. In seconds, zipper down, panties aside, the head of him pushing at the opening of her.

"Roman—"

"I've been hard for you all day." He lifted his hips and plunged inside her wetness.

Akira moved her hips forward to take more of him. She groped at his sweater; he let her kiss that space between his nipples.

Roman's fingers climbed down her thighs, past her knees, down to her ankles. He pulled her forward, making her take in more of him. When there was no more to take, he stationed her on his lap; knees bent, pressed against the sofa while he grabbed her behind and pulled her closer. He held her as he propelled upward into her pocket with a wicked thrust of his hips. He pressed his lips to hers to stifle her cry.

They rocked together, fulfilling the lust that had been building all day.

"All day," Roman confessed, "I...watched...you... walk...around...

in...this...dress...and...I...wanted...to—"

Akira shimmied her hips, froze, and trembled in his arms.

Roman let her catch her breath before he laid her on the carpet and anchored himself to her deepest point. He pushed

168

with hard punctuation. Grunted and pumped—wild for her, hungry for her. Understanding his need, Akira wrapped her legs around his back and allowed him to take what he required.

He climbed into her safe place and buried himself there.

Akira pulled him down to her and used her mouth to consume his growl.

Chapter 20

Lara skied like a pro. Before long, Butch had her standing on her skis and moving down the mountain with little assistance. Akira, on the other hand, had the most trouble mastering standing up for longer than thirty seconds.

Lara tired of Akira slowing them down. "Butch, let's go ahead of them."

"We'll meet you at the bottom."

Lara teased her friend. "We'll meet you back at the cabin."

Akira watched them ski away. "I'll never get this."

"Yes, you will." Roman sat next to her in the snow. "By the end of the weekend, you'll be an expert skier."

"Ha. I doubt it seriously."

"Ready to try again?"

"I've had enough." Her body ached from the falls. "Do you mind if I head back? You can still catch up with Butch and Lara."

Roman stood and extended his hands. "I'm not going without you. If you go back to the cabin, I go back to the cabin."

Akira blew up a puff of air as she took his hands. "Alright. Is there going to be a time when *I* can be *your* support?"

"Hey, don't talk like that. I do for you because I want to. I don't expect anything in return. Every minute you spend with me, you give me something I need. Believe that."

Akira inhaled the scent of him and warmed inside.

"I have something for you." Roman removed his gloves and dug through layers of winter gear to pull out a small box.

"I thought we agreed, no gifts this year. We haven't been dating very long and—"

Roman hushed her by putting a finger to her lips. "This is for both of us. Mostly me."

Akira opened the box and briefly studied the finely crafted piece of erotic jewelry. She agreed. This would bring pleasure to the both of them.

Roman greeted her uplifted eyes with a wicked grin framed by both dimples. "Let's head back and maybe we can try it out before Butch and Lara return."

***

"Turn off the TV, and turn on the stereo." Roman went to put away their skiwear.

They kept the television on, even when they left the cabin, to scare away small animals. Akira fumbled with the buttons on the remote until the reporter mentioned Power & Power. She froze, heart thumping, trying to piece together the news story.

The reporter stood outside the skyscraper building that housed Power & Power Pharmaceuticals giving background information about the company. His frozen breath blew over the microphone as he told the history of the small company and its recent financial trouble. "But now all that is a thing of the past." The government's contribution alone to further its research would bail the company out of debt and keep it running for the next ten years.

"Needless to say, the executives here at Power & Power

Acquisitions

are ecstatic. Finding a vaccine to prevent HIV will save hundreds of thousands of lives."

Roman posted himself between Akira and the television screen.

The missing formula from Greico Enterprises was now in the hands of Power & Power.

They listened to the reporter's summary of the press conference.

"Power & Power has been working on a vaccine against HIV for ten years and announced today that they are close to securing the approval of the FDA to begin testing their new formula."

Akira backed away from the television. "Do you see what's happening?"

Roman shushed her.

"This is bad, Roman."

"Calm down. We knew it would turn up sooner or later. We hoped that someone would try to sell it back to Greico, but this isn't all that surprising."

"No, you don't understand." Akira cried.

Roman turned from the television and focused on her distress. "What is it?"

Butch and Lara entered the cabin, their laughter stopped abruptly as they watched the scene unfold.

"Roman, *Power & Power* has the formula."

Lara rushed around the sofa and joined Akira. "Power & Power has Greico's formula?"

Roman didn't like the shared distress that passed between them. "What the hell is going on?"

"Eric." Lara whispered as if having a revelation.

"Who's Eric?" Butch asked.

Akira's eyes welled with tears.

"Akira!" Roman commanded her attention "What the hell is going on?"

She pulled out of the telepathic conversation with Lara and turned to him. "A guy I dated—he's a sales executive at

172

Power & Power."

A load of bricks knocked the wind out of Roman. "What guy?" He glanced at Lara and knew there was more. "What do you mean you dated him?"

Akira sniffled.

"How serious?"

Akira's gaze dropped to the floor.

Lara looked away.

Roman pressed the issue. "Tell me what the hell you're hiding."

"Roman—" Lara started.

"Right now, Akira."

"It was nothing. We went out a few times."

Roman looked to Lara for confirmation. She tried hard to be devoid of emotion—too hard.

Akira wanted Roman to take her in his arms and comfort her.

He didn't move.

"Akira, are you still seeing this guy?"

"No!"

"The formula is at Power & Power where—what's his name?" Akira didn't answer so he shouted at Lara. "What's his name?"

Lara jumped. "Eric."

"The formula turns up at *Eric's* job. Eric, the man you use to date."

"Roman, I'm scared."

And he felt scared too. Scared he doubted her this easily. Scared he couldn't save her.

"I didn't do it," Akira pleaded. "I didn't."

Butch stepped between them. "We know where the formula is, and that gives us direction. Let's find out how it got there."

Akira pleaded, "Roman?" She broke their eye contact long enough to blink, sending two tears down her cheek. "Everything's out of control."

Acquisitions

Butch spoke in measured tones, "Akira, let's talk. Client to attorney." He grasped her upper arm and pulled her away from Roman's heated gaze.

She jerked away, swinging back around to face Roman. "Ask me."

Roman's words came back to haunt him. They provided the jolt he needed to pull him out of silent reverie. It had to be coincidence, he told himself. They had moved past all the trust issues. Akira had honor. She wouldn't lie about a sexual harassment case. She wouldn't steal from Greico. She wouldn't be involved with another man. She wouldn't use him to cover it all up.

"Ask me, Roman! You know you want to."

As Roman watched fear and desperation cross Akira's face, he cursed himself for entertaining his doubts. He knew her as he knew himself. Akira wouldn't do it—steal the formula, fabricate the sexual harassment claim, see another man behind his back, use him. She wouldn't.

His voice sounded deceivingly calm and sure. "No, Akira. I don't want to. I don't have to." He bent and placed a kiss in the slope of her nose.

Akira sank into the safety of his arms. As she laid sobbing into his chest, he understood the connection between them. This is why he needed Akira in his life, because she needed him as much as he needed her.

Chapter 21

Akira gripped the cold knob of Roman's bedroom door. He had been shut up in his room—coming out only to eat dinner with them in brooding silence—since they returned from skiing. Since the formula had been found. Since she told him about Eric. Without knocking, she turned the knob in one smooth motion and entered his haven.

"Roman, you've been in here a long time. What are you doing?"

In the middle of the bed, he sat surrounded by neatly organized stacks of paper.

She came closer. "Can I come in?"

Roman slid to the edge of the bed. "Come here."

She found her place next to him and pulled his head against her chest. "What are you doing?" Her fingertips stroked his wavy hair.

Roman closed his eyes and let her soothe him. "This is the file from my investigation. I brought it along for Butch to go over—before he talked with you."

The gown she wore, even though it was made of heavy cotton to fight the cold weather, did little to contain the fleshy

Acquisitions

cushion of her breasts. He wrapped his arms around her waist in search of evidence of her undergarments. His fingers confirmed a panty line before wandering downward over the curve of her bottom.

"Roman, do you believe me?"

"Yes." He locked her in with the vise grip of his arms.

"For a minute, you doubted me. I saw it in your eyes."

"That's not what you saw." He kissed her belly as he worked the gown up over her hips and his fingers inside her panties.

"What did I see?"

He lifted his head, breaking the contact between her fingers and his hair. "The realization that you cared for a man before me, that you might still care for him."

Akira felt embarrassingly exposed with her gown crumpled above her waist in Roman's hands and her past relationship in his eyes. "I didn't make up the story about Mr. Johnson."

He rubbed his cheek against her belly.

"I didn't have anything to do with the missing formula."

He rubbed the other cheek.

"I've never felt like this about any other man," she said.

His tongue swirled inside her navel cavern.

Akira's head fell back, her eyes closed. "Do you believe me, Roman?"

He pulled the gown over her head and tossed it to the floor.

"Do you?"

He filled his hands with her breasts, massaging them leisurely.

"Roman," Akira panted, "do you believe me?" Usually, the sex came fast and furious, leaving no time for playing with her breasts. Her nipples hardened, begging for his tongue's kiss.

He pushed her down on the mattress, on top of the papers that made up her file.

She swept them off the bed. "Roman, answer me, please. Do you believe me?"

He branded her flesh with his, pressing his bare chest against hers. "I do."

He licked the length of her breast, flicking his tongue against her nipple, biting it roughly but sensuously. "Don't ask again."

His mustache scarred her flesh as he kissed and licked various parts of her body in random order: her thighs, her neck, her lips, her breasts, and the back of her knees.

"Everywhere," Akira breathed deeply, relishing in his touch. Every nerve of her body tingled simultaneously at his lavish caress. He seemed to move with the accelerated speed of Superman, but at the same time, as slow as a snail. His touch felt both hard and soft, his bites both cruel and passionate. Her mind reeled at the surreal pleasure.

"Everywhere," Roman kneeled between her thighs. His massive hands roughly pushed her legs apart, clearing his path.

Akira's eyes fluttered open long enough to see his head dip down out of sight. She grabbed the sheets and arched her back with the first pierce of his tongue. She made a moan-groan-sigh sound that encouraged him to withdraw and lap at the opening between her folds.

Roman's head moved back and forth in the opposite direction of his tongue. She thrashed uncontrollably. He grabbed her thighs, not allowing her to back away. She would take every drop of pleasure he could give and she would like it.

"Roman...." A shiver moved over her like jumping in a cold pool on a hot day.

His tongue went deeper...in...out...slower...faster...slower.

Unable to stand being submerged in the ice cold swimming pool of Roman's desire, she backed away to the head of the bed. He grabbed her behind with both hands and pulled her onto his tongue in one swift move.

Acquisitions

"Roman. Please." She was consumed by pleasure so good that it caused pain.

His tongue flicked against her swollen, dripping nub. She screamed. Her legs flailed wildly, and her hips rotated right and left. Her body jerked, convulsed. Tension gripped her and then left her body limp, like a rag doll. Roman rode out the waves with his tongue swirling through her wispy curls.

"What are you trying to do to me?" Akira asked, reaching for him.

"I'm trying to make you feel me."

His lips were on hers before she could say another word. He covered his body with hers. She still had not caught her breath from the body-rocking ecstasy when he kissed her.

Roman led her with his tongue. Showed her when to be tender and when to be passionate.

Akira moved her hands between them, jerking at the drawstrings of his pajamas. He wiggled out, kicking one leg at a time until they joined her gown on the floor.

The heat between them was unprecedented. They had done wicked things together, the lust between having grown to a boil, forcing them to take pleasure quickly, to extinguish the need. This time was different. He played with her body with the same meticulous detail he put into his work. He sampled all of her the way he sampled each food on his plate. He showed his appreciation with his moans. He displayed his need with his moans. No matter how much tension built up in her body, he controlled their pace, never letting her push him to advance before he was ready. His power over her body astonished her. When had he learned all of her needs and desires?

Akira opened her eyes and found him gazing deeply at her. She asked, "What are you doing to me?"

Roman pressed his lips next to her ear. "I want you to feel what I feel for you." He planted kisses on her neckline. "Do you feel me?" He guided himself into the heated wetness awaiting his penetration.

178

"Roman," she sighed.

"Do you?"

Lightheaded, she couldn't answer with words.

Roman pushed into her warmth with unfamiliar force.

Hot wisps of air seared Akira's cheek. She could smell the result of her desire on his tongue.

Roman whispered, "Do you feel me, Akira?"

"Yes."

"How do I feel to you?" His stroke became deep, slow and deliberate. "How?" He switched his rhythm. Fast, shallow, and wicked. He pushed until she stiffened. Pulled back until she raised her hips to chase him.

Unable to stand the agony tormenting her body and hurling her in a world of bliss, Akira screamed.

His hand clamped over her mouth. "Shh," he comforted her as she breeched the portal separating sanity and insanity. He found the rocking rhythm that applied the amount of pressure needed to push her into delirium. "Do you feel me here?" He placed a finger on her heart.

Akira's head exploded in a supernova of colors too brilliant to look at with the naked eye. Her mind hurled through all regions of rational thought. She felt lost and afraid, but safe and secure. The wall constructed around her heart crumbled, leaving her open to Roman's manipulations.

His rumbling laughter filled the room. "Shh. You're going to wake Butch and Lara." He kissed her neck. "Quiet."

He kissed her forehead, cheeks and breasts, "Shh."

Slowly, he removed his hand, "Shh."

Roman began with an unhurried, comfortable rocking. His movements were sleek and sensuous inside her satiny tunnel. It was now his turn to experience the surreal pleasure that transcended reality. He pressed his forehead to hers. Their breathing synchronized. His penetration became more concentrated, focused.

His jaw seesawed back and forth. "Do you feel what I feel for you?"

Acquisitions

"Yes," Akira answered, "I do."

"What? What do you feel?"

"I love you."

Roman froze on the down stroke. His eyes glittered. "Say it again."

"I love you, Roman."

His hips rocked. "Again."

"I love you, Roman."

He threw his head back and exploded.

Akira cupped his face in her hands as his body jerked, "I love you." She wiped away the perspiration dripping into his eyes, off the bridge of his nose, onto her chest. "I love you."

His body released the last of its juices. Collapsing on top of her, he remained silent while he struggled to catch his breath.

Roman rolled next to her and pulled the blankets up over them both.

"Are you okay?" Akira asked, wiping his face again.

He caught her hand and kissed the palm. He didn't answer.

"Roman, there's too much distance between what I feel for you and what we have together."

He pulled her back against his chest and enveloped her with his body, his thigh draped over hers.

"Am I asking for too much?"

If he told her yes, she would curl up and die.

"At Thanksgiving," his voice husky, "I considered walking away. Considering the position starting a relationship with you would put us in at work, I thought it would be best. I questioned if you were as important as my job." His hand fell in the dip of her waist, "I'm sorry for being selfish."

She had to ask, "Are you sure your doubts only had to do with work?"

"It must sound crazy to you. If it weren't for you risking your job, we wouldn't be here now." He bit her shoulder, kissed away the sting. "Understand, *thinking* about you not being in my life makes me crazy. So when you say, are you asking too much, I ask what do you need?"

"You."

"Akira, I love you."

A great relief washed over her. She felt mentally exhausted. Physically drained.

"You knew that."

Her eyes drifted closed. She had wished for it.

"I need you as much as you need me."

"Roman—"

"Shh." He massaged her back. "Just say you love me."

Chapter 22

Roman sat behind his desk, his chin resting on his knuckles, when Columbia walked into his office.

"I thought you weren't coming in today."

"Changed my mind. Needed to catch up on work." After the weekend at the cabin, his life's mission became clearing Akira's name. Still working in secrecy, he searched for ways to prove her innocence and bring down Johnson.

"Okay." Columbia eyed him, noting the choppy answer to her question. "Is there anything I can do to help?"

"Leave me alone for a while. Please. I need to find my direction."

"I'll order lunch in."

"Columbia," Roman called her before she backed out of his office, "where are those files I had you pull around Thanksgiving?"

"I returned the ones you reviewed to the records department. The others are at my desk."

"Bring them in before you order lunch."

Roman stood and absentmindedly moved to his file cabinet. A vital piece of information was missing. An obvious clue stared him in the face, and he couldn't see it, but his devotion to Akira would keep him at the daunting task until he uncovered it.

Akira had called earlier, the after-effects of their lovemaking lingering in the satiated softness of her voice. He pictured her eyes sparkling like they had when he guided her hips and showed her how to take every inch of him inside. She sounded afraid when she asked if she demanded too much from him.

"Not enough," he reprimanded himself for not solving the mystery of the missing formula.

The afternoon started immediately after gulping down the deli sandwich, fries and slice of chocolate mousse cake that Columbia ordered for lunch. Not one loose thread in any of the files. He searched them over and over, reading until his eyes ached from the strain.

His next move—recall the witnesses in Akira's case. If Johnson ever suspected what he was up to, he'd go to Lawson. Then Roman would have to explain his continued interest in an unsubstantiated case that had been disposed of weeks ago.

Roman decided to take a mental break. He strolled down the hall to the vending area. The Pepsi representative knelt in front of the open machine stocking it with sixteen-ounce plastic bottles of soda. Without thinking, Roman took the stairwell down five flights to the break room on the sixth floor. He loitered unnoticed at the soda machine listening to bits and pieces of conversations. Nothing out of the norm. What client is a pain? Who wanted free samples, but never placed an order? Roman pushed the vending machine button that delivered an ice-cold bottle of Mountain Dew before taking a seat on a sofa near by.

Roman popped the top on his second Mountain Dew when Candace's long legs stirred the air, commanding the atmosphere to part and accommodate her. She tossed her strawberry hair over her shoulder, narrowed her eyes seductively in Roman's direction, and bent at the waist to pull out a chair. To his surprise, she turned the chair in a complete circle until it

Acquisitions

faced him, then dipped into the seat. She crossed her bare legs, exposing a great deal of thigh through the slit of her skirt.

"Are you looking for me, Roman Miller?" Candace's manicured fingertips glided through her hair while her smoky voice tried to seduce him.

Roman cleared his throat, stalling. Reading her body language came easily, the message too erotic to say aloud. "No, I wasn't looking for you," he unfolded his body to its full height and approached her, "but since you're here, maybe I can ask you a few questions."

Candace rose from the chair, straightened her skirt and looked up into his face. "You can ask me anything you want."

Roman's conscience made him take a step backward. "I'm following up on the Reed case. Things have been insane in the office for the last month or so. Anything different since all of the commotion?"

"Different?" Candace smiled as if they were sharing a secret language.

"Yeah, different." He relaxed his posture and lowered his voice. He could tantalize a woman as well as Candace could tease a man. "You know, new rules, people coming forward with stories. After something like this happens, people love to tell you-know-what-happened-to-me-one-time stories."

Candace flipped around on her heels, taking long strides to the vending machine. "The people in this office are backwoods. They have nothing interesting to tell. My last job was in Chicago. Now that's a classy city. It's a miracle I've stayed here as long as I have. The only one with even a touch of class is Barry, and that's only because I demand it."

Roman joined her at the machine, gladly dropping the change in the slot to purchase her soda. "I heard something about you and Johnson being an item."

Candace looked over his face and chose to remain silent while she selected her soda of choice.

"Aren't there rules restricting the boss dating one of his employees?"

She watched him skeptically. "Maybe. Are you here to bust me?

"No. You know," Roman laughed, "I try to picture you and Johnson as a couple, but I can't see it. You're so—so—well," he took a step back and gave her body an open assessment.

Candace laughed, twisting at her middle like a shy child might. "I hear that all the time."

Roman cupped his chin, still giving her body his full attention. "Really?"

Candace struggled with the soda top.

Roman removed the bottle from her hand and opened it. "Explain it to me. And with him in trouble with the sexual harassment case. He doesn't even respect what he has. I know plenty of men who would kill to be in his shoes."

Candace's top lip tensed. "Can you believe that? I was livid when I got wind of that. I let Barry have it good. I would have walked away too, but he bought me this gorgeous diamond necklace, and I forgave him. How awful is it that he would go after that pork chop when he has me? He had to work hard for me to get over that transgression."

Finally a bit of the truth, confirmation of Akira's charges. Roman felt as if he had found the last word in a New York Time's crossword puzzle.

Candace licked her lips before turning the soda bottle up to her mouth. "You and I are a lot alike."

"How's that?" Roman crossed his arms over his chest and waited for her to deliver a flirtatious punch line.

"We both do what's needed to get over. Even if we have to date beneath us."

He dropped his arms to his side. "Meaning?"

Candace leaned in and whispered, "I know about you and Akira."

"What about me and Ms. Reed?"

"I came to your office after hours to talk to you. I saw you kissing."

Acquisitions

A punch to the gut.

An interruption saved Roman. "Candace, you have a phone call." Danisha waved at him.

Candace exhaled loudly. "See what I mean about the people working here?"

Chapter 23

"Butch, I'm sorry. I didn't know where else to go."

"Sit down, Akira. What is it?"

She clutched her purse. "They took all my money. All of it."

"Who took your money? Slow down. You're not making sense." Butch rounded the desk and sat on the edge directly in front of her.

"My landlord came knocking on my door early this morning and accused me of writing a bad check. I called the bank, and they refused to give me information about my own account. I drove down there—that's where I'm coming from—and the manager told me that the police seized my accounts." She went into her purse and produced an abused document. "The manager gave me a copy of this. The police left it."

Butch silently scanned the legal document.

"I don't understand what's going on. If they had questions about how much money I have, why didn't they ask, or call the bank for my account information? They didn't have to freeze my money. I can't pay my bills. How am I supposed to live

Acquisitions

until this investigation is over?"

Butch returned to his seat as Akira continued to ramble. He pushed a button to call his secretary and requested she dial the assistant district attorney responsible for acquiring the subpoena.

"He's not available," Butch said after hanging up the phone.

"What am I going to do?" Akira's panic spilled over in tears.

"The first thing you have to do is calm down. Some of what's happening to you is the police and assistant DA's way of getting their revenge on my firm. We're not well liked by those folks. They're probably watching you. They want to see if you have money hidden. If they freeze your funds, will you magically come up with more money? It's all a game."

"My landlord is coming back in the morning. I have no way of paying him. My parents are still overseas with my brother."

"The firm has an emergency fund for occasions like this. I'll have my secretary draft a check to cover your rent and your expenses. You can pay it back when this is over and you have access to your accounts again. I don't anticipate that will be long." He paused to jot down a note. "When is your vacation up?"

"Tomorrow. Why?"

Apprehensive about what might happen once she returned to work, Butch wanted to advise her to take additional time off. She made it clear her finances couldn't withstand that. "We need to discuss the atmosphere at Greico with Roman."

"Do you think they have something to do with what the police did?"

"I don't know." Butch offered her a Kleenex.

"What am I going to do now?"

Butch pushed himself up from his chair. "It's time to go to the police. Play their game on their turf."

***

Akira sat in Butch's Suburban with the motor running to provide heat. The last time she sat in the truck had been two days ago on their ride back from the ski trip. If every day could be as carefree as their time in the mountains, her life would be perfect.

Filing the sexual harassment charges against Mr. Johnson had sent her life spiraling out of control. It would have been easier to overlook what he had done. But the one thing that shattered her life had also brought the most happiness she'd ever known. As she tried to find meaning behind what she was going through, she focused on the fact that if not for the sexual harassment complaint, she would have never met Roman Miller.

And Lara would have never met Butch Vance. As closed-mouthed as Lara tried to be, Akira picked up the vibe between them at the cabin. The intensity of the arguments diminished as their time alone increased. When the four of them did get into a debate, Roman often found himself outnumbered because Butch began to agree with Lara's perspective on life.

Butch thought he was being subtle when he asked Akira about Lara at their strategy sessions. He had hinted several times that she should give him Lara's phone number so he could give her a call—to catch up. He said he had heard something that would challenge her or prove a point they had debated at the cabin. Akira read between the lines and offered Lara's number gladly.

Butch hopped inside the SUV. "The detectives will see us now."

"Can you try Roman again?"

Butch hit the speed dial button on his cell. After a minute he said, "Still not answering. I'll be with you. Follow my lead."

Akira nodded, wearing a mask of confidence.

They went inside the police station and were escorted into a sparsely furnished room. Butch opened his briefcase on top of the table and prepared for the interview. His mild-mannered

Acquisitions

features transformed into those of an assertive, but poised attorney.

Detective Casser joined Butch and Akira in the two-way mirrored room with a cup of coffee in hand. His suit looked sharper than Akira remembered from their prior two meetings, except for an ugly green and yellow tie, no doubt, a Christmas gift he felt obligated to wear.

Butch stood up and addressed him, well aware of the tactics of the police. "I don't appreciate you keeping me and my client waiting. We came here as a gesture of good faith."

Detective Casser took his seat. He looked over at his partner, Detective Downs, who entered the room and sat next to him. "Who is this guy?"

Butch and the lawyers at his firm were not a welcome sight at the police station. They had won too many cases and gotten too many criminals off. Many, unfortunately, only to commit the same crimes again.

Butch took the stocky detective's cue and returned to his chair. He would change his behavior to mimic that of the detective with too much attitude.

Detective Downs handed his partner Butch's card. "This is Ms. Reed's lawyer."

Detective Casser looked over Butch's credentials. "Senior partner? Haven't we advanced up the corporate ladder of cutthroats?"

Butch stared the detective down. "Can we get on with this?"

"We can start our questioning right there," Detective Casser said. "I've seen how much income you generate in a year Ms. Reed, how can you afford a big-shot attorney like Mr. Vance here?"

Akira's stomach sank. She thought they would start with easy questions about the stolen formula and build up in intensity. Instead, Casser was going for a quick kill.

Butch stepped in to buffer the situation. "How I came to represent Ms. Reed is not the issue here. If you persist on being inappropriate with your demeanor and your questions, I will take Ms. Reed out of here and you can talk to her again when you have a warrant for her arrest."

Detective Casser lowered his coffee mug without taking the intended sip. Detective Downs intervened. "Let's begin at the top. Tell us about the events leading up to you filing a sexual harassment complaint against your boss."

Akira understood why they would be interested in that night—it was the night when the formula had been stolen—but she didn't want to relive it. She would never be able to move on if she had to keep reciting a story no one believed anyway.

"Haven't you questioned my client about that night before?" Butch asked Downs.

"Yes."

"Then don't waste our time."

Casser's annoyance reeked in his tone. "We need to clear up a few details."

"Ask a specific question, Detective Casser."

"What was your purpose in coming down here, Vance? Are you going to allow your client to answer any questions?"

"Ms. Reed needs to return to work to earn a living. She doesn't have time to waste here with you answering irrelevant questions. I wouldn't be a very good attorney if I allowed that, would I?"

Detective Downs became the fence between the two barking dogs. "I think we have a good picture of what you say went on that night."

Detective Casser removed his jacket. His elbows were rooted on the table, his body leaning toward Akira. "Now tell us about your relationship with Eric Dodson."

Butch looked up from his notepad with poorly masked confusion. "Be more specific with your question, Detective."

"How did you meet?"

"I met him at a trade show. Our booths were next to each other. By the end of the day, we both thought it was stupid for us to act like we hated each other because we worked for com-

Acquisitions

peting companies. We had never even seen each other before. He asked me out for dinner, and we started dating."

"He asked you out?"

"Yes." Akira did not understand the implication.

Butch did not miss the undertone of the question. "Move on."

Detective Casser attacked. "You knew he was an executive at Power & Power but went out with him anyway? Isn't there a company policy against that sort of thing?"

"Not that I know of," Akira answered honestly.

"Did you tell anyone at work about your relationship?"

"No."

"How serious were you?"

"We dated. That's all."

"I guess you could see that if you and Mr. Dodson were seriously involved, it might look bad for you. It might look like you and he were working together to steal the formula and sell it to the highest bidder. It sure would explain why you can afford Mr. Vance here."

Butch's eyes narrowed in the detective's direction. "You don't seem to be able to leave that issue alone. You've had all her assets frozen, isn't that enough?"

Casser shot back, "It irks me that Ms. Reed is using stolen money to pay for her defense. A lawyer who would use every trick he knows to get her off with the crime."

"Question, Detective?" Butch stared across the table at the grimacing cop.

"My question," the detective blurted out, "is why you're sitting here lying, Ms. Reed? What do you have to cover up?"

"I don't understand," Akira answered.

Detective Downs broke his long silence and tried to calm the escalating confrontation. "We talked to Mr. Dodson, Ms. Reed, and he tells us a slightly different story."

Butch looked over at Akira, completely in the dark about where the detectives were going with this line of questioning.

Detective Casser took over with his abrasive attitude.

"Mr. Dodson tells us that it was <u>very</u> serious between you. He says you were engaged until recently."

The shock registering on Akira's face alarmed Butch. He didn't know the meaning of it. She had not mentioned being engaged to Dodson. He couldn't lose control of the interview. He pushed his chair back and stood abruptly. "This is over." He grabbed Akira's arm and pulled her up.

Casser sneered. "Don't leave town—again—Ms. Reed," he called as they left the room.

***

Akira followed Butch into his office to see Roman sitting at Butch's desk, his foot thumping nervously against the carpet. He rushed to her, helping her into the chair next to him. "I got your messages. What's going on?"

Butch closed the door with a bang.

"What happened?" Roman asked Butch while grabbing Akira's hand.

Butch hurled his briefcase on top of his desk with as much force as he had slammed the door. "I don't like being caught off guard." His words were tight, his face tense with anger.

Akira opened her mouth to apologize, but Butch cut her off with his raised voice.

"I should drop you *right now*." He pounded the top of his briefcase with his fist. "Don't ever lie to me. When I say tell me *everything* that's exactly what I mean, *everything*! Do you know how much damage you've done to the case I'm trying to put together?"

Roman stood, matching Butch's height and the menacing tone of his voice. "Don't yell at her like that."

Butch didn't hear Roman over his anger. "Your case is flimsy at best, but I thought I could string something together to clear you. If you keep lying or hiding little secrets, I can't do that. Do you understand?"

"Hey, Butch," Roman's anger began to surface, "bring it down a notch."

"This is between me and my client, Roman. If you can't

Acquisitions

understand that, then wait out in the reception area."

"I said don't talk to Akira like that."

Akira grabbed Roman's arm and encouraged him to sit down.

Butch sank behind his desk.

"What happened?" Roman asked Akira.

Akira looked from him to Butch, then back.

"Is it true?" Butch snapped the clasp on his briefcase and removed her file. His anger wasn't as sharp, but it remained.

"Is what true?" Roman asked.

Akira looked to Butch.

Butch remembered that his friend loved Akira. He couldn't treat her like an ordinary client. He didn't want to hurt his friend unnecessarily, but he had a job to do. A job that he was doing at Roman's request. "The police are under the impression that Akira was recently engaged to Eric Dodson." Roman's head snapped in Akira's direction.

Her eyes fell to her lap.

After a moment of disturbing silence, Butch stood. "I'll give you a few minutes."

At the sound of the door clicking shut, Roman challenged Akira. "I asked you directly what was between you and Eric. You told me you dated casually. Did you lie to me?"

"The police twisted everything around to make it sound more serious than it actually was between Eric and me."

"What is the truth?" Roman shifted his entire body in the chair, giving Akira his full attention.

"I told you the truth—about everything."

Roman's bottom lip dropped slightly. Mistrust filled his eyes. "I don't like this. Who does Eric think he is to you? Did he love you? Is he still in love with you?" He slowly lifted his frame from the chair and stepped away from Akira. "I want to know everything. Right now. I'm not going to wait until you feel it's convenient. I want to hear it all, now."

"It's not what you think."

"I sure hope not because you wouldn't believe what I'm thinking. I'm thinking that this whole thing has been a lie. The sexual harassment complaint—everything. All one big lie to cover up what you did. Pretty smart to get me involved. I could buffer what's happening at work. And connect you with Butch—all at my expense I might add—no paper trail. You'd get away clean and run off with Eric, laughing at me all the while. So, as you can see, I have an active imagination. I hope it's not what the hell I think it is."

Tears stung Akira's eyes, these more potent than the ones earlier. "Where is all this coming from? We talked at the cabin. You said you believed me. You said we didn't have to discuss it again."

The trouble surrounding every aspect of Akira's life made her too confused to think. Trying to sort it all out—the sexual harassment, the stolen formula, Eric—made her head throb with pain.

She wanted to quit her job. Never see Mr. Johnson again. Financial need ruined that plan. Instead, she continued to work, pretending that her life wasn't shattering into a million pieces. The police had to look favorably on it. They would realize she wasn't financially stable enough to quit working, therefore, she hadn't collected a large sum of money from selling stolen property.

Akira kept from falling apart by anchoring to Roman. She saw the concern behind his eyes when he sat in his den going over her case at all hours of the night. He was terrible at his efforts to conceal his worry. Night after night of finding no solution, he climbed into bed behind her and whispered that everything would work out. Now he stood an emotionally safe distance away from her, questioning her innocence.

Seeing her tears, Roman rubbed his hand over the shadow on his jaw and forced himself to calm down. Jealousy, mistrust, frustration, it all wore heavily on a man's soul. "I do believe you. I shouldn't have said that."

He remained a safe distance away when she needed his

Acquisitions

arms wrapped around her.

"Candace knows about us," he blurted out.

"What?"

"She thinks she saw me kiss you in my office. It must have been her that you heard in the corridor the day I interviewed you."

"What does this mean to my case? To us?"

"Eric provided a link between you and Power & Power. If Candace tells Johnson or Lawson about us..." His long legs propelled him across the room. He dropped in the chair next to her. "Candace hasn't told Johnson yet. That's a good sign. I figure she doesn't want to bring attention to her and Johnson, so she's keeping quiet."

Candace would never do her a favor.

Roman asked, holding his breath, "There's nothing left between you and Eric?"

"Nothing. I love *you*."

Akira held her arms out to him and he pulled her close. "Roman, I'm scared."

"Butch and I will handle it. I'm going to take care of you. I promise."

***

Roman jumped at the ringing phone.

"Mr. Miller," Columbia's voice chimed over the phone line. "You have a call on line one and there's someone here to see you."

"Do I have an appointment?" He scanned his calendar.

"No, but there's a young woman here who says she needs to see you right away."

"Okay, tell her to wait just a minute. I'll see her after I take this call."

Roman glanced at the clock. He never scheduled meetings this late in the afternoon. He clicked to the waiting line. "Roman Miller."

"Roman, it's Tabrinsky, the security supervisor."

"How are you, Mr. Tabrinsky? Is there something I can do

for you?"

"I remembered the work you've been doing with the missing formula, and I thought I should call. Mr. Lawton had me send two of my guys up to the sixth floor. They must've found something on Ms. Reed because he asked to have her escorted out of the building."

"Thank you. I owe you." Roman put the phone down and grabbed his jacket.

The phone buzzed again. "Are you ready for me to send in the young lady?" Columbia asked.

"Take her name and make an appointment. I have an emergency."

Roman rushed out of the office to the elevator. Immediately, he regretted not taking the stairs. The car stopped three times on the way down to the sixth floor. The people shuffling on and off did not value the precious time they stole from him.

He needed to get to Akira.

He could only imagine what had happened. Candace could have told Johnson about his relationship with Akira. The police might be handcuffing her. Wild images of the gruff Detective Casser dragging her away made him sprint through the cubicles.

A crowd gathered near Akira's closed office door. Roman stopped outside and forced himself to take on the role of detached lawyer before he knocked.

Mr. Lawton's voice granted him entrance. "Mr. Miller, what can I do for you?"

"I'm looking for Ms. Reed. I have a few questions for her in order to close the harassment case."

Mr. Lawton busied himself going through her desk. Candace eagerly assisted.

"Ms. Reed is no longer with Greico Enterprises."

"What happened?"

"The police assure me she is the person we're looking for. They're close to proving she stole the HIV vaccine. I fired her

Acquisitions

immediately."

"I'm investing this case. Why wasn't I informed before her dismissal?"

"I was coming up to speak with you. I had to act quickly. I didn't want Ms. Reed in this building with the opportunity to steal another valuable formula."

Candace stood erect and placed her hand on her hip. She gave Roman a smile that chilled his bones.

Chapter 24

When Akira did not answer her phone or the continuous ringing of her doorbell, Roman started to knock impatiently. She couldn't blame him for this. Why did she refuse to answer her door? Her car sat in her assigned parking space, so she had come home. Where would she have gone if not home?

Of course she was upset about losing her job. She probably panicked.

"Aww, man. Not *you* again." Luke, the young man with the oversized jogging pants, appeared at Roman's side. "What is it with you? What you got against a brotha getting some sleep so he can go out and earn a honest living? I'm young, but I got responsibilities. I got three kids and two babies' mamas to keep happy."

"Sorry, man." Roman grew embarrassed by the chastisement of a man much younger than himself. Grandma Dixon would have a field day with the whole scene. She'd get in his face about setting an example for young men without positive black male role models.

The man yawned and scratched his bare chest. "Akira ain't here anyway."

Acquisitions

"I saw her car outside."

"She left a few minutes ago with her friend. The healthy girl with the long hair—I forget her name."

"Lara," Roman offered.

"Yeah, Lara. Akira left with her." "You know where they were going?"

The young man raised his eyebrows. "Do I look like I keep tabs on my neighbors? Even if I did know, I wouldn't tell *you*. I don't know if Akira wants to see you. From what I can tell, she's always trying *not* to see you." He read the scorched look on Roman's face. "*And, if* I'm wrong, why are you always on *this* side of the door?"

The young man turned and headed back to his apartment, mumbling all the way. "Lay down the law. I'd make her give me a key. I wouldn't be standing out in the hallway making a scene, disturbing her neighbors."

Roman watched the young man stalk away. He wanted to tell him that they were in love. Their relationship started off when things were rocky for Akira, and things weren't getting better. Then he realized that the man didn't care about the status of their relationship. He wanted him to stop knocking on her door and disturbing his sleep.

Roman wrestled with his pride and contained his ego until he convinced himself that he needed to go home and wait for Akira's call. The thought did cross his mind to drive by Lara's house and see if Akira was there. He discarded the idea. If she wanted his help, she would come to him. Obviously she needed to be with her friend right now and not him. She hadn't even called to tell him she'd been fired.

It bothered him that she had not run to him. He couldn't deny it. He was in the business of saving her. They belonged to each other. He loved her and she loved him. He should be everything to her. *Why didn't she come directly to me?*

You're doing it again. He would never admit it, but he had the strong suspicion this was the reason Sherry had run away. She had to cut him off cold. Didn't leave him any way of contacting her because that's exactly what he would have done. Many times she had pleaded with him to back off. She felt smothered, she said. He was always there trying to fix everything. She could take care of herself.

So, Roman had backed off. Deferred to Sherry on important matters. Became her lap dog. Followed her direction and helped her attain her dreams. Loved her in the only way he knew how—however she wanted.

He loved her too much. Loved her more than he loved himself. Gave up every shred of pride he had to keep her from leaving.

Now he was in danger of loving Akira too much.

No matter how badly he wanted to roam the city until he found her, he would go home and wait.

The difference between Akira and Sherry—Akira needed him. She would come to him. She always did.

***

Columbia entered Roman's office after knocking to gain entrance. "Your eight o'clock is here."

"Eight o'clock?" Roman flipped the pages of his desk calendar. "I don't have an appointment on my schedule."

"Remember the young lady from yesterday? You told me to schedule an appointment for her right before you ran out the office."

"Oh, yeah. Send her in."

Columbia turned to leave the office.

Roman called out, stopping her. "Did I get any phone calls this morning?"

"I cleared your voicemail when I came in this morning. They're on the corner of your desk. No calls since then."

"Thank you." Roman reached for the message slips. Akira had called around seven and asked that he call her. He couldn't sleep all night for worrying about her, thinking of her crying on Lara's shoulder.

"Mr. Miller?" a hesitant voice asked. "I'm Danisha Marshall."

Acquisitions

Roman nodded, remembering completely. "Sit down. Please."

She shifted nervously in her seat.

"What can I do for you, Ms. Marshall?"

"Danisha."

She crossed her legs, flashing the firmness of her thighs. *Why do all of the women on the sixth floor have visible assets?*

Watching Danisha made Roman miss Akira. That's where he wanted to be. Eating ice cream in bed with Akira. There is always someone richer, smarter, prettier, funnier, or with a better body. But there would never be anyone more special to him. No matter what the temptation, he would never stray from what Akira offered because she was the whole package. Her flaws endeared her to him. Her willingness to accept his faults won her a permanent spot with him as long as she wanted to be there. And he wanted her to be with him forever.

Danisha asked, "Are you still looking into the trouble with Mr. Johnson?"

Roman nodded while grabbing a pen and pad to take notes. "Did you remember something about the case?"

"Not exactly." Danisha shifted again. "I know what Mr. Johnson did to me."

Roman's head snapped up. He had thousands of questions he wanted to fire at her. He might isolate her. She'd pull away. He anxiously waited for her to continue at her own pace.

"Mr. Johnson is the kinda man that puts on a big front when the boss is around. When he gets you alone, he's a totally different person. He has this way of looking at you and saying things that by themselves don't mean anything, but they still make you feel dirty."

Roman recalled Akira expressing the same sentiment. "I know this is uncomfortable, but I need you to be more specific."

"I only started here four months ago. From the first day I got here, Mr. Johnson was saying stuff like; 'I bet your boyfriend stays in you all night long'. Then in front of everyone he'd say, 'Danisha, you look tired. Didn't you get any sleep last night?' That's how he is—sneaky. He keeps you confused, and you don't know if he's a nice guy who doesn't know he's being offensive or if he really is trying to insult you."

Danisha paused to change her position again. Her anger made her more comfortable. "That's how it all got started, him saying little things now and then. After the trouble started with Akira, he seemed to start bothering me more. I was in the break room heating my lunch in the microwave and he brushed past me real casual like except that he stopped long enough to rub his *thing* on my butt."

Roman wrote fiercely, interjecting only to ask for other possible witnesses, dates and times. Unable to keep up with her flow of words, he pulled his tape recorder from the drawer.

"I let him keep touching me and rubbing up against me so I wouldn't lose my job. I have a new baby at home that I'm taking care of all by myself. I'm only twenty years old. Nobody was willing to hire me and pay me what Mr. Johnson does. But I can't take it anymore. Not after last week. After I saw how he got rid of Akira, I got scared. I know I'll be next now that she's gone."

"What happened last week, Danisha?"

She straightened in her chair and looked Roman directly in the eyes. "He gave me extra work to do, and I had to stay late to finish it. Once everyone was gone for the night, he came back. He was creeping around on the sixth floor. Scared me to death. The next thing I know, he's jumping out at me. He grabbed me around the waist. He was all over me. I fought him off." Her eyes shifted. "But not before he got my skirt up and his pants down."

"Did he force you to—?"

"No! I kneed him and left him rolling around on the floor. He caught up with me at the elevator and told me if I said anything he'd get rid of me like he was going to do to Akira. He

Acquisitions

said I should be like everyone else and go with the flow."

"He said 'like everyone else'?"

"That's what he said. I told people I thought were my friends, and they told me to keep quiet about it. They said it wasn't that bad. 'If Mr. Johnson likes you, you make more money than the other secretaries', they told me."

Roman's hand moved at double speed as he tried to note Danisha's every word. He retained a calm exterior as he finished his questions. "Did anybody see any of this?"

Danisha nodded and folded her arms across her chest. "His nasty girlfriend, Candace, stepped off the elevator after I kneed him."

"This is a big risk you're taking by coming forward. You're more mature than a lot of people around here."

"I know what people think about me. Men always think I'm easy. Women always think I'm after their man. I'm not like that at all. I can't help that I was blessed in some departments," she looked openly at her hefty breasts, "but I'm not a bimbo. I'm in school trying to finish my degree, and when I do, I'm getting my master's degree in international business. I'm sick of people thinking that they can have me because they want me. Mr. Johnson is a dirty dog and I'm not going to let him do whatever he wants to me. Besides, Akira is one of the only people in this place that talks to me like I'm an intelligent person. When I started here, she didn't whisper behind my back. She helped me learn the ropes. I don't want her to go down because of Mr. Johnson."

"You aren't making this up to help Ms. Reed, are you?"

"No! I'll give you the names of the other people I know he's hit on. Ask them, if you don't believe me."

After Roman completed a formal tape-recorded statement with Danisha, he called Columbia in and gave her the list of women to call down to his office. It didn't take Johnson long to catch on and give him a call to inquire about why he needed to see them.

Roman instructed Columbia, "I'm not in the position to

explain myself to Johnson. Tell him I'm unavailable." Lawton would be calling as soon as Johnson could speed dial his office. "Tell Lawton the same thing."

Roman spent most of the day interviewing the women about their involvement with Johnson. After two more women broke down in tears and told of the abuse they had been suffering, the rest opened up. Some, like Candace, refused to implicate him. Roman didn't push their misguided loyalty. He had enough witnesses to substantiate Akira's claims.

Mr. Lawton appeared at Roman's door as he was finishing his sixth statement of the day.

"Roman," he entered wearing a fake smile. "I've been trying to reach you all day."

"I've been very busy, but I'm glad you're here. You can accompany me and the security team up to Johnson's office."

"Security? To Barry's office? What's going on here?"

Columbia slipped out to make the necessary phone calls to the security supervisor.

"Six women have come forward this morning with stories of sexual harassment involving Barry Johnson."

Mr. Lawton's dusky face paled. "Six? It sounds like they may have gotten together to exact a vendetta against Barry."

"I can see where you would think that, but I took all of the statements, and it is obvious they're true. *And*, I believe that if I make it known that these women can come forth without repercussions, more will make statements."

Mr. Lawton dropped down in the nearest chair. "Barry is a good friend. I know he's a little overzealous with the women, but I can't fire him for that."

"Overzealous? I have stories on tape from women who were forced physically and mentally to have sex with him for fear they would be fired. And it goes further than that. He befriended these women and learned their secrets and personal problems. If the threat of losing their job wasn't enough, he threatened to use the information against them. The man has problems."

Acquisitions

Mr. Lawton shook his head. "I can't believe this. Barry and I have been friends for years. When I was promoted into the regional vice president position over the most popular man up for the job, Barry stood behind me. He came to help me fight many battles—if not for his support I might have left Greico before I even had a chance to prove myself. Over the years he's become not only a co-worker and golf buddy, he's my friend."

Roman sympathized with Mr. Lawton's devastation. He and Johnson were good friends, but he would have to do the right thing regardless of friendship. "I'm sorry, but the evidence is indisputable."

"Barry," Mr. Lawton mumbled. "What have you done?"

"I see no way out of this for Greico Enterprises. We'll be lucky if none of the women want to file lawsuits. You have to fire him."

Chapter 25

Akira came to the door in jeans and a t-shirt. She smoothed her hair down at the temples when she saw Roman standing there. The aroma of pot roast and baked potatoes floated over her shoulder.

"What's this for?" Akira lifted the bottle of champagne from Roman's hands.

"We're going to celebrate." He removed his coat as he stepped inside.

"Celebrate what? I lost my job yesterday."

Newspapers were scattered across the sofa.

"I know, but that's all changed."

"Roman, you've lost me."

He embraced her around the waist and planted a wet kiss on her cheek. "Guess what your man spent his afternoon doing?" He twirled her in an elaborate circle. "I helped Mr. Barry Johnson clean out his office."

"What? What happened?" Her eyes lit up.

They moved into the kitchen, and Akira sat at the table while Roman alternated bites of dinner with the details of how Mr. Johnson had been exposed. She couldn't return to work

Acquisitions

with the formula theft still unsolved, but at least she had been partially vindicated.

"You did it." Akira whispered, watching Roman dreamily. "You said you wouldn't let me down, and you didn't."

Dimples in full bloom, Roman lifted his glass of champagne and waited for Akira do the same. "To long awaited victory."

Akira clinked her glass to his, took a quick sip, and continued to watch him eat.

"Unfortunately, Mr. Lawton refused to fire Johnson. What'll happen next will depend on if criminal charges are filed. These kinds of cases are hard to convict, but some of the things I heard today are unquestionably criminal." He glanced up at her. "You'll probably be called to give another statement. I turned over a copy of everything I had from my investigation. Let's hope the police don't bother dragging everyone through this again."

Akira nodded. At least everyone knew the truth about Mr. Johnson. That would make telling her story again much easier.

"You should be very proud of yourself." Roman looked deep into her eyes. "Johnson has been suspended because you hung in there and fought everything that came your way. A weaker person would have walked away a long time ago. Or never come forward in the first place."

After the warm blush left her cheeks, Akira chuckled at memories that seemed long ago and far away. Here she sat—at her own kitchen table—feeding a man who she would have sworn her enemy only weeks ago.

"What's funny?" Roman finished the last of his drink.

"Us."

"Meaning?"

"Us—being together like this. Not too long ago, you were ready to dismiss my sexual harassment claim—and me. And I was ready to tear your head off."

"Yeah," Roman looked miles into the past. "You know,

our story isn't all that unique. A lot of couples don't like each other when they first meet, but then go on to have a long, loving relationship. The sparks are too strong at first and the chemistry acts in opposition."

"Dr. Roman Miller, relationship expert."

"Let's hear it." He pointed his fork in her direction.

"You want to hear my philosophy about relationships?" She sat back in her chair. "It's hard to put into words. Might be too much for you to understand."

"Try me." He said dryly, unsuccessfully giving her his best frown.

"Good relationships are made from mental compatibility, sexual attraction and commitment."

"Is one element more important than the other?"

Akira shrugged. "It varies from couple to couple."

"And with us?"

"We have it all."

His face took on a strange expression.

"What did I say?"

Roman shook his head.

"You look confused."

"Not confusion, Akira. Maddening love."

***

Roman rested, eyes shut, with his head against the back of the tub. He listened to Akira move around her apartment. Her satisfaction with his job well done justified every struggle in his life.

Soon Butch would clear her in the theft of the drug formula, and then he and Akira could go about the business of furthering their relationship. They had come a long way in a short time, but their future together was only beginning. So much to share. They had spent many hours dreaming. There were many complicated layers to peel back. He had not yet met her parents or brother. When she spoke of them, there was no doubt they were very dear to her.

Acquisitions

He pictured himself sitting behind his desk with a pen in hand writing a list of his intentions. Intentions with Akira Reed. Picturing her as his wife was not difficult. Picturing himself as her husband, near impossible. And what about children? They had never talked about whether or not they wanted kids.

Roman feared he didn't know how to be a good father. He had no example to follow. That brought on the anxiety associated with his parents. Would he introduce Akira to them? Would she be offended if he didn't? He knew women didn't want to be excluded from a man's family life.

"Roman," Akira called, "can I come in?"

Roman opened his eyes and waited for her to enter. She scurried in, picked up his suit, and disappeared again. He listened to her working in her bedroom, cleaning. The brief sound of the vacuum in the hallway. Dishes clanged in the kitchen.

A little while later, Akira rejoined him. "You've been in here a long time." Sitting on the rim of the tub, she handed him a glass of wine.

"Thinking."

"I knew that." She stuck her chest out with pride in her knowledge of his routines. "You like to have a glass of white wine and a heaping bowl of French vanilla ice cream while lying in the bed at night watching television."

"Oh, you think you know me."

Akira nodded. "I also know you contemplate situations and make important decisions in a bathtub filled with steaming hot water and overflowing with bubbles." She grabbed a fistful of the bubbles and blew them at his face. "What's on your mind?"

He swatted at the bubbles and reciprocated the gesture. "When did you realize you loved me?"

"You're borderline arrogant," she scolded him with a smile.

"Just borderline? I was striving for much more."

210

"I'm outta here."

"Wait." He managed to grab her hand, stopping her. The soapy water made a barrier between them of soft, silky wetness. "I want to know. I'm really not arrogant, only a little insecure."

Akira kneeled next to him. "Insecure? I doubt it. Arrogance and conceit are rearing their ugly heads."

"Maybe a little. Tell me anyway."

"It crept up on me. I can't pinpoint the moment it all came together. I opened my eyes one day and realized I was in trouble." Akira's hand dipped into the warm water again finding his thigh. "I still can't believe what's happening between us. When we're together, it's so *right* that it seems like I made it up in my mind—like a screenwriter would do. When you leave, I always have to ask myself if you were really here or if I dreamt the whole thing."

A huge smile sent his dimples into action. She took it as a cue to continue her underwater journey across the cords of his outer thigh to the firm flesh of his inner thigh. Her love play turned erotic when she began to massage his manhood.

"Remember," Roman laughed, "things seem smaller in water."

"That's it, Ol' Arrogant One, I'm stopping." She withdrew her hand.

"No," he caught her before she could go far, "finish what you started."

She took a sip of his wine before searching like a blind woman reading Braille for where she left off on the exploration of his body.

She asked, "Do you know when you fell in love with me?"

He nodded and answered what he knew would be her next question. "The day I kissed you in my office. That day, I knew I had to have you in my life because you were my key to happiness."

"What's wrong with you?" She gave him a love tap to the back of his head.

Acquisitions

"What do you mean?"

"Real men don't think, like you think and they certainly don't talk the way you talk."

"Real men *do* talk and think like me. It's the brothers out there perpetrating that give us a bad name. A real man goes out and makes his place in the community and in the world, and when he does, he wants nothing more than to have a good woman beside him. It's women that don't allow us to express ourselves the way we'd like. You call us *weak*."

"Don't go Butch on me." Akira laughed, referring to the debates at the cabin.

"Hey." Roman grinned. "Butch gets it right now and then. I speak the truth. Do you disagree? Women don't call a sensitive man a weak man?"

"If a man is with a woman who calls him weak because he expresses his genuine emotions, then he is weak. No man would allow *anyone* to disrespect him in that way—man or woman."

"Point taken."

"Now get out of the tub before the water gets cold." Akira moved to the door. "I'll meet you in my bedroom with another glass of wine and a bowl of French vanilla ice cream."

Roman treated her with another dimple-laced smile before she closed the door.

***

"I thought I'd wear the gown you gave me." Akira greeted Roman's towel-clad body at the foot of her bed with his boxers in hand.

Roman fell easily into the game. "What do you have on your mind?"

"For what I have in mind, you won't be needin' these." She tossed the boxers over her shoulder.

Roman moved to her with the cool easiness of an over-confident gangster. "You started something while I was in the tub."

She perched herself on her knees at the edge of the bed.

212

She pulled away his towel. Her eyes traveled over his body, taking in every incredible inch. From the top of his shiny waves to the bottom of his size twelve feet, Roman was flawless.

His lashes dipped. "You can touch me."

"I know."

Her hands cascaded down his freshly oiled body. His moans encouraged her to continue her aggressiveness. She wrapped her fingers around his shaft, barely covering half of it. Starting at the base, she stroked upward. His body came forward. Downward. He sucked in a deep breath. Again—up and down, his body moving back and forth to her rhythm.

Roman's fingers weaved through her hair, grasping the back of her head. His other hand lightly stroked Akira's cheek with the same rhythm she used on his eager manhood. He dipped to meet her lips, careful not to disturb her stroke.

"Ask me," he whispered as he wildly planted kisses on her neck.

Akira used her thumb to smear the liquid pearl down his shaft.

"Ask me, Akira," Roman pleaded between ragged breaths. "Ask me."

"Can I taste you?"

His fingers tightened against the back of her head. He placed his other hand on her shoulder. Using both hands, he guided her mouth to her answer.

Her tongue discovered his weak areas—the places that made his knees buckle. Timid at first, she licked and stroked. His uninhibited response made her swallow more and more. All of him out, and all of him back in. He responded most violently to the flicking of her tongue. The twin sacs between his thighs lifted and tightened.

Akira pulled away, the saliva of her tongue mixed with the cool air to shock him into reality. "Ask me."

"Damn." He pushed her onto the bed, pinning her wrists to the mattress.

Acquisitions

Akira devoured him with her kisses.

He reached between them, his blunt tip puncturing her mound.

"Ask me, Roman."

He gathered her wrists again and pinned her to the bed. Breathing hard, he stared into her eyes. "I have you where I want you."

"I'll settle for no less than begging."

"Damn." He flipped onto his back, carrying Akira with him.

She settled between his thighs, her breasts meshed with his chest. "Ask me."

"Make love to me, Akira."

Akira's eyes never left his as she lowered herself down the length of him. She loved this man more than she had ever loved anyone in her life. Fulfilling his request was her privilege. She placed a hand on each of his shoulders, balancing herself. He would not let her fall—not ever—he'd allow her freedom, but be nearby to catch her if she should fall. She moved slowly, making the sensation last. Usually overwhelmed with passion, taking it slow was not something they did during their lovemaking. The pressure built and swelled. Roman consumed her body and captured her mind.

"Make love to me." Roman repeated until Akira ruptured in an explosion of tremors. He flipped her onto her back.

"Do you love me?" Roman asked as she shook beneath him.

"Yes. I love you."

Roman returned to the moist heat, riding Akira to his salacious conclusion. His dark lashes beat, his eyes locked on hers, telling her he loved her. Slowly, rocking. Sharing kisses. Bringing her to climax again—with him, sharing that ultimate bond. Giving all he had, begging her to take his offering.

***

Detective Downs lifted a cup of steaming hot coffee to his lips. "What are the chances that the lawyer went home last night and beat us back here this morning?"

Detective Casser cracked his window to help clear the foggy windshield of the unmarked police car. "You have a better chance of flying home with newly sprouted wings."

"I never figured him in on this whole mess. Do you think she might be telling the truth?"

"I doubt it," Casser said coldly. "I think she seduced them both—Dodson and the lawyer. She's covering all her bases. Dodson moved the formula for Reed, giving her the big payoff. Either the lawyer's in on it, or he's been so busy defending her, he hasn't had any time to see what she's really doing."

"I don't know. I don't figure her for the type." This from Downs, who always wanted to believe the best of people. "If she has all the money, why hasn't she jumped on a plane and taken off? We have a tail on Dodson, and he hasn't gone near her. If I had several million dollars stashed somewhere, I wouldn't trust anyone to hold it without keeping contact with them. Especially if they're both sleeping with someone else. Jealousy has ruined many perfect crimes."

"I don't know all the answers. Maybe we should question Dodson again. Make him think that Reed's getting ready to leave the country with all of the money. See how that shakes him."

Chapter 26

Columbia skirted down the corridor to meet Roman as he stepped off the elevator. "Mr. Miller, I tried to call your cell phone."

"What is it?" Roman touched her arm to absorb the panic twisting her face.

"Mr. Lawton is here—and he brought security with him."

Roman looked toward his open office door. "It's alright, Columbia, I can handle this." He gave her a half-hearted smile. "You go back to work and don't worry." He escorted her to her desk, grounded himself, and walked into his office.

Mr. Tabrinsky and one of his officers stood near the door.

Mr. Lawton looked up from behind his desk. "I need to speak with you, Roman." He gestured to the two security officers and they left the room.

Roman placed his briefcase at his feet. "What's the problem?"

"Well, I've learned some disturbing news, and I hoped you could clear it all up. Explain the misunderstanding."

He wanted to get to the point. "I will if I can."

"Early this morning, I had a visit from the two detectives

investigating the stolen formula. They told me they observed you at Ms. Reed's home—all night. Is that true?" Mr. Lawton braced the corners of the desk.

Roman answered without shame, "That is true."

"Why? It had something to do with the investigation, right? Trying to win her trust and make her confess?"

Standing at a crossroad, Roman searched his options. Mr. Lawton pleaded with him to make up a story that would save his job. But the choice was much grander than Mr. Lawton could know.

Did he lie about his relationship with Akira to save his job? His future? The promotion to a partnership position that he had been coveting for years?

Or did he tell the truth? Honor what he had with Akira, the consequences bring what they may?

Lying would mean he felt ashamed of Akira and what they shared, that he valued his work far more than their future. Because once Akira Reed learned that he had lied—covered up their relationship to save his job—she'd drop him faster than he could count to three. He had no idea how they would survive with both of them out of work, but at this point, he didn't care. As long as they were struggling together.

"Mr. Lawton, I'm in love with Akira Reed."

Mr. Lawton's thin lips parted, his eyes widened, his jaw went slack. After regaining his composure and donning a stern expression, he continued. "The police are also questioning whether or not the two of you are in all of this together. They think the sexual harassment claim was a sham, all a way of covering up the theft."

"Sir, I can't control what the police think. I did fall in love with Akira during the investigation, that's true. I promise you I didn't act on my feelings until the case was closed. Is this all an elaborate plot to steal from Greico? Absolutely not. I have too much at stake. Akira is an honest person. I don't know who sold the formula to Power & Power, but I'm working hard to find out."

217

Acquisitions

"That's what you say, but I can't take that chance. All the people at Greico that I've trusted...I don't trust any of you anymore." Mr. Lawton stood slowly, wearily. "Security," he called, "you may enter now."

Chapter 27

Average height and medium build, he possessed dark, strong features. He wasn't supermodel handsome, but had infectious sex appeal that left women at the mercy of his sleepy eyes.

Old feelings came back with the vengeance of an artic wind.

I should have never, ever called him. Akira fudged the truth, "I'm glad you came."

Removing his coat, Eric stepped into Akira's apartment. He touched several items, reacquainting himself with the surroundings. He smiled at familiar pictures on the end tables.

"God, it's good to see you again." His powerfully thundering voice commanded the attention of those he sold to. "I wish it didn't have to be under these circumstances."

"You know why I called?" Akira invited him to sit down with a flourish of her hand.

"Yes, it wasn't hard to put together."

Good. Because Akira had no idea why she invited the pain of her past back into her life.

When Akira called Eric, it was with the intent to aid in her

Acquisitions

defense. Eric being this close, filling her head with past visions of sitting on her sofa, touching and laughing in the dark, she wasn't sure she had done the right thing. Butch had spoken to Eric and gotten nowhere. She hoped their history would afford her more information.

Akira started right in, hoping to distract her mind from images of their past. "You told the police we were engaged?"

"No," he turned to her, propping one leg up on the sofa. "I told the police the truth. We dated, but it didn't work out."

"They told me different."

"That doesn't surprise me. The two detectives that came to see me accused me of all kinds of things. Accused *us* of all kinds of things. Everything I said, they twisted around to mean something else. They threatened to arrest me in connection with the HIV vaccine that Power & Power recently acquired. And they said I had something to do with a sexual harassment case over at Greico Enterprises involving you." He stood up and paced back and forth in front of her. "Hell, by the time they were done with me, I was scared to death I'd lose *my* job."

"I *have* lost my job."

Eric stopped suddenly. The lamp made seductive shadows dance off the sharp features of his face. "I hadn't heard that. I'm sorry."

Akira nodded her thanks then caught the meaning of his words. "You hadn't heard that? How would you have?"

Eric's body tightened with the realization that he had said too much. "I—I asked around after the police came. You know this business. Every salesperson knows what every other salesperson is doing. I was worried."

Akira watched for any sign of a lie. Eric's fatal flaw, known only by those close to him, was in his complete inability to lie without showing a telling sign. As she scrutinized his demeanor, the sign came. A simple gesture of shoving his hands in his pockets told Akira all that she feared might be true.

***

"What do you think?" Detective Downs stared out the window, across the street to Akira's apartment building.

"I think I'm sick of this stupid case," Detective Casser answered bitterly. "I'm sick of all of the players involved. And most of all, I'm sick of freezing my ass off in front of this broad's building every night."

Downs looked over at his partner, not bothering to shield his annoyance. "Eric has been inside for about an hour."

"Making plans to run?"

"I wouldn't have thought it."

Casser picked up the hand-held radio. "Let's go ahead and bring them in for questioning. Before that Vance character shows up."

***

Roman joined Butch at the distal end of the bar. They were both starving and regretted coming to the restaurant at peak time for the dinner seating. The waitress sympathized with the men and directed them to a small table in the bar area where they could order from the full menu. It was not as flashy at the main seating areas, but two hungry men could care less about the decor.

"Greico fired you?"

Roman twisted the cap off his beer. "Those two detectives following Akira's case couldn't wait to tell Lawton they saw my car parked at her place overnight. Lawton couldn't be sure I didn't have anything to do with the stolen formula. He had to let me go."

"You're more understanding than I would be."

"I knew the risks when I became involved with Akira." Roman downed a swig of beer. "Don't mention this to her. I want to tell her face-to-face tonight."

Butch nodded. "What are you going to do?"

"After we figure out who really stole the formula, I want to take Akira and get away from all this madness. Then I'll start looking for work."

Acquisitions

"You know there's always a place for you at my firm."

Roman shook his head. "Practicing trial law is too intense for me. I'm thinking about starting my own practice like Grandma Dixon has been telling me for years. Maybe dabble in divorce law or work with sexual harassment cases. I have to think it all over. Talk to Akira."

Butch nodded.

The two men paused in their conversation long enough to eat from the newly presented tray of assorted appetizers.

"What did you need to talk to me about?" Roman asked when the hunger pangs were under control.

"A couple of things."

"Like?"

Butch downed his drink for added support. "What do you think about Lara?"

"Akira's friend?"

Butch nodded, ignoring the inquisitive look on his friend's face.

"She's nice, I like her."

"What do you know about her?"

"Personally?"

Butch nodded again before stuffing a crab cake into his mouth.

"She broke up with her boyfriend last year because he treated her badly. I guess she was really crazy over this guy Clifton because she went into a deep depression and started overeating." Roman paused to taste another sampling of the food tray. "She gained a lot of weight—fifty or a hundred pounds—I can't remember. Anyway, she's finally coming out of it. She's in an exercise program and sees a doctor about her diet. But you know about that from the weekend at the cabin— all the special foods she ate. Why the questions about Lara?"

Butch watched Roman's expression while he asked the next question. "What do you think about me and her getting together?"

"You and Lara? I had no idea you were interested in each

other the way you spent the entire time at the cabin fighting."

Butch reached for another crab cake. "It's crazy, isn't it?"

"She did know how to handle you. You've been seeing her? Akira didn't mention it."

"I've called her a couple times since we've been back, but that's about it. I really like her—as a friend first. I can hold a conversation with her and not worry about her holding up her end. She can keep up with me on everything. You saw how easily she caught on to skiing. Not like your clumsy girlfriend."

"Hey."

They laughed together before Butch continued. "She's like that about everything. Hell, most times she's teaching me things."

"I don't understand the problem."

Butch's eyes darted around the room before he continued. "She's a large size woman."

"What? You can't be with someone who you can't drape over your arm and brag about her modeling career? That's messed up, man."

"I didn't say I wasn't going to be with her. I'm my own man. I make my own decisions."

Roman waited for him to go on.

"It's that I've never *been* with a woman…"

Roman laughed as he lifted the beer bottle to his lips.

"Why are you making a joke of this?"

"Because it's stupid. If you like Lara, be with Lara. Besides, who said Lara wanted you?"

The delivery of their entrees interrupted the conversation.

"There's something else I need to talk to you about," Butch said.

Roman glanced up at him, but after the foolish discussion they had just finished, he refused to give Butch his undivided attention.

"Sherry called today."

Roman dropped his fork. The noise of it falling to the

Acquisitions

floor sounded like the chime of a grandfather clock. A waitress hurried over with another.

Butch went on, delivering the message as if it were an eulogy. "She has a client that committed a crime here in Michigan, but fled to New York. He's been extradited, and she fully expects there to be a trial. She asked me to sit second chair because she's not familiar with any Michigan criminal laws that might impact the case. She flew in this afternoon."

Roman continued to watch his friend, unable to gather his thoughts. His mind whirled out of control. He still had hundreds of questions to ask her, and they all fought for first-string positioning. He had searched for her for so long, and now that he was finally getting her out of his head, she calls out of the blue.

Butch knew what he wanted to know. "She asked about you."

"What did she ask?"

"She hopes that she can go out to dinner with you tomorrow." Butch went inside the breast pocket of his suit and gave him a piece of paper with Sherry's hotel information.

Roman took the paper and stared at the numbers, unable to digest any of it. The clamor of the other patrons annoyed him. He needed to think.

"I feel like dirt doing this. I know you're with Akira now. I don't want to be the cause of you two having any troubles, but I thought you'd be mad if I didn't tell you."

"I would have." Roman spat. "Are you going to work the case with her?"

"I'll hear her out, but then I'll probably refer her to one of our other attorneys."

Roman nodded and put the piece of paper inside his wallet.

"You don't *have* to call her."

"That's ridiculous. Of course I have to call her. I love her."

Butch's jaw dropped. "You love her?"

Roman sank down in his seat when he realized his slip of tongue. "That's not what I meant."

"What exactly did you mean?"

"Man, don't push me. I'm surprised that Sherry's asking to see me after all this time. It caught me off guard."

"Why *would* she want to see you after all of this time? You've moved on with your life. Leave her alone to move on with hers."

"I didn't ask for your advice."

"Why are you mad at me?"

Roman looked around noticing the attention he had drawn to their table. "Sorry, man."

"I don't think it's me you need to apologize to. It's Akira. Remember her? The woman you've been running around telling you love *her*?"

"Don't be a smart-ass." Roman motioned for the waitress to bring their bill.

"What are you going to do? Drop Akira now that Sherry's in town? You forget how badly she treated you?"

Roman pulled bills from his wallet to cover the tab. "The first thing I'm going to do is see what Sherry wants. I don't even know if she wants me back." Roman pulled on his coat. "I'll catch up with you later."

"Roman, think about this first," Butch called after him, but Roman was already walking to his doom.

Chapter 28

Roman pushed every single thought and image of Akira out of his head as he made his way downtown to Sherry's hotel. He convinced himself that seeing Sherry had nothing to do with his relationship with Akira. He dreamt of the day he would receive answers to his questions. Answers that would allow him closure to what seemed an ancient part of his life. He tried to be angry with Sherry, but the only emotion he could muster made his groin stir with memories.

Both parties fully understood the reason for their meeting. The outcome would be no surprise. Roman would demand explanations. Sherry would give answers that could never satisfy him.

Knowing that Sherry could never erase the feelings of abandonment she planted deep down in his soul, Roman wondered why he found himself trekking in the snow to see her.

Simple, everyone wants to be wanted.

From the day he began to understand the magnitude of his parents leaving him and his sister, he wanted to be loved. Not only loved out of obligation, as he sometimes wrongfully believed Grandma Dixon had done, but loved and desired because he was a good man.

Confused emotions swirled inside Roman as he drove toward downtown. Sherry should have wanted him as much as he wanted her. But she didn't, and he had to know why not. More than that, he had to make her want him one last time. Then he could walk away knowing that he had ended things on his terms.

The memories surrounded him on the wings of every snowflake that hit his windshield. Beautiful Sherry. He had fallen in love with her in the Bahamas—an impulsive vacation they decided to take together. During those seven days, she stole his heart.

As he searched the corridor for her room number, his heart pounded with anticipation. Could she be more beautiful than he remembered? How would they greet each other? Would he be a disappointment to her? How much of their time together did she remember?

He was fantasizing about jumping on a plane with her to fly back to New York where they would start their new life together when he found her door.

He removed his coat and straightened his tie before he knocked.

***

"Three hours!" Butch pounded his briefcase as he yelled at the desk sergeant. "Three hours you held my client before allowing her to make a phone call. Let me tell you, I will be looking into this thoroughly, and if I find one thing out of order, I'll be back."

Butch snatched up his briefcase and turned to Akira. "Let's go." He cupped her elbow in his palm and guided her to the door.

"Did you say anything?" Butch asked once they were inside his Suburban, moving slowly down the slippery highway.

"No. What's going to happen to Eric?"

"I don't know, and I don't care—he's not my client. What

Acquisitions

were you doing with him anyway?"

Akira explained why she invited him over to talk. "He didn't tell me much, but I get the feeling he is involved in this mess somehow."

Butch questioned her about her accusation.

"He told me that he's been keeping tabs on me. How could he be doing that? I asked him, but he wouldn't say. He admitted he started seeing someone at Greico shortly after we broke up."

"Did he give you any clue as to who?"

Akira shook her head. "None. It wouldn't be hard to find out. Only the people on the sixth floor would know who I am. Roman and I could narrow the list down to the eligible females for you."

Butch became uncharacteristically quiet. He had not yelled at her for interfering. He never said she was crazy for inviting Eric to her apartment. He wasn't on his cell phone making calls and planning his next move. He sat in the driver's seat gripping the steering wheel, concentrating on the road.

"Butch?" Akira waited for his reluctant glance. "Where's Roman? How come he isn't with you?"

He fiddled with the heating.

"Call him."

"I can't, Akira."

"Why not?"

"He wouldn't answer."

"Tell me what's going on."

Butch's answer rocked her heart.

Helpless, she could only cry. Roman fired from Greico. *Sherry back in town.* Akira felt as if she was reading snippets out of the local newspaper describing a stranger's life.

"Akira, I didn't tell you because I want to listen to you cry. I want you to go to the hotel and stop Roman. He loves you, I'm sure of that. For some unknown reason, he's certifiable when it comes to Sherry. If you love him, go to the hotel."

"I'm not going to belittle myself by fighting over a man. I've been through enough humiliation."

"You're not going to fight *over* a man, you're going to fight *for* your man."

"Why did he go there?"

"I don't know," Butch admitted. "He should have burned the paper. I guess he has something to prove."

"What could he have to prove to her?"

"He's not thinking clearly."

"What if he doesn't want me? How will I feel if he tells me to go away?"

"I guarantee he won't do that."

***

As Akira stood outside Sherry's door, she regretted coming. She should have never let Butch push her into this confrontation. She could always leave, walk away from Roman and all his meaningless words, but something stopped her. At least this way she would know exactly where she stood. She lifted her hand and tapped lightly on the door. Too lightly—no one heard her. Wild thoughts raged in her head. What if they were in the middle of something intimate? The vision angered her into knocking louder.

Akira sucked in a deep breath.

Sherry answered the door in a floor-length, pink negligee covered with a sheer wrap.

***

Lara turned on Butch. "You shouldn't have sent my friend to that hotel. What if Roman rejects her? It'll destroy her."

"He won't reject Akira. He loves her."

"That's what's wrong with you men. You do whatever you want without any regard for other people's feelings. He shouldn't be there with this woman if he loves Akira. He should have thrown her number out. Why did you give it to him anyway?"

"I couldn't keep it from him. He would find out if I decide to work with her."

Acquisitions

"And that's another thing, why are you even considering taking that case?"

"It's my job." As Butch tried to explain, but the excuse sounded lame.

"You have a suck job."

Butch stood toe to toe with Lara as she looked up into his face demanding answers.

"Take me to the hotel," she demanded.

"What good would that do? This is between Roman and Akira. We shouldn't get in the middle of it."

"Why did you come here to tell me all of this if you didn't want me to do anything about it?" Lara pulled her robe tightly around her waist.

Butch hesitated with his answer. Any reason he could call her, he would use. Any task that would lead him to see her, he would undertake. "I needed an excuse to see you."

"An excuse to see *me*?"

"Yes, I needed a reason to come here."

Butch dipped his head before he lost his courage. His palms enveloped Lara's face and he kissed her lips. The ringing of his cell phone caused them to separate. He turned his back on Lara as he answered, too embarrassed to see the expression on her face.

"What is it?" Lara asked once he ended the call.

"That was a friend at the ninth precinct. The detectives released Eric Dodson."

***

"Yes?" Sherry asked with a huge grin on her face. Modesty didn't make her close her wrap. Her bosom overflowed from the negligee. She wore little make-up, only a neutral colored lipstick. Her hair flowed with a soft curl onto her shoulders. Her perfume was light and seductive. Her toenails were perfectly manicured.

Why had she come back to town? Akira couldn't fight against their history. If Sherry wanted Roman, she would have him.

230

Akira stood speechless at the door.

"Can I help you?"

"Roman Miller, please." Akira requested, sounding as if she were standing at the desk of his receptionist instead of the hotel room of his ex-lover.

Sherry wrinkled her nose, not attempting to hide her displeasure with the interruption. "You know Roman?"

Akira nodded.

"This must be about business?"

Sherry's arrogance reminded Akira of the café waitress. "Is he here?"

"Roman, there's someone here to see you." Sherry stepped aside, allowing her to enter the hotel room.

Akira didn't wait for Roman to appear. She moved through the outer room into the bedroom. She found him sitting at the foot of the bed without his suit jacket and tie, his shirt unbuttoned.

Sherry nipped at her heels. Akira ignored her questions.

Roman leapt to his feet. "Akira, what are you doing here?"

"Who *is* this, Roman?" Sherry moved to his side. She looked at Akira as if she were a dirty orphan fresh out of the gutter.

The sound of Roman's name floating from Sherry's lips chilled her. She crooned his name as if they were in the heat of making love. It had a distinct familiarity that had not been long forgotten.

Roman addressed Akira as if she were a complete stranger. "I don't understand why you're here."

"You don't?"

"No, I don't."

"That's it. I'm calling security." Sherry moved to the phone.

Akira looked at Roman with questioning eyes. Would he allow her to be carted off by hotel security?

"Don't, Sherry." Roman's voice had the same lyrical

Acquisitions

quality when he said her name.

She stopped, and then turned to continue watching the scene unfold.

"What did you think would happen if you came here?" Roman asked.

"I don't know." Akira glanced over at Sherry. "I wanted to see—for myself." She locked her eyes on Roman's exposed chest.

He began to button his shirt.

"I thought you were ready for me to love you."

Sherry stepped closer to the two of them. "*Who* are you?"

Akira turned her eyes to Sherry. "I'm his girlfriend."

Sherry took in a long head to toe look at Akira before she smirked. "I doubt that very seriously."

Akira looked to Roman.

"Sherry, leave her alone. This is not her fault. This is all my doing."

"You're really seeing *her*?" Sherry snorted.

"He's seeing me only if he leaves here right now." Akira turned her wrath on Roman. "You are *my* man. You are in love with *me*. Why are you here?"

Roman dropped his lashes, and Akira wanted to stroke them.

"Let's go." Akira hated the pleading quality her voice had taken on. She repeated herself more definitively, "Let's go."

Akira turned and started to the door hoping that Roman would be behind her when she reached the elevator. Either way, she was not stopping. She had given them both enough to laugh at after she left. She had come to bring him home. Now it fell to Roman to make a decision.

Akira didn't look back. She stepped onto the elevator and went directly to her car. Once inside, she laid her head against the steering wheel and let her tears flow freely. The flash of oncoming headlights broke her reverie of tears. She started her engine and drove to Roman's house to await the outcome of her actions.

232

Chapter 29

Akira boldly used the garage code to enter Roman's home through the mudroom. He had given her the access number weeks ago. Tonight she used it for the first time.

Akira went into the den, the room closest to the garage entrance, and sat down in the chair that had brought her much comfort over the last few weeks. Her hands shook uncontrollably. She mused about how she would not be able to enjoy the comfort of the small, warm space anymore, but she quickly remembered she would be losing much more.

Akira rose when she heard Roman's footsteps coming toward her. He stopped in the doorway of the den and stood silent, his face absent of emotions.

"I'd like an apology," Akira stated with authority.

"I'm sorry. I have a past. I can't change that. Not even for you."

"I don't want that piece of apology!" she shouted.

It came too quickly. He only said what she wanted to hear. There were no heartfelt emotions behind it. He only hoped to put a quick end to their argument.

Roman removed his coat and placed it neatly over the arm

of the loveseat. He stopped a few feet from Akira and waited for her to continue.

Akira inhaled the woodsy fragrance of his cologne. Cologne he applied to please Sherry. She attacked with the viciousness of a wolf drawn by the smell of fresh blood. "I want you to apologize for being a liar. I want it to be so eloquently stated that I understand why I just caught my boyfriend—the man who said he loves me—in a hotel room half dressed with his ex."

"I bet I can thank Butch for that."

She ignored his sarcasm. "I want you to apologize and mean it. When I leave here, I should feel good about myself and be able to move on without you. I want you to grovel so that the next man I decide to get serious with won't have to deal with the baggage you left behind."

"There won't be another man after me because I'm not going anywhere."

"I didn't ask you to stay."

"You told me I was staying."

Akira's fists were clenched. She wanted to jump across the short distance separating them and punch him in the face for what he had done and the nonchalant way he handled the whole scene. "Do you understand what's happening here?"

Roman stared at her, confused.

"We're breaking up. Why don't you act like you care?"

Exasperated, "We're not breaking up, Akira."

"Yes," she shouted, "we are."

"No, we're not. You told me to leave Sherry's hotel if I wanted to be with you, and I did. We're not breaking up."

"That was before."

"Before what?" He lifted his palms in question.

Before he arrogantly stepped into the house and acted like *he* had been wronged. Before he couldn't give her the apology she deserved. Before she smelled the cologne he wore to make her hot on the skin Sherry had caressed.

She asked, "Why don't you care?"

"I do care, it's a lot to deal with right now."

"*I'm* the one who should be saying that. Don't turn this around and try to make yourself the victim."

"Akira, I know I'm not the victim. Okay? I'm tired, and I don't want to deal with this right now."

"When would you like to deal with it?"

He sounded defeated. "I don't know—not now."

"Every time I want to talk about your relationship with Sherry you tell me later. When, Roman? How about over dinner? Or after you tell me you love me? What about after I take you in my mouth and you call me by her name?"

He turned away. "You're out of control."

"Would it have been a better time if I hadn't showed up at that hotel?" Akira stepped closer, forcing him to face her. "What were you going to do? Have sex with her?"

Roman looked away.

Akira covered her heart in an attempt to keep the shattered pieces inside her chest. Her voice trembled with the tears she refused to shed. "What were you going to do, Roman?"

His silence told her all she needed to know. She grabbed her coat and headed out the way she came. "I will never forgive you for making me trust myself enough to love you and then destroying that trust without one bit of remorse."

Roman snapped out of his daze and ran to catch her, stepping in front of her. "Don't leave."

"I can't stay."

"You have to. You love me, and you know I love you." He placed his hands on her shoulders. "I was confused. Sherry appeared out of the blue after all of this time. There's so much unfinished business between her and me. I don't know—I had to see her."

Akira listened to the explanation because she was entitled to hear it, but she was in no way obligated to believe it. She hoped she didn't believe it because then she could walk away from him and their relationship filled with hate and anger, and

Acquisitions

that would make it much easier to get over him.

"I was stupid. I don't know how far things would have gone between Sherry and me if you hadn't come. I hope that I would have come to my senses before I made the biggest mistake of my life. All I know is that you *did* come, and I *did* walk away from her to be with you."

Roman pried Akira's coat from her hands and placed it on the nearest chair. "I thought Sherry was the greatest thing in the world, but I realized as I looked at you standing beside her that she's nothing but a memory. A memory that I've built up to be more than it ever was. She never really loved me because she loved herself too much. And I never really loved *her*. I loved the *chase* of her. When I thought I had one last chance at winning the game, I went running—without any regard to you or what we've built together. For that, I am truly sorry."

Akira hunted for sincerity.

"It's you that I love without a doubt. I love you because you love me. I love you because of who you are. I <u>am</u> sorry. I'll get down on my knees and beg if you want. Don't leave."

Akira looked up into eyes that reflected unbridled pain and remorse. Still, no matter how badly she wanted to run to him, love him, go on as if the night had never happened, she couldn't. "I don't believe you."

"You have to believe me. It's true."

"I don't have to do anything when it comes to you anymore." Akira clutched her coat to her breast and started for the door again.

"Yes, you do!" Roman shouted, his massive palm encircled her arm and pulled her down the hallway to his bedroom. "You say you love me, well you have to allow me to make a mistake. I'm trying to fix that mistake the only way I know how."

Akira pulled away from him. "Why do I have to allow you a mistake? Do you think this is a game show and you get one freebie? You're an adult; you know that actions have consequences. You should have thought about what you were doing before you did it."

"Akira, I'm not perfect. How can you deny me the right to be human?"

"I've given you chance after chance. You've betrayed me every time." She counted off his treacheries on her fingers. "Your findings in the sexual harassment case. You're siding with Greico when they accused me of stealing the HIV vaccine. Your part in my dismissal."

"You're hanging all of that on me? I stood by you. You know my hands were tied."

"I've been back and forth about all of this since our first kiss. One minute I trust you, the next I'm suspicious. All of my doubts were cleared up tonight."

The silence engulfing the room placed a wedge between them. A twinge of regret moved through Akira's gut as she wondered if she had said too much—gone too far. She discarded that fear. Roman was in the wrong. She refused to take any responsibility for his running to Sherry.

The controlled, arrogant attorney returned. "We're going to calm down and discuss this rationally. I'm not letting you leave until we do."

"Okay. Let's start with this." Akira rushed to his dresser and lifted one of the gold trimmed picture frames. "You know this makes me uncomfortable, but they're still here. I didn't push the issue because I wanted you to remove them in your own time. When you were ready to let the past go. I didn't want you to take the pictures down and hide them to please me. I wanted you to love me and not her."

Roman stalked over to his "Shrine of Sherry" as Akira had secretly come to call it. "You want the pictures gone?" He plucked the frame from her fingers, dropped it to the ground, and smashed it beneath his boot. "These pictures don't mean more to me than you do." He picked up the picture frames one by one and slammed them to floor. The glass in the frames broke into tiny pieces and shot through the air like stray bullets.

Acquisitions

The more Roman pummeled the photos, the better he felt, the freer he became from Sherry's influence. When all of the frames were broken, he went inside his dresser and removed the photo albums. He ripped the pages from the books and tore them to shreds, releasing all the pent-up frustration he had regarding Sherry.

Akira backed away from the flying glass and let Roman take the steps he felt necessary to relieve his pain and release the past.

Roman's chest heaved with his every breath. He turned to Akira. "That's how much Sherry means to me. I want to be with you."

"Is that supposed to erase from my mind the fact that less than an hour ago you were undressed with Sherry?"

"You told me to leave the hotel—I left the hotel. You wanted me to take down these pictures—I destroyed them. Everything you ask, I do. Anything to keep you in my life. What else do you want from me?"

"I want to not have to ask."

Her words stung deeply. His words back to haunt him again. Words he used to cleverly seduce—make her beg for his touch, on more than one occasion—would now cause his demise.

He let silence bring the tone of their argument down a notch. "You told me we were okay if I left the hotel. Now you're saying that we're finished. I walked away from Sherry to save us."

"You walked away from Sherry to save us? If you wanted to save us, you should have never gone to the hotel."

"Don't leave," he barely whispered. But Akira heard him. And she saw the pain in his eyes shining bright with the glimmer of tears.

Akira considered staying, but staying would not work. It would mean she could never leave. She would be committing to the relationship forever, no matter what problems occurred between them. She could not accept the burden of that decision. It was not her fault he was hurting. He had gone to the hotel room—not her. He took on the responsibility of loving her and had fallen short.

"Akira, how can I fix this?"

"I don't know that you can."

"I made a mistake. Why won't you forgive me?"

"The worst thing a man can do to a woman is disappointing her."

Akira did what she had to do.

She turned and walked away.

Chapter 30

February 21

The click of Akira's heels sounded seconds after her feet actually hit the shiny, dark wood. She dragged in long, deep breaths to keep from unraveling. Butch squeezed her arm, as he guided her to the courtroom.

"Remember, this will be a closed hearing. An attorney is serving as mediator. For all intent, he'll perform the role of a judge." He leaned down and whispered his reminder. "There won't be too many people in the gallery. Only the people directly connected with the case. If you get nervous, focus on me."

Akira nodded. Not too many people, but Roman would be there.

In the center of the wood floors of the courthouse was painted the scales—a symbol of justice. *How ironic*, she thought, the wood floors were the last thing she remembered seeing before she fled Roman's house for the last time.

"Ready?" Butch's confidence calmed her. "I'll be right up front. I'll object if I don't want you to answer. Give me a second to do so before you answer."

"This isn't a trial. You can't object," Akira said.

"Watch me."

Akira nodded, trying to display the same level of confidence he harbored.

"Lara is already in there. Look to one of us if you need support."

Butch grabbed the elaborately carved door handle and pulled it open. Akira smoothed the seam of her dress, patted the wayward locks of her hair into place, pushed her shoulders back, and looked up into his face for one last boast of courage before she stepped inside.

Immediately, the few in the gallery turned with doubting eyes to greet her. Lara, all smiles, gave her the thumbs up. She also gave Butch a heated glance that made his step falter.

Akira inhaled Roman's unique scent as she passed him sitting in the first row across from the witness stand. He looked sexier than ever in the midnight blue suit, powder blue shirt and multi-patterned tie. She could feel his immaculately trimmed moustache tickling her thigh. If she could position him on his back and nibble his full top lip, all would be right in the world.

When their eyes met, he scooted to the edge of the bench. His long lashes flickered.

No dimples today. His face appeared hard, unreadable.

He hung on her every word, his lips separating, whispering encouragement.

Mr. Johnson had never turned around as she approached the stand and never looked at her during her testimony. By the time Akira took the stand, ten women employed at Greico had told their stories. Many had been dismissed under suspicious circumstances well before Mr. Johnson's assault on Akira. A few tales were as mild as dirty cartoons, while others were worse than a horror movie. Her story fell toward the middle of the scale. The twist that made hers compelling had to do with the stolen drug formula and how it tied into the dynamics of her charges.

Acquisitions

"You did good." Butch patted her shoulder as she joined him in the bench behind the prosecutor's table.

"Are you sure?"

He nodded.

While they whispered, the attorney-mediator called the court to recess until after lunch. Lara joined them as Butch explained what he believed would happen next.

"Basically, Akira, your testimony is the icing on the cake. I'd think Johnson's attorney would advise him to accept the terms of his dismissal. He may be hesitant because Greico's legal team will disassociate themselves from him. That'll leave Johnson open to any lawsuits his victims might file. Greico will move to settle quickly. Legally, and financially for the company, it's the best scenario."

Lara embraced Akira. "This is almost over. I'm proud of you for coming this far."

"I'm proud of you, too." Roman's voice wafted over Lara's shoulder. The timbre rolled over Akira's body, bathing her in liquid heat.

Lara mumbled to Butch, and they disappeared with the rest of the people filing out to lunch.

"Good to finally end this madness," Roman stated tentatively. His hands were tucked deep inside the pockets of his tapered suit. He rocked back on the balls of his feet.

"Yeah." Akira's eyes moved over the room to avoid the depth of Roman's. "It's almost over."

"Don't lump me into the memories of this. They'll be bad memories. What we had was wonderful."

Still too good looking to be real. His polished complexion glistened under the harsh lighting. His square reading glasses were tucked inside the pocket of his jacket. Noticing them made Akira feel they were sharing an intimacy—his secret dislike of wearing glasses. She remembered his confession that wearing reading glasses made him feel old. During her interviews, he removed them every chance he got. Funny how she remembered the tiniest details since he wasn't around anymore.

Akira tried to lighten the mood. "What do they say? What doesn't kill us makes us stronger."

"That's what they say." Roman rocked forward, disrupting the pattern Akira had settled into. "But what they say is wrong." He relaxed. "Because not being together is killing me."

A lump formed in Akira's throat taking all of the moisture of her mouth into its reserve. "Roman, not here. Don't make this day any harder for me."

"It doesn't have to be hard."

"Please," she said softly, "don't."

"All you have to do is forgive me. Forgive me, and I can stand beside you through this. Beside you is where I should be, Akira."

"I'm not ready. I don't know if I'll ever be ready." Her heart crumbled. Upholding one's convictions can be torturous.

"I miss the wine and ice cream. I miss laughing and watching television together. I miss you."

Akira started for the door.

Roman blocked her path. "You can't leave."

"Don't do this. Please."

"We need to talk."

"What did we think was going to happen? It had to end. I hoped it wouldn't be like this—I wanted us to be friends."

Shock distorted his features. "It had to end? It's not over. We've hit a rough patch. We have to stop this before it goes too far, and we can't fix it."

Akira touched his cheek, pressing the palm of her hand firmly to his face, releasing the love she still felt for him. "This *is* settled."

Her steps, the click of her heels followed.

"Akira," Roman called. "Are you wearing my Christmas gift?"

Her steps faltered. She tripped on the runner. She waved

Acquisitions

him away and righted herself. He couldn't save her—it wasn't his job anymore. She held her head high and sauntered out of the courtroom, his erotic Christmas gift dangling from her body.

***

March 1

"We have to stop meeting like this." Butch pulled out a conference room chair for Akira to sit next to him.

"One more time, then I'll be through with you," she joked.

Butch dropped his voice as the conference room door swung open. "This will be a piece of cake."

Negotiator extraordinaire, Akira thought as Butch haggled the finer details of her settlement. Details that never occurred to her, he added. Clauses that seemed fair, he fought to have removed. He found the loopholes and made them impassable. He read every syllable of the fine print with a magnifying glass. Greico's legal representatives were worn to exhaustion by the first break of the day.

"I guess this is what you wanted." Mr. Johnson stormed into the conference room, sneering.

Butch placed a protective hand on her back. "These proceedings are closed. What are you doing here?"

"I have business with Greico."

"Conveniently scheduled to coincide with the time of Akira's settlement talks. Don't speak to my client. If you need to say something, talk with your attorney, who will, in turn, talk to me."

Akira stepped up. "No, Butch. I want to hear what he has to say. Leave us alone for a minute."

Butch moved to the corner of the conference room, giving them limited privacy. His stoic expression told Akira to be happy for the little space he allowed.

"It's over now, Mr. Johnson. What do you have to say?" Akira had dreamt of this final confrontation in many ways. Her favorite scenario had to do with a pair of scissors and certain parts of the male anatomy that Mr. Johnson would be

244

forced to part with. But this could be as good. A chance to clear the air, tell him the things she held inside when her job was in jeopardy.

"This is what you've always been about—money and jealousy. Candace told me how badly you want to be in her place. You'd sink to any level to get what you want." Mr. Johnson moved around the table until he stood directly in front of her. "I know about it all. You played Miller. You led me on. You tried to win the sales leader position, and when you saw that there was no way that would happen, you stole the HIV vaccine from Greico."

Akira shook her head in disbelief. "If you believe one word of what you've said, you're sicker than I ever imagined. You have a problem. You use your authority to intimidate women into sleeping with you. Can't you see that's wrong?"

Mr. Johnson turned away and crossed the room. "What I did isn't any different from what millions of businessmen do. People use their power to get what they want everyday."

"And that makes it right?"

"Does it make it wrong?"

"You almost ruined my life. You took our working relationship and turned it into something vile and dirty. Because of you, I've been implicated in stealing the HIV vaccine. I could go to prison—" The reality of the statement made Akira pause. "I'm scared to death to think that I could be wasting away in prison for a crime I had nothing to do with. All because you can't control your sexual urges. What do you keep Candace around for?"

"What Candace and I have is special. *You're* making a big deal out of nothing." He glanced over at Butch and tapered his words. "*If* I came on to you, that's all it was—and I still believe you asked for it. What's the difference between what I did and you carrying on with Miller?"

Akira's mouth dropped. She had compared Roman's motives to this man's? "What Roman and I had was real." Even as she said the words, she questioned their truth. She had

Acquisitions

doubts about Roman's intentions at first. Sure, she'd caught him with another woman. Despite it all, she felt Roman had truly loved her.

Mr. Johnson dismissed her declaration with a guttural moan. "Because of your hysterics, I'm going to lose everything." He trembled with anger, spittle wetting his beard. "I've been fired. Candace is angry. I can't afford the legal fees and settlement costs." His face twisted. "But money won't be a problem for you, will it? Not having a big, fancy attorney and a pack of liars to back you up." He took a menacing step forward. "What you need to do is come to your senses and forget this nonsense."

Butch pushed off the corner, ready to intervene. Akira stilled him with a gesture of hand. "What you need to do, Mr. Johnson, is find the root of your problems. You have serious issues you need to deal with before you hurt any more people."

Mr. Johnson fumed. "Who are you to speak to me like that?"

"I'm the one who is responsible for bringing you down. And don't ever forget that. Don't forget the one you least suspect can do you harm beyond belief. Strength doesn't have to be flashy and loud."

"That sounds like a threat."

"Oh, it is. It most definitely is a threat. Your stunts have torn my life apart, but I will recover and I will be stronger because of what you've put me through. You're right, I do want you to pay. And I'll enjoy spending every cent of your money. Because the only thing a man like, understands is money, which makes it my mission to take every dime I can get from you." She dropped her voice. "When I'm done with you, you'll be penniless."

Mr. Johnson shook, tightening his fists.

Fearlessly, Akira sauntered up to him. "If you ever mess with me again, you can say hello to the soup kitchen."

***

"Akira," Roman's voice rang out from her answering

machine, "are you there?"

With all of the excitement, Akira hadn't checked her messages until she crawled into bed and noticed the blinking light. She listened as Roman called her name several more times. The tranquility of his voice lifted her and floated her around the room like a falling leaf.

"Akira," Roman continued, "Butch told me you had your first settlement negotiation today...I wanted to make sure that seeing Johnson didn't upset you too much. If there's anything I can do to make things better—you know where I am." He paused, and she could hear him sigh.

God, how she wished he were there to hold her and repleni her strength. Seeing Mr. Johnson helped give her closure, but she was upset by his bizarre accusations. If he could believe the stories Candace fed him, so would the authorities.

"I miss you so much, Akira." Only those who knew Roman well would have detected the hitch between his words. "I love you."

He recovered with a deep chuckle. "I can't sleep at night without you here next to me."

The line went dead. The dial tone buzzed for what seemed like forever before the machine beeped, signaling the end of the recording. As the next messages played on, Akira toyed with the idea of picking up the phone and dialing Roman's number. She made excuse after excuse why she should do it. Then she made excuse after excuse why she should not. Sleep fell on her like a shroud, ending the debate and rocking her into a fitful sleep.

***

"Butch said things went well, but you look terrible." Lara entered Akira's apartment all smiles the next afternoon. "Here's the purse I borrowed from you."

"How'd dinner with Butch's partners go?" Akira returned to her recliner, pulling a comforter over her feet.

Lara dropped to the sofa, beaming like a cat burglar after a big heist. "It went wonderfully. It's rocky between Butch

Acquisitions

and me, but we're working on it. We both have baggage that we'd like to get rid of before we get serious."

"Serious?" Akira smiled her approval.

Lara nodded.

Akira thought of Roman and his inability to turn his back on Sherry. She didn't want to see her friend hurt again. "What kind of baggage?"

"Butch is a successful, intelligent, wealthy black man. He's used to women flocking to him, doing his bidding, accepting whatever he dishes out."

Akira raised a knowing eyebrow.

"That's right. I'm not the one. My past with Clifton taught me a valuable lesson. In this relationship, Butch will have to do the chasing." She laughed, her face displaying remembrance of a private moment. "Everything is a great debate between us while we try to fit into our roles. Butch isn't the type of man you can let run around unchecked. He needs to be kept in line."

"And who better to do it than you?"

"Exactly," Lara laughed. "I keep tabs on him. He fusses about having to answer to me. But he loves every minute of it, and I do, too."

Akira shook her head. "You two deserve each other."

"I hope we do. I'm making it sound like there's never any peace between us. There is. Oh," she sucked in a deep breath while clutching her chest, "when we get intimate, he is the most passionate, tender man I've ever known."

"Intimate already?"

"Intimate as in talking, kissing, caressing. Spending quality time together without words. I've been open with him about everything. I told him I don't want to have sex until there's a commitment. He hasn't pushed me. He's really into knowing me for who I am."

"I'm happy for you, Lara. You deserve it, and Butch does, too." Akira openly surveyed her friend. "I've notice that you've lost more weight."

"Doing it my way, on my own time. I'm still eating right and exercising. Butch comes over almost every morning and works out with me."

Akira joined her friend on the sofa for a tight squeeze. "You keep at it. Things are going your way."

Lara set her friend away from her. "What about you? Like I said, you don't look like a woman who can sleep in all day and pamper herself."

"I haven't been sleeping well."

Lara watched Akira settle on the sofa and focus on the television screen. "Roman looks sad, almost pitiful. He tries to put on a good front. It doesn't work. You're both miserable, why don't you give him another chance?"

"I'm not ready."

"Why not?"

"This from you?" Akira reminded her, "Weren't you the one who called him an opportunist?"

"That was before I knew him. He's good for you, Akira. And you're good for him. Why are you so adamant about pushing him away?"

Every day that passed Akira missed Roman more and more, making it harder for her to stand by her principles. Akira didn't want to explain her feelings again; Lara always tried to convince her to change her decision. The doorbell rang, preventing her from answering.

"Roman. What are you doing here?" Akira turned accusing eyes to Lara.

"I didn't have anything to do with it."

"She didn't," Roman assured her. "Hi, Lara." He gave her a weak smile.

"I better go." Lara patted Akira's shoulder as she left the apartment.

Roman filled the doorway with his height. He rested against the frame, shuffling his leather gloves back and forth. "I tried to stay away. I couldn't. We can only work this out if we talk."

249

Acquisitions

"Roman, I can't go over this again." Akira moved away from his overpowering presence.

"Let me ask you one question." Roman pushed the door closed with the heel of his boot.

Akira studied the details of his face. Underneath his eyes were shadows she didn't recall. His forehead wrinkled with deep contemplation. The strength in his dark eyes was hidden by doubt.

"Yes?"

"Why did you come to the hotel that night?"

She stood speechless.

"Why did you come for me?"

She backed away from the growing closeness in the room. The intimacy left behind by their time spent lounging in the living room seemed to jump up and stand behind Roman, taking his side in their fight.

"Why, Akira?" His hands dusted her shoulders.

"You know why. It won't help to go over it again."

"Why, Akira?"

She squared her shoulders and faced the source of her broken heart. "I came because I love you. I wanted to stop you. Save us."

"Then what changed? Between driving to the hotel and meeting me at my house afterwards—to this moment—what has changed?"

"Seeing you with Sherry changed everything. If what we had is so fragile, how can I trust it? Seeing you in Sherry's space looked too natural. You were too comfortable. In one visit, you were at the level of intimacy it took us weeks to achieve. How can I compete with that? I can't."

Roman raised his voice in frustration. "I don't want you to compete. You've thought that from the beginning—no matter how many times I tell you differently. You've always viewed my past with Sherry as a hurdle, a contest of some sort. I want to be with you, not her."

"You made me compete for you the second you decided to

go to her. I chose not to. And if you still can't see you have issues with Sherry and your break-up, how can I have a relationship with you?"

"Can't you understand I needed closure in order to be with you completely, without past history in the way?"

"Closure? How were you going to achieve that?"

"I needed to talk things out with her."

Roman sitting on Sherry's bed, half dressed replayed vividly before Akira's eyes. "And did you achieve that?"

Roman's thick lashes dipped.

"You were going to sleep with her. You *would* have slept with her if I hadn't come."

Roman's lashes flashed.

"Tell me what I'm saying isn't true. Tell me, Roman, and things can go back to the way they were. We'll forget about that night in the hotel, never mention it again. Tell me that you love me too much to have even *considered* making love to another woman. Please, tell me, Roman."

Chapter 31

"You staying for dinner?" Grandma Dixon shuffled around the kitchen. She had replaced her fancy church dress and wide brim hat with a fluffy pink robe and matching slippers.

"No, Grandma. I'm heading home to change out of this suit. Need anything before I go?"

"You okay, boy?" Her voice took on a tenderness he hadn't heard in a very long time.

"I'm fine."

Grandma Dixon pulled out a chair at the kitchen table and instructed Roman to sit with her pointing finger. He noticed the enlarged joints and crooked appearance of her hand. When he stopped paying attention, she had aged. It saddened him to see her, his only mother figure, transformed into an old woman overnight.

"I want you to sit right there," Grandma Dixon said as she began to pull food from the refrigerator. "I like having you here while I cook. It reminds me of the days when you and Gayle used to run around the kitchen, getting in trouble. Waiting for me to spank your legs. Seems like you two begged for attention any way you could get it."

Grandma Dixon's statement was innocent, but it hurt just the same.

"What is it?" she watched him over her shoulder. "And don't tell me that it's nothing."

"Gayle and I did want attention any way we could get it, Grandma. You loved us, but we needed our parents."

Grandma Dixon's face puckered in anger. "You trying to say I didn't do a good job with the two of you?"

"You did a great job with us." He stood next to her at the kitchen counter and started mocking her chopping action on the celery stalks. "But we needed our parents."

"Your parents were young when they had you."

"You always make excuses for them, Grandma. If that's true, that they needed to grow up themselves before taking care of us, where have they been the last ten years of our lives? We're grown. They still aren't in our lives."

The arthritic hands moved swiftly to chop the onion into equal pieces.

"Look at everything that has happened in my life—graduating from high school, college, and then law school. They weren't there to see any of it. Not even a phone call."

"Roman, what's past is past. I can't explain why your mother and father are the way they are. They weren't ready for kids. But they went and had two. Still, to this day, they haven't learned to live up to their responsibilities."

Roman slapped the knife down on the counter and paced to the center of the kitchen. "This goes way beyond living up to responsibilities. Gayle and I are both too old to be considered someone's responsibility. I'm talking about loving your kids. Plain and simple, they don't love us. Never did."

Grandma Dixon slammed her weather beaten hand down on the counter sending bits of onion flying to the floor. "You wait a minute." She turned her body around to face him. "Your parents love you very much. I know you're hurting because of everything going on in your life right now, but you

Acquisitions

watch your mouth. I've never allowed you or your sister to badmouth your parents, and I'm not starting today."

Roman matched her passionate stance. "You can't go on defending them forever. They've done damage to us that can never be repaired."

"I don't see Gayle standing in my kitchen spouting off, sounding ungrateful for everything I've given you. She's living her life out there in sunny California. She doesn't complain about things that can't be changed."

"Gayle, my big sister, climbed into bed with me many nights, crying—the both of us crying because we had been deserted. We never came to you because we were afraid you'd send us away, too."

Grandma Dixon absorbed the blow. She stared through him as if she was trying to recall nights when this could have occurred. She softened her tone, "Roman, why are you talking about all this? What do you think can be done about it all these years later?"

Roman again matched her emotional posture. "I've screwed up my life."

"What?" Before she could go to him and hug his hurt away, Roman stepped back and dropped into the kitchen chair. "What are you talking about?"

"Everything that I thought was important means nothing. I've screwed up everything." When he found the courage to look up at Grandma Dixon's face, tears were already pooling at the rims of his eyes.

"I don't like to hear you talk foolishness like this. Especially when it ain't true."

"Is there something wrong when a man who wants nothing but to be loved ruins it when he finally finds the only woman who can ever give him what he needs?"

"What are you talking about, child?"

Roman rested his elbows on his knees, keeping his head down until he could control the threat of his emotions.

Receiving no response, Grandma Dixon grabbed a chair

and placed it squarely in front of him. She positioned herself, dipping her head low, so that she could see his hidden face. "Butch told me that gal came back to town." She spread unspoken love to him by brushing his hair with her fingertips. "Every time she comes around, you end up like this. She's not the one for you. Love doesn't make you feel this way."

"I don't love Sherry." He rubbed his eyes before lifting his head. "I love Akira. Akira doesn't love me anymore. I messed up big time."

"That's crazy. If Akira loves you, she loves you. She might be mad at you, but—"

"You don't understand," Roman snapped. "I hurt her. I hurt her and, she's gone. I've apologized. I've promised her I've changed. I've done everything I can think of, except lie to her. I couldn't lie to her no matter how badly I wanted to." When Akira had asked—begged—him to say that he had no intentions on sleeping with Sherry again, he couldn't give her the answer she wanted. The truth was, he didn't know if he was strong enough at the time to tell Sherry no.

Grandma Dixon shook her head. "I don't understand how one mistake can make her stop loving you."

"Ever since Sherry walked out on me, I've been trying to get her back. Everything I've done with my life has been connected to winning Sherry back. I stayed at Greico Enterprises doing a job I hated because it was my best chance at advancing up the corporate ladder and becoming a partner. Becoming a partner to prove to Sherry that I could be successful if that's what she needed to come back to me."

"You said you don't love her anymore."

"I don't. I see that now. Too late to save what I had with Akira. All my attention has been focused on getting Sherry back. When the opportunity presented itself, I jumped at it. I forgot about Akira and how much she means to me and went to Sherry."

"I can't say that I approve of that. No matter that you're my grandson. When your grandfather was alive, we had prob-

Acquisitions

lems like any married couple, but fooling around was out of bounds."

"I went to Sherry the minute she called. We talked. For a minute, things were like they used to be. She kissed me. I should have never allowed it to go that far, but I did. The next thing I know, we're getting into something that I know is wrong. Wrong because of how much I love Akira. Wrong because I don't have the same feelings for Sherry that I had years ago.

"I swear I was getting ready to leave. I came to get answers about why she left me, and things had gone way too far. We were talking—Sherry never could explain to me why money and prestige were more important to her than me. I wanted Sherry to want me for who I am. I wanted her to know that I lost my job at Greico and I wanted her to accept me despite that; the ultimate sacrifice for her. But it was the same old Sherry. I was getting ready to leave when Akira showed up."

"What happened?"

Roman visualized the scene in the hotel room. "She did what any woman would have done."

Grandma Dixon touched his knee when his voice began to waver.

"The thing is, I'm sorry. I'm really sorry."

"Do you think Akira is wrong to let you go?"

"Yes. We love each other. We're good together. Everybody is entitled to a mistake. She's wrong because we're right."

Grandma Dixon recognized the return of her arrogant grandson. She pushed her chair back and returned to the counter where she resumed her chopping. "Do you hear yourself, boy? If this is how you apologized to me, I wouldn't take you back either. You had no business going to see that gal. She's always been trouble."

Roman paced the room not wanting to listen to his own faults described by the family that should take his side, no matter if he's wrong.

"This is one of the silliest things you've ever done. Now you want to blame everybody for Akira having the good sense to walk away from somebody she can't trust. You're pulling stuff from way back—criticizing your parents—to keep from shouldering the blame. What did Akira say about giving you another chance?

He stood behind her. "She said she can't do it right now."

"Didn't say she wouldn't do it. Said she can't right now. She can't right now because she needs a reason to. What reason you give her? You got caught? Sherry walked away again? What reason you give her to trust you again?"

Grandma Dixon turned to him. "Listening to you today gave me a new perspective about your life. I've learned something when I thought I knew all there was to know. Matter of fact, I'm calling Gayle tonight to see if she's walkin' around with this same pain.

"And, I'm going to give you that your parents weren't all they should have been. Might not be too late for you to pursue that. You should give your parents a call and talk to them—work it out.

"I'm even going to give you that being left probably made you more sensitive about being loved. But what you done to Akira was nothing but destructive. If she really loves you, seeing you with another woman is tough.

"I guess what I'm saying is that, you made a mess of things. Don't justify it with what happened in your past. Live up to it. Fix what you done. Prove your love for Akira how she needs it proved—not how you think is best. I raised you to be a man—stop whining and blaming—take care of your business. Be a man."

***

Roman let the darkness of his home cloak his guilt as he removed his winter gear and placed it in the hall closet. He flipped the switch that operated the recess lights in the foyer and hallway. The quietness of his home had always been a

Acquisitions

welcome retreat after a day of listening to vindictive sexual harassment allegations at Greico. However, he didn't have work to fill his days anymore. Or Akira to bring him peace at night.

Time to stop moping and make serious decisions, Roman thought as he filled the tub with hot bubbly water. Before stepping in his bath, he filled a glass with white wine and placed the remainder of the bottle on the floor next to the tub. Akira would not be there to give him refills if he needed.

Grandma Dixon's harshly honest words haunted him as he sipped his second glass of wine. He could not deny that she had been correct in her assessment of his life.

Money would not be a problem for a while. Grandma Dixon taught him to be thrifty at an early age—an age when having enough food to feed a woman and two small children had been an ongoing challenge. He'd never return to those days, or let his grandmother want for anything. Struggling had made him wiser, more compassionate. He'd learned that lesson and never wanted to see those days again.

The fourth glass of wine gave him the courage to vow to leave a voicemail message for his mentor at Greico. Having no notice he would be fired, he'd left several ends untied—retirement, pension, unpaid benefits owed. The best thing to do would be to finish his business with Greico and move on.

Move on to what?

He downed his sixth glass of wine, still searching for the answer to that question.

There were many decisions screaming for his attention. The option of starting a law practice seemed most viable. Actually, it wasn't a bad idea. Grandma Dixon would be proud. He'd be able to weed out the cases he wanted to work. Not be dictated to anymore without any input into his own career passions.

As his mind's ability to reason began to fog, and thoughts of Akira surfaced, he drained the tub. Standing up and becoming light-headed served as notice that it wasn't his habit to drink an entire bottle of wine alone.

Akira would have laughed to see him swagger down the hallway holding onto the wall as he made his way to his bed. He took the time to dry off, but opted not to walk to the dresser for pajamas. A few seconds of fluttering eyelids, and he was asleep.

***

The chime of the doorbell made Roman sit straight up in the bed. An instant throbbing headache made him massage his temples. He grabbed his robe and made his way down the hallway.

"Hey, baby." Sherry stood on his front porch, a scarf covering her head and draped around her neck. "Let me in."

Roman stepped back. He used the few seconds it took for him to close the door to squeeze his eyes together. When he turned around, he fully expected Sherry to be gone. Disappeared. Another wild dream brought on by his guilt.

"You look like you've seen a ghost." Sherry stepped up to him boldly, her high heel boots allowing her to match his height. "Oh, I see. You've been drinking."

Before Roman could ask why she was there, Sherry peeled off her coat and draped it over the nearest chair.

"I'm leaving town in two days." The tone of her voice showed no emotion. The look in her eyes as they scanned his half nude body revealed her agenda.

Roman moved around Sherry, leading her into the living room where he sat on the sofa. "Going back to New York?" he said, still groggy.

"Yes, my work here is done, as they say. Butch will clean up the paperwork." Sherry sat next to him, turning up on her haunches so that she leaned into him. "I didn't want you accusing me of leaving town without talking with you first."

Roman nodded. He considered himself a strong man, but Sherry's closeness rattled him. Maybe because it was time to end their connection and she wouldn't like it.

"My work will be bringing me here more often." Sherry's

Acquisitions

hands found the collar of his robe. "My firm is opening an office here. We'll work closely with Butch's. They want me to be active in getting it up and running."

Roman removed her wandering hands from his chest. "That should be a good opportunity for you."

"For us, baby."

"Meaning?"

"We can spend more time together now that I'll be flying in and out on a regular basis."

"You're joking, right?" The words surprised him as much as they did Sherry.

Her eyes widened at his response. "Isn't that what you've wanted all this time? All the time you've been looking for me? Trying to contact me?"

"You know about that?"

Sherry denied without lying. "I thought this would be good for both of us, baby. Part of the reason I accepted the challenge was for us to give it another try."

"I'm not about that anymore." Roman stood to move away from her. Suddenly her beauty faded. "You aren't coming back here because you love me and want to be with me. You're here tonight to set up a relationship that will be convenient for you. I need more than that."

"I wonder what that means." Sherry matched his height. That made him uncomfortable. He should be taller than his woman. He was her protector. "Could it have something to do with how you ran out of my hotel room when that woman came looking for you?"

"Actually, it does, but not how you're thinking. Akira taught me that love doesn't work this way. It isn't a convenience. One person doesn't get used while the other is doing what they damn well please. Love is about two people working together through the hard times, toward the same goals."

Roman took another step back before he continued. "You and I have never had the same goals. Even tonight, as drunk

260

as I am, I know that what you're proposing isn't enough. See, Sherry, I want the whole package—commitment, kids. And I don't want that with you."

Sherry's heels clicked rapidly against the wood as she stomped her way to the foyer, snatched up her coat, and shoved her arms forcefully into the sleeves. "You think that homely woman can give you what you need? She's not your style." She fit the zipper together and gave it a tug. "You like the flash, the glamour. You may say you don't want the life I want, but you do." She threw her scarf around her neck. "Never once did you complain when I dragged you along to the parties with the politicians or the celebrities. You liked it as much as I did."

"I endured it because I wanted to hold onto you. But I lost *myself*. I was miserable. If I'm not happy, I can't offer happiness to anyone else. I know what I want out of life and who can give it to me."

Roman held the door open for her. "Maybe if you had stayed, things might be different. But right about now, I'm glad you did leave. I finally know what my life should be about and I'm going to go after what I want—who I want."

Chapter 32

"I added a clause in the settlement that I haven't mentioned yet," Butch said, as he and Akira stood alone in the elevator, their heads tilted upward, watching the numbers flash by on the way to the twelfth floor.

"What kind of clause?"

"Greico Enterprises will pay for any counseling you need, for as long as you need."

"You think I'm crazy?" Akira asked.

The elevator settled at the twelfth floor, and the doors slid open inviting new occupants aboard. They exited the car. As they passed an open, empty office, Butch grabbed Akira's arm and pulled her inside. Once the door was closed insuring privacy, he began to explain. "Akira, honey, there's no way I think you're crazy."

"Then why add a clause like that? Especially without telling me?"

"No one should suffer the mental anguish Barry Johnson caused you. The least Greico owes you is resources to work through it. Look, I know you try to be tough, fight the world all by yourself, but we all need support systems. Right now,

Kimberley White

all of your family is overseas, and when they come home they'll be on the other side of the country. You and Roman are apart…" Butch tried to lighten the conversation with a smile. "Lara is a good listener. I've bent her ear many times myself, but you need a professional."

"I appreciate you looking out for me, but I don't need to see a shrink, really."

He nodded, surrendering. "Well, if you ever do need it, all you'll have to do is ask."

"Butch," she hesitated, "how is he?"

"Roman?" He placed his briefcase on the empty desk. "Okay, all things considered. Having a hard time dealing with your break-up."

Akira nodded.

"This is the first time you've asked about him. What's going on? Missing him a little?"

Akira nodded. She grew angry with herself when the thought of Roman made her eyes glaze over with tears. She held them back. With all of her might, she held onto her tears. She refused to let Butch see her cry over a man. She had remained strong up to this point. Breaking down over Roman would have to wait until she passed through all of her crises.

"Sit down." Butch waited until she was seated behind the desk, and he had perched himself on the desktop in front of her before he spoke. "What Roman did was not right. Everybody knows that, including Roman. Honey, you can let that go now and go back to him. No one is going to judge you or say you gave in."

"I'm not worried about what people think."

"Oh, c'mon. You're worried people will say you're giving in. You insist on keeping up this stoic front, trying to prove that nothing can get you down. I admire it. In certain circumstances, you need to do that. That coping mechanism brought you this far in the sexual harassment case." Butch gave her a brief squeeze on the shoulder. "But how long do you plan on keeping up that hard exterior? When it comes to relationships

263

Acquisitions

and being in love, you have to let your guard down."

"I let my guard down with Roman too many times. Every time, I was hit in the head with a brick." Akira swiped at an escaped tear before it ran down her cheek. "I want to be with Roman, I admit that, but I can't. Whenever I see him, I picture him sitting on that bed with Sherry standing over him."

"Let me tell you, Roman had a lot of issues with Sherry and the way they broke up. Guess what? Poof, all gone. He's taken care of that situation. I'm sorry it hurt you, but he needed to work through his past. What you have to remember is that nothing happened between him and Sherry."

"Because I stopped it."

"Akira, honey," he said as if explaining a simple concept to a child, "don't you see that if Roman wanted to sleep with Sherry that night, nothing you could have done would have stopped him? Why did he leave her and follow you to his house? Because he wanted Sherry? I know her. For him to leave her standing there, not giving her what she wanted, well, that was putting an end to whatever might have been."

Butch let that sink in before continuing. "And what about now? You're not together anymore, why doesn't he run to her now? Why did he send her away to be with you when you keep telling him it's over?"

"I don't know." And she truly didn't.

"If I didn't know that you and Roman are good for each other, that you make each other happy, I wouldn't get involved. But I see you sad and hiding it. I see Roman miserable and trying to smile. There's something unnatural about what you two are doing. Maybe, when all the legal trouble is over, you'll take the time to sit down and think about everything. We all know that you and Roman belong together. There's no good sense in hurting when you don't have to."

"You don't understand."

"Talk to me." His gold bracelet shimmered when he crossed his arms over his chest.

"I told you the truth about Eric, but I didn't tell you everything. We weren't engaged, and we weren't serious. Not because I didn't want to be. I fell hard for him. I focused on all the good things in our relationship, and ignored how destructive it was. I wanted a committed relationship, but he told me he couldn't have one with me because I wasn't the type of wife he needed to further his career."

"What did he mean by that?"

"He wanted a corporate trophy wife. One he could dress in slinky outfits and parade in front of his bosses. My full figure wasn't what he was looking for."

Butch kept his eyes trained on her as she crossed the room.

"The first time I saw Roman, I wanted him. I believed he was out of my league, so I didn't dare get my hopes up. Then he starts throwing me these signals and I think he may feel a connection, too. He kissed me and made all types of promises. He told me I made him happy."

"And then Sherry came back," Butch added, fully understanding. "You think Sherry fits the mold of Roman's dream girl."

"If he had gone to the hotel and talked with Sherry, I would have been mad, but we would still be together. Roman did more than that. I found him on her bed half dressed."

"Roman says nothing happened, and I believe him."

"Butch, something did happen. There came a moment when Roman had to choose between sleeping with Sherry or coming home to me, and our relationship wasn't strong enough for him to leave."

Butch didn't reply.

"When I barged into the bedroom, he didn't jump off the bed and run to me to explain. He didn't show any remorse. Roman looked directly at me and asked why I had came."

***

As the attorney had informed Roman, Johnson had returned to Greico Enterprises for another meeting regarding the sexual harassment charges. Unbelievably, Johnson thought he could save his job.

Acquisitions

Roman stood in the shadows near Johnson's car dressed in black jeans, a black turtleneck sweater, and a black jacket. A few people came and went between the parking garage and the office building, but it was early morning and most were settling in until lunch.

Johnson pulled his keys from his pocket and flipped through them, pressing the button that disarmed his alarm.

Roman stepped out, "Johnson."

"Miller," Barry clutched his chest, "you nearly gave me a heart attack."

"I'd like to talk to you."

"I think you've done enough talking. I can't believe you listened to what those women had to say. They're lying. I thought you understood how things worked, but I guess we're in the same boat now."

Roman stepped in front of him, stopping him from walking away.

"Is there a problem?" Johnson asked, worry narrowing his eyes to slits.

"Actually, there is."

"I don't have time for this."

Roman pressed his massive hand into Johnson's chest. "You'll make time. It won't take long."

"What's wrong with you?" Fear made a clear sheen appear across his forehead.

"You messed with someone I love. Now is the time to back down. Or you'll have to deal with me."

"What are you talking about?" Johnson sputtered.

"Talk with your lawyers and put a stop to this. You can't work here anymore. You've done enough to ruin Akira's life."

"Akira Reed? You're in love with— I can see a having a little sex, but love?"

"I love her more than anything in the world, and I won't stand by and watch while you make her miserable. All she wants is for his whole thing to end. Talk with your lawyers and admit what you've done. Greico will negotiate a reasonable settlement, you'll find a new job, and everyone wins."

"You can't threaten me."

"I'm not threatening you. I'm appealing to what decent bones you have left in your body." Roman tightened the noose of Johnson's tie. "I knew you and I would have a showdown over this—I hope this is as confrontational as I have to get. Do the right thing. Or see me again."

Acquisitions

Chapter 33

Time to make serious decisions, Akira thought as she walked toward her apartment. Her legal battles were far from over; she understood that. Still, she couldn't wait for everything to be resolved before planning her future.

"Hey, Akira." Luke jogged down the hall. He held a small brown box in one hand and the band of his oversized jogging pants in the other. "That dude left this for you."

"What dude?" Akira mocked his terminology.

"Tall guy. Always outside looking in." He flashed his smile. "He was ringing your bell when I came home. One look at my tired behind, and he knew it wasn't the day to be raisin' the roof. He asked me to give you this box."

"You didn't get nasty with him, did you?"

"Never. I give the man a hard time for standing out here waking everybody up, but the truth is, I feel what he's about. Many times I stood on the outside trying to plead my case. He's alright."

Akira took the box. "What is it?"

"Do you think I opened it?"

Akira gave him a playful arch of her eyebrow. The size and shape of the package left little to the imagination. Clearly, inside she would find a cassette tape.

Luke crossed his arms over his bare chest, the sounds of a crying baby coming from his apartment. "Number two is over for the weekend." Pride crinkled the corners of his eyes. A chronic complainer about his social situation with his three kids and their mothers, he could never hide the joy he felt when they came around—the kids and their mothers.

"Anyway, I talked to dude for a little while. He told me he messed up real bad with you and that he's trying to get you back. That true? Or was he runnin' a game?"

Akira kept her eyes glued to the box, turning it over inside her palm. "True."

"He sure looked lovesick. You've been looking down, too."

She felt low all the time without Roman around.

Luke laughed, "I've seen the two of you going at it when you thought nobody was lookin'."

"Luke!"

"Ain't nuthin' wrong with handling your business. He seemed straight, Akira. I don't know many men who would spend their time standing in a hallway trying to win a woman." He nodded toward the box, "Better study what's in there pretty hard."

Akira held off listening to the tape until the end of her evening. Butch and Lara, two people she'd grown to trust as much as family, agreed she should forgive Roman, chalk his weakness with Sherry up to a momentary lapse of judgment. Even Luke told her to consider Roman's words carefully.

Deep inside, Akira believed him to be a good man. Why she couldn't forgive him was hard to rationalize. All of the turmoil of the past several months played a large part in that choice. Her emotions were off-center. Her future dangled in the air until the theft of the formula was resolved. Her finances needed to be straightened out. With all of that to deal with, she

Acquisitions

had to be surrounded with people she could trust.

The image of Roman sitting on the side of Sherry's bed made another ghostly appearance. He seemed helpless, torn, confused. Why? Why should he feel those things when it was all clear? *Love me, honor me, and be with me.* Simple. Did he have the right to be perplexed after he gave her the green light to love him?

Well, she had asked those questions night after night. She still had no concrete answers. Pride and jealousy influenced her decision. If Roman had the right to be confused about their relationship, she certainly had the right to question his loyalty.

With a long sigh, Akira pushed the play button on her stereo.

"There are things I need you to hear." Faint static provided background noise on the tape. Where had Roman been when he recorded it? What had he been wearing? Did he do this at night or early morning? Did he have the square reading glasses he hated perched on the bridge of his nose?

"Akira, what I did to you was completely wrong and totally unacceptable. I'm sorry for disappointing you. If I had it to do over, I would. I don't know what you need me to do to regain your confidence. If I did, I would've done it by now. I have no right to ask you to forgive me. I understand that. All I can say is that I love you, and I want to be with you. Being with anyone else after finding you is completely unsatisfactory."

Akira grinned; the lawyer in Roman made him say that.

"I know you fairly well, Akira, and I know that you'll come around when and if you're ready. It takes a long time to rebuild trust. There's no point in me chasing you or trying to push you before then. So I won't."

Akira's heart sank. Dread twisted her stomach into knots. Eternal loss shot sharp pains through her skull.

Roman continued after a short pause. "Know that I'll be here waiting for you for as long as it takes. All you have to do is pick up the phone, and I'll be right there. Ready to do whatever you need to fix this mess I made."

Another short pause. "I love you, Akira. I have big plans for our future." His voice lifted when he said that. "All you have to do is ask me. I'll be waiting."

Akira waited a minute before stopping the tape player. She didn't want to miss one word. Without thinking, she jumped from the bed and went for the phone.

"Hello?" Butch said when Akira placed the phone to her ear. "Akira, are you there?"

"Yeah, I'm here."

Butch chuckled. "The phone didn't ring on my end. Anyhow, I need to talk to you. Is this a bad time to call?"

Deflated, she settled on the edge of the bed. "No, go ahead."

"A friend tells me that Detectives Casser and Downs are hunting around Eric Dodson. We need to put the pressure on him to spill whatever he knows. Any chance you could get him in my office?"

"I can try. Can't you subpoena him or something?"

"He'll be more apt to help you if it's his choice. Call him and let me know."

"Okay."

"Honey, you sound funny. You alright?"

"I'm fine. A little tired."

"Get some rest, but we need to do this as soon as possible. Before the police pick him up for questioning again."

Chapter 34

"Mr. Vance," Detective Casser put down his half eaten sandwich and stood behind his desk, "what brings you here? Come to turn in your client? Make a statement?"

"Always good to see you, Casser," Butch sneered. "My client and I would like to speak with you."

"Downs," Casser called across the bustling squad room, "put Vance and Reed in a room." He grabbed a napkin and dabbed at the corners of his mouth.

Downs looked up from his telephone conversation, surprised to see Akira and Butch at the station voluntarily.

After sitting in an interrogation room for fifteen minutes, Butch stood and paced the length of the small, dimly lit space. "We'll wait here for exactly five more minutes, and then we're out of here. That Casser is such a—"

"Sorry about the wait," Casser apologized insincerely as he entered the room with Downs closely behind. He sat across from Akira with a cup of coffee in hand. "Would either of you like coffee?"

"No," Butch answered. "We'd like to get on with this."

Downs sat across from Butch poised to take notes on a

legal pad. His dark hair had been trimmed, but nervous habit made him continue to finger-sweep the unruly hairs.

"You came to see us." Casser sipped his coffee.

"Sources tell me that you're looking at Dodson's involvement with the stolen formula and that you'll be making arrests soon."

"Maybe," Casser answered coolly.

"I believe he knows more than he's admitting."

"Maybe," Casser retorted. "Maybe your client knows more than she's admitting, too."

Downs entered the conversation. "Do you know anything Ms. Reed? Has Dodson said something we should know about?"

Akira looked to Butch before she answered. "Nothing, but I know Eric, and I know that he's hiding something. I tried to talk to him, or have him talk with Butch, but he wouldn't do it."

"At my request," Butch clarified.

"Why are you here wasting my time with this, Vance?" Casser asked.

"I want to know what you know. My firm has more resources than this department will ever have. Share the information. I can have my private investigators on it immediately. We both want the same things: to solve this crime, and to have no more contact with each other. Work with me, and I give you my guarantee we'll work with you."

Casser leaned forward and placed his puffy hands flat on the table in front of him. His negative energy made the interrogation room stuffier. "Am I supposed to trust you, counselor? Remember the Herman case? I won't be burned again. I was wet behind the ears then, now I know better."

Downs spoke up. "There may be a way we can work together."

Casser threw him a look. "Let's talk outside."

Downs continued, ignoring Casser. "Wear a wire, Ms. Reed. Dodson trusts you. He holds you in high regard—that

Acquisitions

was evident when we questioned him. Get him to talk about what he knows. Get us anything we can use to clear up this case."

"Absolutely, not." Butch stood, lifting his briefcase from the table. "We're done."

Akira stopped him with a touch to his forearm. "I'll do it."

"No, you won't. Akira, honey, wearing a wire is dangerous. The people involved in this stand to lose a lot of money and their freedom. If they catch you wired, I don't know what they'll do."

"I can't keep going on like this. I want this investigation to end. If Eric knows something that might help solve it, I have to get it out of him. I know Eric, he'd never hurt me."

A depraved smile lit Casser's eyes. "Looks like your client is finally smartening up, Vance."

***

Roman relaxed in the first class seat of the 747. He'd flown out to see Gayle knowing that contacting his parents would only be successful if she supported him on it. She told him it wouldn't change anything. She reminded him of her turmoil after visiting them a year ago. She made him promise to think about it more and to call her before making his final decision.

Roman knew what had to be done. He would call Gayle afterward; she'd only try to talk him out of going, and this decision had been too long in coming. No matter what the outcome, he needed to exorcise the demons.

The California lifestyle suited Gayle. She looked good. Had a bronzed man hanging on her arm willing to please. Working hard to make her mark in the design world. Already she had designed wardrobes for two up-and-coming hip-hop artists.

Gayle had encouraged him to move out to California with her. Starting a law practice there wouldn't be hard, she told him. Star-type people were always looking for legal represen-

274

tation. She could throw a party, invite "her people," and he'd get new clients immediately.

"I could never leave Grandma Dixon alone three thousand miles away," Roman had told Gayle.

"We'd bring Grandma Dixon out here with us. She'd love it. When she came to visit last year, she was in heaven—star gazing, going to work on the set with me, hanging out at any party I could get her to. Grandma Dixon is not ready to sit at home and start knitting. She'd love it here."

Roman ended the debate by promising to think about it.

California did appeal to him. No more snow to shovel. No more winter clothes.

No more Akira. Being three thousand miles away from her would never work.

Roman reclined his seat and closed his eyes to dreams of Akira. Moving to California together wouldn't have been too far-fetched months ago. It would bring her closer to her family in Seattle. Jobless, they could both start again—together. He'd made a taped promise to Akira: he'd give her space and wait for her forgiveness. Right now, he had no idea how long that would take. Passively waiting wasn't his style. But his style had ruined their relationship. He'd do whatever Akira needed him to do to have her back. The hard part was figuring out exactly what she needed. Until he found the key to that mystery, he'd have to lay low.

While he waited, he had things to do to make himself a better person, like clearing the air with his parents, moving forward with opening his law practice, and looking after Grandma Dixon. When Akira came to him, he'd be ready.

Chapter 35

Roman adjusted the bags of newly purchased summer clothing underneath his arm before flipping open his cell phone. "Hello?"

"Grandma?"

"I've got your grandma alright, man."

Roman laughed. "Butch, why are you always at my grandma's house?"

"Because she likes me more than she likes you. I've told you that. Why do you fail to understand?" The kidding stopped, "Especially the way you talked to her."

"She told you about that, huh? Is she still upset?"

"No, I took care of it."

Roman maneuvered around a crowd of tourists. "What's she doing?"

"Old girl fell asleep on the sofa after she cooked this spectacular welcome-home dinner for you. Turkey, roast beef, homemade bread, all the trimmings. I came by to wait with her. Do you need a ride from the airport?"

Roman found a seat near the expansive glass windows where he could watch the ground crew ready his plane for

Kimberley White

take-off. "That's why I called." He positioned his bags under his seat. "I'm about to hop another plane—to New Orleans."

"New Orleans?" Butch's voice sounded with alarm. "You sure?"

"I should've done it a long time ago."

"I can be at the airport in forty minutes."

"No, I'm going to do this alone."

"When did you decide to visit your parents?"

Roman switched the phone to his other ear. "Right before I landed."

"Man—" Butch started, but changed his thought mid-sentence, "if you need a friend—"

"I know. Listen, kiss my grandma for me when she wakes up. Tell her I'll call as soon as I get back home, but don't tell her where I'm going. If things don't go right I'd rather she didn't know I went to New Orleans."

"I'll keep an eye on her."

"Butch?"

"Yeah, man?"

"Keep an eye on Akira, too?"

"I will. Peace."

"Peace out."

***

Butch sat in the surveillance van with Detective Casser as Downs checked the audio quality of Akira's microphone. "As soon as we hear what we need, we're coming in," Downs told Akira, running his fingers through the hairs at the nape of his neck. "It won't be dramatic like the cop shows. We'll come up and ring the bell. If you get in trouble, you say that it's time for you to go. If you can't get out, we'll come get you."

"Don't be a hero," Butch added from the front seat.

"He's right," Downs agreed. "Remember what we told you to say?"

Akira nodded. Fear settled in; she was placing herself in danger. She held her arms up and out for Downs to hide the last wire.

Acquisitions

"I'll be right here," Butch assured her, "listening to every word. If I don't like what I hear, I'm calling everything off."

"Relax, Vance." Casser rolled his eyes. "We've been doing this for a long time. Let us do our jobs without any interference."

"Ready?" Downs placed his hands on Akira's shoulders. She tucked in her shirt. "Ready."

"Your car is parked right behind the van. Get in and drive up the street to Dodson's apartment. Take a deep breath and stay natural. Everything'll be fine."

"Okay." Akira looked to Butch.

"You'll do good, honey."

***

Akira took the deep breath, as instructed, before ringing Eric's doorbell.

It took a minute, but he pulled the door open. "Right on time."

"Wow, you've changed everything."

"Yeah." Eric took her coat. "I did a little redecorating."

"More than a little." Akira wandered around the apartment taking it all in. Every piece of furniture had been replaced. All of the memories they shared were removed.

"Let me check on dinner."

"Dinner?" Akira slid onto the piano bench.

Eric answered, raising his voice as he moved toward the kitchen. "You know I love to cook. I thought it would be nice to stay in."

Akira selectively punched the keys of the piano. She knew nothing about pianos, she never ventured to learn an instrument in school, but the rich tones proved that serious money had been invested in its purchase.

The thick, mouthwatering aromas sailing out of the kitchen reminded her of quieter times—days where she and Eric stole away from work for long lunches at his apartment, or the thrill of going out of town to medical conferences when both of their employers had sponsored booths. It was on one of those trips that they hid in Eric's hotel room, skipping the vendor-sponsored dinner to spend the day in bed.

Those were the things that made her want Eric. She caught herself romanticizing her time with him. She couldn't forget the endless arguments because he wouldn't take her out in public. Or, the rude barbs about her eating habits and lack of a size-two body.

As Akira looked around, she found it hard to believe what she saw. Eric was living well above his means. Unless, he had come across a sudden windfall.

Her first inclination was to run from the apartment before he returned from the kitchen. Although things had not worked out for them romantically, she wanted nothing to do with the possibility of him going to prison. Casser and Downs were unforgiving if they suspected you. How could she bring that wrath down on someone she had a history with?

"Everything looks good." Eric entered the living room, rubbing his hands together for extra emphasis. "We're having tortellini primavera, orange glazed chicken, followed by the best lemon pound cake you've ever tasted." He stood over her with a smile that spread the length of his face. Now that they weren't together, he wasn't restricting her diet.

"I love anything a man is willing to cook for me." Saying the words made her recollect the day Roman stumbled around her kitchen trying to cook breakfast, and the day in the cabin when nobody would allow him to volunteer for kitchen duty.

Eric sat next to her on the piano bench. Their thighs touched. He claimed her smile for his own, not knowing that it was triggered by visions of Roman kneeling over her before they made love.

"I was surprised to hear you wanted to see me."

She rested her fingertips on the piano keys. "Seeing you the other day reminded me of how it used to be between us." Exactly what Downs had instructed her to say.

"Brought back memories for me, too." His voice became smoky, alluring. "I'm sorry for the way I talked to you on the

Acquisitions

phone. I wanted to call you, see you again, but when the police showed up...."

"That was scary."

Eric's arm wrapped around her back in search of the piano keys. "I'm glad it's over. I'm glad you called." His other hand found the piano and he began to play a slow melody.

"I didn't know you played."

"I learned as a kid. I always wanted to be a concert pianist, but that takes a lot of time and pays very little. I promised myself that as soon as I was able, I'd buy myself a baby grand."

"Things going that well at Power & Power?" she asked.

He abruptly ended his melody. Suspicion washed over his face, circled his eyes, and pouted his lips.

Akira covered. "Think they'd hire me?"

Eric lifted his chin as he laughed. "I could get you in to see the right people." He left the piano bench to return to the kitchen, leaving his remark to simmer between them.

Akira sat confused. Was he joking? After a few minutes, he called for her to join him in the dining room for dinner.

***

Roman sighed heavily as he settled back into the ripped vinyl seat of the taxi. *Thank God that was the wrong address.* According to the neighbors, the previous owners had vacated the dilapidated old house nine months ago. After knocking on several doors, only some of which opened, he had been given directions to another neighborhood on the other side of town.

Coming to a rolling stop, the cab driver asked if he should wait again. Roman peered out the side window at a pastel yellow house trimmed with black awnings. Activity in the backyard spilled into the driveway.

"Yes, wait please." He shoved a twenty-dollar bill through the Plexiglas money slot. "Leave the meter running."

"Yes, sir." The cabby stuffed the bill into his pocket and settled back against the seat.

With one deep breath, Roman stepped from the cab. He stood in the front yard admiring the difference between this house and the last. The perfect lawn with well-manicured shrubbery wasn't what he expected. He tried to picture the mother and father he remembered living in family-oriented, suburban neighborhood. The party activity in the rear did ring familiar. While he stood committing the tiniest details of the house to memory, a group of rowdy little boys around eight or ten years old came barreling out of the backyard.

"Hey." He caught hold of one of the boys. "Do Mr. and Mrs. Miller live here?"

"I think they're inside." The boy ran off to catch up with his friends.

Roman glanced over his shoulder to assure himself the availability of a hasty retreat. The cabby had pulled his baseball cap down over his eyes. The motor was still running.

"C'mon in." A man's husky voice called through the unlocked screen door.

Roman hesitated long enough for the man to appear in the foyer. The scent of barbeque chicken and ribs filled the small area. Fresh cakes and bread also assaulted him, reminding him of Grandma Dixon's welcome-home dinner he had missed.

The shocked, mouth-hanging-open, big-eyed look on the man's face told Roman he had the right house.

"Can I help you?"

Roman's shoulders tensed. *He's not sure of who I am.* "It's me, Dad. Roman."

Roman didn't know what he expected to happen. Gayle had not been well received when she tracked them down last year. Why he yearned for his father to yell out for his mother and she to come running, both of them smothering him in lost hugs, he didn't know. What he received was more accurate. His father scratched his head.

"Roman?"

"Yeah, Dad, it's me." Roman felt like a little boy about to be scolded for interrupting adult business.

Acquisitions

His father studied him for recognition. "You grew up to be a handsome man." He took a step closer. "Looks like you're doing well for yourself."

"Is Mom around?" He glanced past his father's shoulder. "She's in the kitchen with her friends."

A roar of laughter swelled up from the backyard.

"What brings you here?"

The in-flight lunch rocked and rolled. "I came to see my parents. Are they here?"

His father's eyes narrowed. The remark angered him.

"I see you're having a party. Should I come back later?"

"No." His father answered too quickly. His expression made it obvious, he never wanted Roman to return. "Wait in here. I'll get your mother."

He led Roman down a hallway, passing several men watching a historic Ali boxing match. The house fluttered with people laughing and having a good time. Roman took a seat in the great room, and waited.

What he had seen of the house was clean and well furnished. The emphasis on entertaining had not changed. The large-screen television where the men watched the boxing match was equipped with a sound system that would rival any movie theater. The sounds of music thumping from the back of the house and the shouts of the partygoers chilled him. How many nights had he laid in bed with his hands over his ears trying to go to sleep?

His father's hair was a little long for a man his age. The wavy pattern turned into tight curls that covered the nape of his neck. He remained the tall, well built man Roman remembered. His belly more prominent, but his stylish dress hid it well.

Roman rose from the sofa when first his father, and then his mother entered the room.

"Hi, Mom."

"Roman." She tried to smile.

He wanted to push past them and run out of the house ridding them of their torturous disappointment.

"Your Dad said you were here, but I didn't believe it." She dutifully held out her arms for an embrace.

Roman stepped into his mother's arm span and held her tight. His lashes fluttered as he inhaled the scent of a mother's love. It was awkwardly unfamiliar to him. He waited for her embrace to match his own. When she stepped away, he released her.

"What brings you here?" she asked.

"It's been a long time—I thought I should look you up."

His mother moved to the sofa, his father sat on the arm next to her. She wore her hair in a tight, shiny ponytail tied with a burgundy scarf. The flowers patterning her shirt matched the scarf perfectly. The shirt and form fitting pants were meant for a trendy younger woman, but his mother wore the ensemble well.

"You in trouble?" his father asked, certainty of the answer scrunching his nose.

"No, Dad, I needed to see you."

"Why?" his mother asked, skeptical of his visit.

"Because you're my parents, and I haven't seen you since I was ten years old."

His mother and father looked at each other. Disappointment showed on their faces. They watched him as if he was the wayward son who had fouled up again.

"This isn't a good time," his father officially informed him.

"When would be a better time? Twenty or thirty more years?"

His father rose from his place next to his mother. "Enough of the mouth. I won't have you showing up on my doorstep uninvited to mouth off at me. I am your father."

Before Roman could speak to that lame remark, the door flew open, and one of the rowdy boys from outside ran in.

"Mom, I'm hungry."

The shock that gripped Roman made him sway on his feet.

Acquisitions

He watched as the boy climbed onto his mother's lap. *His mother's lap*, not this little boy's. She smoothed the wavy pattern of his hair.

"Go in the kitchen and ask someone to help you." She dusted off the knees of his pants.

"Mom," the boy whined.

Roman had never been allowed to whine.

"Scott, do what your mother told you to do," his father said.

Having received the expected response from his father, the boy scurried out the room.

"Is that my brother?" Roman asked, but the answer was painfully obvious.

His father looked at him as if he were retarded.

Roman addressed his mother. "You have a whole other family?"

She looked down at the expensive plush carpeting.

"After you left Gayle and me, you started another family." He quickly did the math. "When I was about twenty-five, you—who never even picked up the phone to congratulate me on graduating from law school—had another kid? Are there any more?"

"Scott wasn't planned," his mother offered as an apology.

"Gayle and I were?"

"Not exactly."

"But you kept Scott. You gave Gayle and me away. Why?"

"We were older when Scott came along."

Then you should have known better. Saying this aloud would have found him lying on the front lawn. Confusion made Roman want to fall at his mother's feet and beg her for an answer he could understand. Anger made him ball his fists and press them against the seam of his pants legs. "You never told us. Does Grandma Dixon know about this?"

His parents looked at each other, bewildered.

His mother answered, "We thought Gayle would have told

you both."

"What?"

Now it all made sense. Big sister Gayle had found out when she visited last year, hence the need for the shrinks. That's why she wanted to talk to him before he made the trip.

"Why does he get to stay? I needed a mother and father, too." Roman detested himself for the whiny quality of his voice. He felt ten years old again. He remembered staring out of Grandma Dixon's window watching the driveway for signs of his father's old Ford station wagon.

His parents looked at each other again, bewildered.

His mother's voice broke; her face showed remorse for the first time. "Why are you asking all of these questions?"

"Roman," his father stood and approached him, "don't you know we couldn't keep you?"

Everyone around him had secrets.

His father continued. "The state took you and Gayle away from us. You were on the way to foster care until your grandmother stepped in and took custody of you. I can't believe Dixon never told you. Or Gayle. We explained this to her when she came."

"Wait," Roman lifted his hand to stop the attack of words, "why did the state want to take us away from our parents?"

Tears streamed from his mother's eyes. His father sighed. "Listen, this is painful for your mother."

"It is for me too, but I deserve to hear it."

His father sighed again. "Your mother and I were young when we had you and Gayle. We were about having a good time, being free. The neighbors realized we weren't taking proper care of you and your sister. Your teachers caught on and turned us in." He went to the sofa and comforted his wife. "It's a good thing they did. I can't imagine what might have happened if someone didn't step in and take control."

"You never fought for us?"

"Fight for you? We were high out of our minds most of

Acquisitions

the time. That's how we dealt with our problems. We partied and drank too much."

"You never came back for us?"

No reply.

"The state can't keep you from visiting."

His mother sniffled.

Roman ran his fingers over his waves. He wished Akira were there to soothe him. "Once you got yourselves together, you didn't come back. You started a new family?"

"You have any kids?" his father demanded.

Roman shook his head. His little brother was young enough to be his son.

"When you have kids, you ask yourself how in the world you could stand by and watch someone else raise them for you, not have any say in what they do, how they dress, what school they go to." He tightened his grip around his wife's shoulders as she sobbed. "You cock that self-righteous attitude with yourself when you have to pull your wife kicking and screaming out of the courtroom. And you try to explain it to your kids when they ask you over and over again when you're coming for them. You live a day in my shoes, then stand before me looking down on me like I'm dirt."

***

Roman had wanted to understand. He had needed to know.

He waved the flight attendant away as she approached. Like an adopted child, he had just met his missing parents and unknown little brother. He redirected his attention on the school picture his parents had given him of Scott before he left their home. He pulled out his wallet and removed a picture of him sharing Santa Claus' lap with Gayle when he was Scott's age. After an hour of supposing and wondering, hating and forgiving, he placed both photos back inside the sleeve of his wallet.

His first angry reaction had made him pull his cell phone out in the cab before reaching the airport and dial Gayle's number. He had planned to demand answers. She knew about their parents and Scott, so why hadn't she told him? He remembered the confused, depressed state Gayle returned home in last year after her visit. Sparing him the same pain was all she could do.

His anger then turned to Grandma Dixon, the keeper of her daughter's secrets. Lies. Why hadn't she told him? He wondered if she knew of her other grandson, Scott. Roman highly doubted it. She never would have tolerated being kept away from her family. If Gayle hadn't told him, she hadn't told Grandma Dixon.

Roman imagined the pain Grandma Dixon would experience once he told her about Scott and the pastel yellow house in New Orleans. Why would he inflict such hurt upon her? She had never fully explained why his parents couldn't reclaim him, but what did it matter now?

Why upset Grandma Dixon? Roman knew he couldn't torture himself. He had enough turmoil mucking up his life right now. The emotional unsteadiness of his parents could not be his problem. He refused to internalize it. He had learned a great deal of information that he should discuss with his sister and grandmother, but why? To open up more wounds? To point fingers and assign guilt? No solid bonds would come from forcing himself back into his parents' lives. Accusing Gayle and Grandma Dixon of being the source of his pain would be unfair and a lie.

He reminded himself again that he only wanted to know. To clear the air. To get answers. He had.

Now it was time to move on with his life.

Chapter 36

"Why is it taking so long?" Butch asked Detective Casser.

"Because she's not doing what we asked her to do. For the last hour, they've done nothing but eat dinner and talk about old times. Like I keep saying, she's in this with him. This whole set up has been to prove him innocent, not to help with the investigation."

"Listen, Casser—"

"No, you listen, Vance—"

Downs jettisoned his body between the two front seats. "Both of you shut up. Ms. Reed isn't a professional. She's doing okay. She has to win Dodson over, make him comfortable enough to trust her. We need to listen closely for whatever we can use, and I can't do that if you two keep bickering like little school girls!"

***

"This has been really great, Akira." Eric settled next to her on the black leather sofa after placing a Whitney Houston CD in the deck. "We should do it more often."

"I don't know if that'll be possible with the police hounding me." She looked up into his eyes in search of guilt or remorse. "They're going to arrest me any day."

Eric placed his arm across her shoulders and pulled her to him. "That's never going to happen. You know and I know you didn't do it."

"You're one of the few people who believe that. My lawyer says there's not much he can do now. We have to wait for the police to make the next move. When they do, my lawyer says he'll do his best, but...the evidence is stacked against me. I might get hard time for something I didn't do."

Eric guided her head into the crook of his neck. "I'm never going to let that happen to you. I care about you too much to stand by and watch you go to jail. Things didn't work out between us, but you've always been in my corner. I'll stand by you."

Akira lifted her face to him. "What can you do?"

"Don't worry about it. I'd take care of it if I had to."

Before Akira could contemplate proper police informant etiquette, Eric's lips were caressing hers, his tongue roaming inside her mouth. She forced herself to relax into his kiss— one kiss to make him confess it all.

"Oh God, I missed you," Eric exhaled into her ear; his hand went up to her breast as he pushed her back on the sofa.

The ringing doorbell interrupted an uncomfortable situation. No doubt, Butch demanded that one of the detectives come up and bail Akira out. Playing this role did not suit her. She wanted to push Eric away, but needed to win his confidence. She couldn't recall exactly how much give she had on the hidden wires. Knowing that Butch could hear her making out also didn't make the best of circumstances.

"Wait right here," Eric said as he straightened his shirt. "I'll get rid of whoever it is."

Akira sat upright, waiting for her cue. She hoped the microphone had not been dislodged. The wires felt bulky underneath her breast.

"What took you so long?" Like a gust of wind blowing south from a fish cannery, Candace burst into Eric's apartment.

Acquisitions

"What are *you* doing here?"

Akira rose from the sofa, wanting to ask the same question. They both turned to Eric.

He spoke to Candace. "I told you I had something to do tonight. Why are you here?"

"Something to do?" Candace crossed her arms over her cleavage and turned to Akira. "That about sums it up."

"Eric," Akira stayed calm—Eric hated confrontational women, "you know Candace? How?"

"Shut up." Candace dropped her purse to the floor. "I'm the only one who's going to get answers today."

"Don't tell me to shut up." Akira had withstood Candace's mouth one too many times.

"Candace," Eric's patience wore thin, "there's no need to all do this."

"All of what?" She whipped around to face him, her long strawberry mane following a second later. "We don't need her anymore. Why is she here?"

Akira's mouth parted slightly, she needed more information, but their argument was heating up, which left no room for her questions.

"Would you be quiet before you say too much?" Eric ordered.

"You don't tell me what to do. I get it now, this is a double cross." Candace placed one hand on her hip and the other she jabbed in the air to make her point. "You and Akira are still seeing each other, that's why you insisted on giving me only part of my payoff. You were supposed to send it to the Caribbean so that it would be there, drawing interest, when we arrived. You said it was safer for you to hide the money, but I see now."

Candace marched up to Akira. "No wonder you got so angry when Barry rejected you. I knew there was no way in the world he could want you when he had me. But you know what? You can have both those losers." She turned on Eric again. "Give me my money, every cent. I'm out of here, and

I don't ever want to see your face again."

"You're too stupid to be believed. Will you keep your mouth shut until we can talk?"

"Listen," Candace yelled. "I had to sleep with Barry—that pig—not you. If it wasn't for me, we'd never have gotten the location or combination to the vault. You were sitting in the parking garage listening to the stereo while I had to break into Greico and snatch the formula. I'm the one who has been taking all the risks. The only thing you've done is deliver the formula to the execs at Power & Power. I could have done that myself if I had known you'd try to cheat me."

Having reached his boiling point, knowing that everything had been revealed, Eric snatched Candace up by her arms and wrestled her toward his bedroom.

Akira jumped out of the way as they tripped over Candace's purse and tumbled to the floor. The amount of struggle Candace was able to put up against Eric's brawn shocked her. Perched up on the sofa, she watched, her heart racing, as Candace wrapped her long, milky legs around Eric's middle. Words of deceit flew between them as they rolled around, knocking over expensive art pieces.

Akira heard the door bang against the wall before the sound of Eric striking Candace across her face. She raked her long nails down his cheek, drawing blood.

"Hold it!" Downs ran into the room and wrestled to separate them.

Casser stood in the doorway laughing. "She gives as good as she gets, doesn't she?" He moved to help his partner. "You should have thought twice about getting tangled up with her, Dodson."

Butch's eyes widened as Casser held a wildly kicking Candace in his arms. She towered over him by at least four inches, but he effortlessly restrained her as Downs handcuffed Eric.

Akira rushed over to Butch. "Did you hear everything?"

"Honey, are you okay?" Butch shielded her as Casser con-

Acquisitions

tinued to struggle with Candace. "Are you alright?"

Akira nodded and asked again, "Did you hear everything? Did you hear how they worked together to steal the formula?"

Butch spoke in soothing tones. "Every word. The police have it all on tape."

Chapter 37

Roman jumped up. His thighs knocked over the chair in Grandma Dixon's kitchen. "I should go to her. Is she okay?"

"Roman," Butch said, "it's cool. Akira is fine."

Grandma Dixon appeared in the doorway.

"Why are you just now telling me this? You should have called me and told me what she was going to do. I would have never allowed her to put herself in that kind of danger."

"No offense, man, but that wasn't your decision to make. Akira wanted to do it. Her having the courage to put herself out there brought an end to this whole mess."

"I'm going to check on her. She's probably alone and afraid."

Butch pushed his plate away and stood to match Roman's height. "Akira isn't at home. She went to spend time with her family in Seattle."

"Seattle?" The announcement hit Roman with the force of a wrecking ball. "How long is she going to be gone?"

"She didn't say."

Grandma Dixon placed a comforting arm around his waist. "Roman, boy, you alright?"

Acquisitions

He glanced in her direction but spoke to Butch. "What else do you know about Akira leaving?"

"There's nothing else to know. She wanted to get away to make sense of everything. She needed to rest. She came by here to see Grandma Dixon before she left; Lara and I drove her to the airport."

"You talked with her, Grandma?"

"Yeah, I did. She seemed fine, a little worn, but okay."

Roman felt better with his grandmother's assurance that Akira was not in trouble, but the fact that she was thousands of miles away choked him with emotions that reminded him of his parents, emotions he never wanted to associate with Akira.

"I need to be alone, Grandma." Roman stooped to kiss her cheek. "I'll call you later."

"You want me to ride with you?" Butch called after him.

"No. I'll catch up with you later. Peace out."

Without any warning, Akira had gone to Seattle. They were no longer a couple; she didn't have to notify him of her plans. Deep down inside, Roman believed that time would help them work out their problems. Akira needed space; time to think and then she would ask him to come back to her. He felt sure of it.

Roman slid into the corner booth of the bar, ordered a beer, and tried to steady his thoughts. As he began to get a handle on his life, and the direction he needed to take, Akira rocked the boat. Butch couldn't even tell him when she planned to return, or if she planned to return at all. Having lost her job and ended their relationship, there was nothing to keep her in Detroit anymore.

Their love had been right. The timing was awful, but what they shared was meant to be. Akira needed a reason to come back to him. She needed to trust him again. He'd have to work hard to regain the level of trust they had before he weakened at Sherry's call, but they'd get there. Akira needed to be won over again. The key would be to make her swoon, remind her of how much love they'd shared. How could he share his vision with her now? He'd have to find a way to give her whatever she had to have to cement their relationship.

In the morning, he would cement his future when he signed the lease to his new office. He had appointments lined up all day. Interior decorators. Office supply stores. Utility companies. Telephone interviews for an assistant and a secretary. Only after everything was in place, would he tell the people most important to him that he had moved forward with opening his own practice. With Gayle's client referrals, his practice would be profitable in no time.

***

The trip to Seattle should have cleared Akira's head enough to point her in the right direction. Just that morning her mother had asked, "What are your plans now that this is over?"

"You have to have direction in your life," her father said.

They'd waited for her to answer. She sat in silence.

"Akira," her father sighed, exasperated.

"Dad, I'm happy to be putting all of this behind me. I have a little time to relax and figure my life out."

As Akira lay on the bed in the guest room of her parent's home, inhaling the scent of honeydew melon scented candles, watching the flickering reflection of the flame dance across the ceiling, she thought about her time with Roman, the love he brought into her life and what she was missing every day they spent apart.

Roman had never taken her on an expensive vacation. They never ate in fancy restaurants where a suit and tie were required. He never offered to buy her jewelry.

What Roman did do was make her happy. He sacrificed his career with Greico to help clear her name. He paid her legal bills that were in the thousands of dollars. He protected her with everything he had, shielded her from those who pronounced her guilty.

And he made love to her. He took his time when they were intimate, biting her inner thighs until the pain became too

Acquisitions

sweet to stand. Kneading her breasts one at a time, smiling when her nipples responded to his touch. Coaxing her to release all inhibitions and call his name when orgasms rushed her body.

What had gone wrong? Akira rolled over and smothered her face in a pillow. The darkness did not shut out all the love and pain she felt because of Roman.

How could they get back to where they were before Sherry waltzed back into the picture? After all these weeks, Roman may not be interested. He had offered—she had refused. It might be too late to straighten out the huge mess they had made of their relationship.

Every trial they had weathered only made their bond stronger. Why had she let Sherry rip them apart? Clearly, they wanted to be together.

The reality, no matter how much she refused to see it, was that their time together had been brief. Now they both had moved on with their lives. She had made a grave mistake pushing Roman away, but too much time had lapsed to repair it.

Chapter 38

June 2

Stepping back into the building that housed Greico Enterprises made Akira flash back to a time filled with both pleasant and sad memories. Remembering all the ups and downs that occurred over the last months was enough to make her stomach churn. Like her parents promised, everything had worked out for the best, and she had not only come out on top, but became a better person because of everything she had endured.

Butch tugged at the cuffs of his suit. "I'm going to the men's room," he announced when the elevator chimed. "I'll meet you in the lobby."

"Don't be long." She stepped onto the elevator, smiling as she descended one last time down to ground level. After today, she would never have a reason to come back.

She had been vindicated, but it did not erase the feelings of betrayal she felt when no one believed Mr. Johnson had violated her. Or the frustration she felt when she was being investigated like a common criminal.

Greico made a formal apology when Eric and Candace

Acquisitions

were busted for selling the formula. They quickly betrayed each other when they were taken into police custody. Selling their souls, this time for freedom, each enthusiastically told different versions of the truth. Plea bargains, trials, and prison time were in their futures.

Akira wanted to see Eric, have him explain the details she needed to hear, but when she asked Butch to set it up, he simply said, "No way." The road in front of Eric and Candace would be hard; she didn't need to be caught up on their runaway train.

Not only did Greico Enterprises give her a public apology for the accusations surrounding the missing formula, they also corrected the situation regarding Mr. Johnson. To avoid a massive civil lawsuit, they offered all of his victims an out-of-court settlement for the mental anguish they had been forced to suffer. The fact that Akira's brother made the Seattle Supersonics helped push them to settle quickly before more lawyers got involved.

Akira still could not believe it had been so easy. She signed a receipt, and they handed her a check with more zeroes than she thought she'd ever see. Of course, Butch had been right there to take his firm's cut. He was a cad, but if it weren't for his support, she would have never made it through the turmoil. She hoped that he hurried down to the lobby so they could tie up their loose ends. She wanted to get out of the building—away from the memories—as soon as possible.

Akira released a well-earned shout of joy into the empty elevator car. Today signified the end of an ordeal. Now she could start living anew, put it all behind her.

Her smile faded. Roman, too, was now behind her.

The two weeks she spent in Seattle helped her deal with their break-up. It had been hard, but as long as she didn't think about him, she could stand the emptiness that had begun to plague her.

The elevator doors opened and a Korean family of three stepped in: a man, his wife, and a newborn baby in a stroller.

They spoke to each other in their native language. Akira peeked into the carriage. The baby, dressed all in blue, slept peacefully.

"Your son?" Akira asked the parents.

"Yes," the man answered, his words heavy with accent. "My son, yes."

The sweet innocence of the baby made Akira want to lift him up against her bosom and kiss his fat cheeks. Give him the love she brimmed over with since she could no longer share it with Roman. She backed away to the left side of the elevator instead and waited to arrive in the lobby.

The elevator stopped to pick up more passengers. Akira kept her eyes glued to the floor when it stopped. The familiar woodsy aroma first caught her attention. She gained the courage to trace the figure's outline, starting at the black wing tips and scanning upward. Roman had joined them at the eleventh floor. He watched her intensely—looking at her as if she was someone he knew but could not quite place.

Still dressed immaculately, Roman was more handsome than ever. Not much about his features had changed. He'd become more trim—thin. Akira instinctively worried he wasn't eating properly. His waves had thickened and appeared blacker than she remembered, but it had been a long time since she ran her fingers across them.

Her eyes flashed away from his. She watched the numbers overhead, counting off the floors until she was free to leave the shrinking space.

Saying, "Hi," like they were casual acquaintances seemed stupid. Ignoring him like he was a stranger, dumber still. But what could she say to her ex-lover after weeks of silence? How would she pick up a conversation that ended too many days ago?

Amazing. The Korean family stood between them and didn't feel the tension in the air. Didn't they know how much she had loved Roman? They were oblivious to the fact that Akira's heart beat so loudly in her ears that she could not hear

Acquisitions

the foreign words the family shared.

Roman turned abruptly to face her. He weaved around the Korean family to reach her. "I can't pretend we don't know each other."

Akira glanced at the family who didn't notice the drama unfolding. "Did you know I would be here today?"

"Butch mentioned it."

"And you thought you'd come here to see me?" She kept her voice down, glancing at the baby carriage. She didn't know if she was flattered by his attempt to see her or upset that Butch had a hand in it.

"I had business to clear up. Things I should have done a long time ago, but decided to take care of today with the hope that I might run into you."

His blunt statement gave her the courage to look up. Emotional sparks stung her face and warmed her cheeks.

He spoke boldly, with confidence. "It's been a long time. I needed to see you."

"Not here. Not now." Coming undone with overwhelming love was not the way she wanted to make her final exit from Greico Enterprises.

Roman tilted his head in confusion. He hesitated then stepped back to his corner of the small box.

Akira watched his back as he stood, hands shoved in his pockets, head titled upward, studying the illuminated numbers overhead. She wanted to run to him. She hungered to have his body envelop her. He was standing only a few feet from her. All she had to do was take one step or call his name or reach out to him. That's all she needed to do to feel whole once again.

Akira lifted her hand.

The elevator came to a jerking stop as it reached the lobby. Roman held the door open as the Korean family slowly made their way out of the elevator.

She waited impatiently, walking closely behind the Korean family.

Roman wedged himself between them.

"I need to get off, please."

He pressed the button that closed the doors.

Akira held her chin up in an attempt to show him she was not playing games. "What are you doing?"

"We need to talk. I knew you'd never come to me." He turned a key in the control panel setting off a loud chorus of ringing bells.

"Where'd you get the access key to control the elevator?"

"Mr. Tabrinsky in security let me borrow it for a while."

The emergency phone rang. Roman held up his hand stopping her chatter. "No, we're fine," he said into the receiver.

The clanging of emergency bells stopped.

"Let me talk to them." Akira reached for the phone, but Roman twisted his body putting it out of reach.

"Take your time. We'll be here." He quickly replaced the receiver in the emergency box.

***

Roman had glanced over his shoulder to pinpoint Akira's location in the elevator. He noticed the woman in the lemon yellow skirt and jacket the moment the elevator doors opened. Did she realize how many cars he had to pass up before finding her? And now she wanted to leave without hearing him out.

Akira was more beautiful than he remembered. Her hair was longer, the auburn tips replaced by light brown curls. The sexy slope of her nose remained the same. The ride to the lobby gave Roman too much time to concentrate on the curves of Akira's hips and the prominence of her cheekbones, rouge colored cheekbones that highlighted the pink blush over her eyelids.

He silently thanked Butch for the call telling him she was on her way down.

With the elevator at a standstill, Roman moved front and

Acquisitions

center of the car. "Akira."

Silence. Her eyes told the truth. She was happy to see him.

"Akira," he crooned. "It's not like I don't see you standing there." In spite of himself, he smiled. "Okay, suit yourself." He faced front.

"I want out of here." The words were faint. "What do you think you're doing?"

Roman turned to face her. He ran his fingers over his freshly cut, oiled waves. He unsuccessfully masked the mischievous lilt in his voice. "This will go a lot better if you're nice to me." He faced front again.

"Roman Miller, I don't know what you think you're doing, but I demand that you unlock the elevator and get it moving." She stepped forward. "I don't want to have to do anything drastic."

He smiled at her defiance. "Something drastic is what I had to do to get your attention." He spread his arms wide, "Don't look for help from the elevator crew. They're in this with me."

"What?"

Roman turned again. "Be nice."

Her voice softened. "Okay."

Roman went to her, standing a breath away. "Do you understand now?"

"No, I don't." Her breathing slowed. Roman didn't know if it was the effect of being stuck in the elevator or of having him near.

He dipped his head next to her ear and whispered, "You wanted romance." He slowly lifted his hand and pushed the hair away from her forehead.

"But—" Akira softened with curiosity and confusion.

Roman glanced up at the flickering lights and guesstimated the time remaining. The elevator crew had promised him ten minutes tops—he didn't have much time. "Akira, I messed up. I'm sorry."

"I know. I've never doubted you were sorry."

He bent at the knees, placing his face directly in line with hers. "You forgive me?"

"I forgive you, Roman. I just can't forget. You walked away from me with the first temptation that came along. Do you understand that I can't risk my heart on you?"

"Do you understand that you're the key to my world?"

His words clouded Akira's mind.

"Do you understand how much I want to pin you against the wall and make love to you right now?"

Her body responded to the image.

"What I did was ridiculous. It was the worst decision I've ever made. But believe me, I've been paying for it by not having you in my life these past few months. It's been hell."

He placed his palms on each side of her face. "I've been waiting for this chance to make you understand." He moved in closer, the heat of his mouth brushed over her lips. "My problems might have involved Sherry, but they started long before I met her. I've confronted my issues and dealt with the past. Now I'm ready to love you like I should have in the first place."

Akira remembered their candid talks late into the night.

"I'm not a *bad* person. I messed up—I've admitted that— but I'm trying to do the right thing. I want to fix us."

The air between them smoldered.

Akira stood helpless, watching, weakening. "I don't know how you can fix this. Once trust is shattered, is it ever possible to get it back?"

"Yes. Yes, it's possible. We'll both have to work at it, but it's possible."

"Roman, I don't know if I can."

"Do you love me?" He pulled her face closer to his, separating them by inches. "Do you love me, Akira?"

Her defenses crumbled.

"Do you love me?"

Acquisitions

Her stomach dropped. "I love you."

Roman's smile was full of liberation and longing. When his dimples appeared, relief overwhelmed her. She was open, wide open to accept whatever would happen next with Roman.

"I love you," Akira repeated. She lifted her hand to touch his face, hoping to catch a dimple before it faded. "I've missed you so much."

Roman tilted his head into her palm.

"What do you want from me?" she asked.

Roman closed his eyes and relished in her touch. "I want you in my bed tonight."

And she wanted to be there.

"I want you to kiss me and show me how much you love me and how much you've missed me. Can you do that?"

"I will do that."

Akira leaned into Roman's arms and they shared a kiss that lasted until her knees buckled.

"Oh, yeah," he pulled his lips from hers after another quick kiss. "I want something else."

"What?" Whatever, she'd give it.

"You know I'm romantically challenged, but you might like this." He tightened his grip around her waist while he pulled a photo out of his back pocket.

In the picture, a clown with multi-colored hair held up a sign that said, "I love you, Akira." He stood outside, above his head a sign: Roman Miller, Attorney at Law.

"He's one of the first clients Gayle directed to my new practice."

"Your own practice?"

He nodded. "Entertainment law. My office is up and running." He kissed the slope of her nose. "I want one more thing."

The elevator jerked.

She grabbed his waist. "Anything."

"It's huge."

"Anything."

"I want you to move with me to California. My practice is there, and I want you by my side." Another jerk. "What do you say?"

Akira's eyes glazed over. "You want me to move to California with you? I can't make a decision this big without thinking it over."

"You love me. I love you. This place has too many bad memories for us. Why not start over? Do this the right way."

A motor hummed.

Roman rushed on, "Your parents are meeting us out there in two months for the wedding. I've made all the arrangements."

"Wait!" Akira stopped his rambling. "A wedding?"

"Grandma Dixon told me that if I wanted you back in my life I had to give you what you needed to be happy. And I've always been willing to give you whatever you wanted. The problem was I couldn't see what you needed. I finally figured it out. You need honesty, trust and most of all, you need to know I love and adore you above everyone else."

An oval shaped diamond ring appeared from nowhere. He slipped it onto her finger. "Everyday, from here on, I'm going to prove to you that I'm trustworthy. Everyday I'm going to make love to you in a way that proves you're the most beautiful woman in the world. Starting today—if you let me—I'm going to take you away from all these bad memories and replace them with nothing but happiness."

He dropped to his knees. "You asked me to save you. I will always be there to catch you."

"Roman—"

"If we want this to work—to last forever—we have to do everything the right way. I'm not going to ask you to move thousands of miles away with me without you knowing what my intentions are. I had a long talk with your father—he was hard to convince. Your brother gave his nod of approval. Your mother says to call her as soon as you get off this elevator and

Acquisitions

let her know what your answer is."

"You talked to my family? They know about this? What—" Akira's voice wavered. "What about Grandma Dixon?"

"Grandma Dixon?" He raised a quizzical brow. "I talked with her. She's crazy about you. I have her blessing with what I'm doing."

"You can't leave her here alone."

Another reason he loved her—because she cared about the people that were important to him. "I told you I've taken care of everything. She's agreed to move to California. Gayle can't wait until we all get there." He kissed the inside of her wrist. "I've handled every single detail you could possibly think of, so stop stalling. Tell me what I want to hear."

"What's that?" Akira teased. Her heart had already succumbed to his charms.

"Tell me that you love me and can't live without me. Tell me that you've been miserable without me. Tell me you miss the way I wake you in the middle of the night. Tell me you want to have my babies. Akira, tell me that you forgive me and want to start over with me…and that you want it to last forever."

"All those things and more."

The elevator jerked and began to descend.

She dropped to her knees putting them at eye level, "Ask me."

"Akira Reed, will you run off to California with me?"

Tears. "Ask me."

"Will you marry me?"

"Again."

"Will you be mine forever? Will you stand by me while I start my practice? Will you trust me to make you happy? Will you have my kids? Will you be my wife? I'll ask you over and over again in any way you need to hear it. No matter how many times I say it, what I want will never change. I want you. I want you in my life forever." He kissed her temple, her cheeks. He tasted the cherry lip-gloss. "Answer me, Akira."

"Yes, I'll marry you." She grabbed him around the neck, throwing her body into his. They landed together on the floor.

The elevator doors parted to a group of worried onlookers.

"Sir, are you alright?" the young engineer with dirty red hair asked.

Akira and Roman righted themselves on the floor.

"We can take it from here." The engineer came to assist Roman who had Akira draped around his neck.

"No," Roman's arms tightened around her waist. "Akira stays with me. She never leaves me again." He directed his words into her ear. "Hold tight, Akira."

Excerpts for future publications

BY DESIGN
by
Barbara Keaton
March 2003

Shari stood at the base of the concrete steps, closed her eyes and inhaled deeply, loving the way the warm June breeze filled her lungs. She opened her eyes, then rubbed her hands briskly .ogether, a wiry smile spread across her face as she looked up at the massive steeple of St. Simon the Apostle Catholic Church—the church she had grown up attending mass at and its attached grammar school. Shari glanced at her watch. She had to laugh, for once she was on time. Had to be for the christening of her best friend's first child.

The smell of incense swept into her nostrils as Shari opened the large wooden doors to the church. She paused at the small marble bowl, dipped her two fingers into the holy water, crossed her self and continued down the long aisle. Shari focused her smoky brown eyes on the large painting ahead, situated behind the wide alter. A black Jesus, draped in a billowing white robe, his arms out stretched, with the hands of God behind him, welcomed her, bright rays of light filtered around the stunning portrait. As she continued, she thought of the countless days spent in the sanctuary and her dream of one day walking down the very aisle toward her husband to be dressed in white. Shari shrugged. She wasn't sure that that dream would ever become a reality; especially since she had no real prospects in her life.

Sandra and his aunts. She paused when her gaze rested on a broad smile that met her. Umph, she thought, as she absorbed the warm chocolate face starring intently at her. He reminded her of a dark angel—warm, protective and inviting. And his eyes. They were the color of light-brown sugar, a stark, but beautiful contrast to his smooth dark complexion. She nodded her head in his direction as she continued toward the front of the church. She felt his eyes on her back and forced herself not to turn around, instead she focused her attention on her best friend as she approach.

"Hey, you made it," Deb pulled Shari into an embrace, then pulled back.

"Now, Deb," Shari began, looking at her best friend, the woman who was actually more like a sister to her. She noticed the brightness in her brown eyes, the comforting glow emitting from her oval shaped warm brown face. She hugged her again. "You know I wouldn't miss this for the world. How could I miss my goddaughters christening?" Shari smiled, then turned to see the chocolate angel watching her. "Where is my baby?" She looked back at Deb, then slipped off her olive green overcoat to reveal a pale pink bolero jacket with a matching skirt that rested inches above her knees, her eyes drifted back toward the dark stranger.

"Darrin has her." Deb pointed to the front of the church, then turned her attention to Shari's distraction. "Cute, isn't he?"

Shari's head snapped around. "Who?"

Deb chuckled. "Hamilton."

"Hamilton?" Shari responded, a slow smile crossing her face.

"Yeah," Deb took Shari by the elbow. "Hamilton Edmunds, Junior. He's Darrin's cousin. On his father's side. Hamilton's mother and Darrin's father are sister and brother."

"Oh," was Shari's only reply as she wondered why she hadn't met him before. She steeled herself against taking another glance at the handsome dark man sitting just feet from her. She turned her attention to the front of the church, and upon finding Darrin, moved past Deb and stood next to Darrin, who was standing among Father John, the parish priest, and his best friend, Mike. Darrin grinned upon seeing Shari. He embraced her, then kissed her on the cheek.

"Deb was so worried you wouldn't make it back from Paris in time for the baptism," Darrin said. "But I know you. I knew nothing would keep you from this day." He handed his daughter over into Shari's arms. Momentarily forgetting Darrin's cousin, Shari snuggled Little Daneda Shari Wilson against her. The chubby 4-month-old cooed warmly as Shari rested her eyes lovingly upon the baby's warm cocoa face. She saw that the baby had her fathers deep, dark eyes and his coloring, but had Deb's small, flat nose and squared chin.

How could she miss this, Shari thought as Father John signaled to the gathering participants to join him so he could begin the Roman Catholic sacrament of baptism. She followed the priest and the others to the altar where the baptism bowl rested upon a matching large grey and white marble stand. She smiled warmly as the baby cooed and gurgled while the priest began the ceremony with the anointing of oils.

Shari looked at Deb, then Darrin who stood immediately to the right of her. Darrin's best friend, Mike, was to her left. Her face flushed as she looked upon the faces of two of the people she loved most in the world. This was a day Shari knew she couldn't miss, even though for the past two years, Shari's job as head buyer for Macy's kept her on the road at least two days out of the week, with nearly two months spent abroad. But she had purposely kept busy, forcing away the reality of not being able to truly connect with one special person. Shari glanced up into the eyes of the large mosaic of Jesus. She prayed silently for peace and solace, followed by her desire to find a true love. She knew, following her break up with her long-time beau, Bruce, that she had never been in love.

310

ORDER FORM

Mail to: Genesis Press, Inc.
315 3rd Avenue North
Columbus, MS 39701

Name _____

Address _____

City/State _____ Zip _____

Telephone _____

Ship to (if different from above)

Name _____

Address _____

City/State _____ Zip _____

Telephone _____

Qty	Author	Title	Price	Total

Use this order form, or call 1-888-INDIGO-1

Total for books _____

Shipping and handling:
    $3 first book, $1 each
    additional book _____
Total S & H _____
Total amount enclosed _____
MS residents add 7% sales tax